FINDING FORGIVENESS

FINDING SERIES #4

SLOANE KENNEDY

CONTENTS

Copyright   v

Finding Forgiveness   vii

Trademark Acknowledgements   ix

Acknowledgments   xi

Series Reading Order   xiii

Series Crossover Chart   xvii

Trigger Warning   xix

Chapter 1   1

Chapter 2   15

Chapter 3   26

Chapter 4   40

Chapter 5   58

Chapter 6   75

Chapter 7   91

Chapter 8   110

Chapter 9   125

Chapter 10   144

Chapter 11   157

Chapter 12   173

Epilogue   194

A Note to Readers   201

About the Author   203

Also by Sloane Kennedy   205

Published in the United States by Sloane Kennedy

Cover Images: © sorali © Subbotina

Cover Design: © Jay Aheer, Simply Defined Art

ISBN-13:
978-1541063419

ISBN-10:
1541063414

FINDING FORGIVENESS

Sloane Kennedy

TRADEMARK ACKNOWLEDGEMENTS

The author acknowledges the trademarked status and trademark owners of the following trademarks mentioned in this work of fiction:

Harley Davidson
Mercedes
Ford
Candy Crush Saga
Marmaduke
Curious George
Mr. Clean
Smurfs
Nike

ACKNOWLEDGMENTS

A big thank you to Missy and for her quick beta read.

Also, thanks to LJ and Beth for giving Roman his name – he wouldn't have been the man he is without it.

SERIES READING ORDER

All of my series cross over with one another so I've provided a couple of recommended reading orders for you. If you want to start with the Protectors books, use the first list. If you want to follow the books according to timing, use the second list. Note that you can skip any of the books (including M/F) as each was written to be a standalone story.

Note that some books may not be readily available on all retail sites

Recommended Reading Order (Use this list if you want to start with "The Protectors" series)
1. Absolution (m/m/m) (The Protectors, #1)
2. Salvation (m/m) (The Protectors, #2)
3. Retribution (m/m) (The Protectors, #3)
4. Gabriel's Rule (m/f) (The Escort Series, #1)
5. Shane's Fall (m/f) (The Escort Series, #2)
6. Logan's Need (m/m) (The Escort Series, #3)
7. Finding Home (m/m/m) (Finding Series, #1)
8. Finding Trust (m/m) (Finding Series, #2)

9. Loving Vin (m/f) (Barretti Security Series, #1)
10. Redeeming Rafe (m/m) (Barretti Security Series, #2)
11. Saving Ren (m/m/m) (Barretti Security Series, #3)
12. Freeing Zane (m/m) (Barretti Security Series, #4)
13. Finding Peace (m/m) (Finding Series, #3)
14. Finding Forgiveness (m/m) (Finding Series, #4)
15. Forsaken (m/m) (The Protectors, #4)
16. Vengeance (m/m/m) (The Protectors, #5)
17. A Protectors Family Christmas (The Protectors, #5.5)
18. Atonement (m/m) (The Protectors, #6)
19. Revelation (m/m) (The Protectors, #7)
20. Redemption (m/m) (The Protectors, #8)
21. Finding Hope (m/m/m) (Finding Series, #5)
22. Defiance (m/m) (The Protectors #9)

***Recommended Reading Order** (Use this list if you want to follow according to timing)*
1. Gabriel's Rule (m/f) (The Escort Series, #1)
2. Shane's Fall (m/f) (The Escort Series, #2)
3. Logan's Need (m/m) (The Escort Series, #3)
4. Finding Home (m/m/m) (Finding Series, #1)
5. Finding Trust (m/m) (Finding Series, #2)
6. Loving Vin (m/f) (Barretti Security Series, #1)
7. Redeeming Rafe (m/m) (Barretti Security Series, #2)
8. Saving Ren (m/m/m) (Barretti Security Series, #3)
9. Freeing Zane (m/m) (Barretti Security Series, #4)
10. Finding Peace (m/m) (Finding Series, #3)
11. Finding Forgiveness (m/m) (Finding Series, #4)
12. Absolution (m/m/m) (The Protectors, #1)
13. Salvation (m/m) (The Protectors, #2)
14. Retribution (m/m) (The Protectors, #3)
15. Forsaken (m/m) (The Protectors, #4)
16. Vengeance (m/m/m) (The Protectors, #5)
17. A Protectors Family Christmas (The Protectors, #5.5)

18. Atonement (m/m) (The Protectors, #6)

19. Revelation (m/m) (The Protectors, #7)

20. Redemption (m/m) (The Protectors, #8)

21. Finding Hope (m/m/m) (Finding Series, #5)

22. Defiance (m/m) (The Protectors #9)

SERIES CROSSOVER CHART

Protectors/Barrettis/Finding Crossover Chart

The Protectors

The Barrettis

Mace (P1)	Ronan (P2)	Hawke (P3)	Mav (P4)
(Cole)	(Seth)	(Tate)	(Eli)
(Jonas)			

A: Matty

Dante (P6)
(Magnus)

Memphis (P5)
(Tristan)
(Brennan)

Vincent (P9)
(Nathan)

Cain (P7)
(Ethan)

Jace (P11)
(Caleb)

Phoenix (P8)
(Levi)

Gage (P10)
(Nash)
(Everett)

Vaughn (P12)
(Aleks)
(coming in 2018)

Matty's grandmother

Dom (E3)
(Logan)
A: Eli
A: Tristan
B: Tanner

Ren(B3)
(Declan)
(Jagger)
B: Sierra
B: Jordan

Rafe (B2)
(Cade)
A: Beck
A: Toby
A: Rebecca

Vin (B1) MF
(Mia)
5 biological children

Zane (B4)
(Connor)
Brennan (brother)
Hannah (sister)
B: Leo

Finding Series

Callan (F1)	Dane (F2)	Gray (F2)	Roman (F4)	Quinn (F5)
(Rhys)	(Jax)	(Luke)	(Hunter)	(Beck)
(Finn)				(Brody)

Escort Series

Gabe (E1) MF
(Riley)

Shane (E1) MF
(Savannah)

Recommended reading order can be found at beginning of my books. Or
check out the bundles called A Family Chosen

Sibling	——————	(Spouse/Partner)	MF = Male/Female book
Friend	——————	A: Adopted Child	
Crossover Relationship	— — — —→	B: Biological Child	
() behind name is Series and book # (i.e. B 1 is book 1 in Barretti)			

TRIGGER WARNING

CHAPTER 1

"What can I get you?"

Roman Blackwell took one look at the bartender's cowboy hat and plaid shirt and guessed he wasn't going to find his favorite brand of whiskey in a place like this so he simply said "Scotch, neat" and then turned around to study the surprisingly busy club. He'd been to more gay clubs than he could count but this one was on the top of his "what were they thinking?" list. There was the obligatory mirror ball above the dance floor but for the life of him, Roman couldn't figure out how it jived with the honky-tonk country music blaring from the antiquated sound system or the dark wood-paneled walls that looked like something you'd find in the house of a 70's sitcom family.

He'd had high hopes when the app on his phone had showed that a club called *Red* was within a few miles of his hotel in the not-so-busy downtown section of Missoula, Montana but when he'd arrived, he'd found that the app had left out a strategic apostrophe as well as an *s* and *Red* was actually *Red's*. The sight of a few Harley Davidsons sitting out front among the half dozen pick-up trucks – two of which were attached to horse trailers – had been the deciding factor in whether he stayed or not. He'd always found bikers to be an interesting bunch

1

when it came to random hook-ups because despite their testosterone-driven demeanors, tattoos and leather wear, they usually ended up being the guys that begged him the loudest to get them off when he had them pinned beneath him.

But despite the Harleys out front, he wasn't seeing any men who looked like they belonged to the Hogs. What he did see was a lot of cowboy hats, bolo neck ties, blue jeans and cowboy boots in all sorts of textures and colors. And then there was the dancing...there wasn't a pole or cage in sight and while there were a few guys who might as well have been fucking on the dance floor considering all the gyrating they were doing, Roman was waiting for the moment when the whole group broke out into a line dance.

"Hey."

Roman glanced to his right and saw a pretty little thing sizing him up. No way the emo guy had been there a minute ago because he certainly would have noticed the full, pouty lips, nose piercing and hint of guy liner framing bright blue eyes. A shot of lust went through Roman and he shifted his weight so he could give the guy his full attention.

"Buy me a drink?" the guy asked as he let his long fingers rub over his hip and down his thigh.

The bartender slid Roman's drink in front of him but instead of ordering the guy a drink, he took a swig of his own. Emo Guy pouted prettily but didn't seem too disappointed because he sidled up even closer to Roman. But when he placed his hand on Roman's thigh and let it travel towards Roman's dick, Roman grabbed his wrist.

"Where is he?" Roman asked coolly as he took in the leather pants and vest the guy was wearing. There was no doubt the guy was linked to the still absent bikers but he definitely wasn't one himself.

"Who?"

Roman turned the guy's arm over and pointed to the tattoo on the guy's forearm. "Cooter," Roman said with a chuckle as he read the name tattooed beneath the words *Property of*.

"He's playing," Emo Guy said, though from the smile on his face, whatever or whoever Cooter was playing with didn't seem to bother him. "Want to go watch?"

While Roman liked fucking bikers, he wasn't really interested in brawling with them over some boy toy that had so far only managed to get him half hard. But curiosity got the best of him so he gave the guy a brief nod and then swallowed the rest of his drink. Emo Guy took his hand and began leading him through the still sedate crowd of cowboys. Several of them openly stared at him and a few even sent him inviting looks but he ignored them. As they drew closer to the far side of the club where a red curtain separated the main room from what he assumed was a private area, Roman could hear hearty laughs and deep, rumbling voices.

As Emo Guy pushed the curtain aside, Roman realized it wasn't a private area – it was just a room with a couple of pool tables. But that wasn't what had his attention. No, it was the half-naked guy bent over one of the pool tables who caught his eye along with the huge guy pounding into him from behind. Several other guys were standing around the table and a couple even had their cocks out and were stroking them as they urged the guy doing the fucking on.

The first thing Roman noticed about the guy getting fucked was how still he was as the biker rammed into him. His hands and cheek were pressed flat against the green felt. His shirt was still on but was pushed up to reveal a slim back and even under the dim light hanging above the table, Roman could see his hair was a startlingly light shade of blond. His body kept jerking as he was brutally fucked but he made absolutely no sound and didn't struggle against the man holding his hips as he thrust into him. His eyes were open and staring in Roman's direction but not looking directly at him.

"Fuck, yeah!" one of the onlookers shouted as the guy doing the fucking cursed as he came. He held himself inside the guy for only a few seconds before pulling out and then another guy was stepping up and slamming into him.

"That's Cooter," Emo Guy said with pride.

Roman shook his head at the sickening sight. As much as it bothered him, especially considering how young the guy pinned to the table looked, the guy wasn't complaining about the harsh treatment and he didn't look drugged or drunk so Roman turned to leave. But just as he reached behind him to pull the curtain back, his eyes once again caught on the guy's and some unnamed emotion went through him when he saw how empty his gaze was – like he wasn't even there. He'd seen that look before and it had fucking haunted him his whole life.

"Such a pretty little slut," Cooter snarled as he fucked into the guy. His big hands reached up and fisted in the guy's hair and he yanked his head up and held it at an unnatural angle as he continued to brutalize him. The guy still didn't make a sound and when Cooter slammed his head back down on the table and pinned it there with his beefy hand, the guy's eyes looked exactly the same. Cooter grunted as he came and Roman felt the bile rise in his throat as he watched the man pull out and a trickle of blood ran down the guy's inner thigh.

"Bleeding just like a bitch," Cooter said in satisfaction and as the next guy moved into position, Roman dropped the curtain and began moving towards the pool table.

One of the bikers stepped in his path and snarled, "You gotta fucking wait your turn, man!"

But Roman just kneed him in the groin and then slammed his hand into his nose. The guy shouted in pain as he hit the ground and then Cooter was coming at him. Adrenaline surged through Roman's blood as he saw a smattering of blood on the guy's condom covered cock and he didn't hesitate to slam his fist into Cooter's bulging neck. Cooter gasped and Roman hoped to God he'd managed to cause permanent damage to the man's trachea. The guy who'd been about to fuck the man on the table stepped back but Roman grabbed him by the balls and squeezed hard. The man screamed like a stuck pig and froze in place. The only two men still standing had enough sense to back off and one of them quickly tucked his own dick back in his pants as if to protect it from Roman's wrath.

"I suggest you take your friend there" – Roman motioned to Cooter who was struggling to draw in air – "and go before I rip your fucking balls from your body and jam them down his throat."

The biker he was holding onto nodded and as soon as Roman released him, he and another guy dragged Cooter to his feet and helped him stumble out of an emergency exit. Roman had no idea if Emo Guy had taken off when the whole thing started and he didn't care. All he cared about was that all the bikers were gone. But he wasn't stupid enough to assume they wouldn't return once they had the chance to regroup. He turned to the pool table and saw that the guy hadn't even moved during the commotion but awareness had returned to his gaze and even though he lifted his head slightly to look over his shoulder at Roman, he didn't move otherwise. When he dropped his head back into the same exact position, a surge of anger went through Roman as he realized the man fully expected him to take the bikers' place. But his rage dissipated as he eyed the blood on the man's thigh.

Roman sucked in a couple of deep breaths and then reached down to pull the man's jeans up. He closed his hand over the man's upper arm and pulled him upright. Shock went through him as he got his first good look at the man's face and he realized that he wasn't a man...he was a fucking kid. Late teens maybe – twenty at the most.

"Do you need medical attention?" Roman asked as the kid finally reached down to zip up the pants that Roman was still holding up around his slim waist. As soon as he was done, he shook Roman's hand off.

"You shouldn't have done that," was all the kid said as he ran a hand through his light hair. Roman didn't miss how striking the young man was but his affect was so fucked up that Roman didn't know what the hell he should do. Maybe if the kid had begged him to take him home or to the ER or even if he'd shown some sign of being intoxicated or drugged, Roman would have had a place to start but the guy was so disconnected from what had just happened that Roman was clueless. He had a very strong suspicion that if he just left him, he'd fold himself back over the pool table for the next guy who walked into the room. That or he'd go looking for the bikers so they could finish him off.

"Is there someone I can call for you?"

The kid shook his head and then pushed past Roman. But when he swayed and nearly fell, Roman grabbed him by the arm and made a decision that he knew he was going to regret come morning. "What's your name?"

"Hunter," came the disinterested response.

"You have two choices, Hunter. Either you tell me who to call to come get you or you're walking out of here with me right now."

Hunter's mossy green eyes looked around the room as if he was finally seeing it and then his gaze went to the pool table. "You," he finally said but he didn't take his eyes off the pool table until Roman pulled him from the room.

~

"Sit," Roman ordered softly as he locked the hotel room door behind him and switched on the lights. Hunter shuffled past him but instead of sitting on the bed, he stood nervously.

"Um, I should shower before you…before we…"

Agitation went through Roman as it dawned on him what was going through the quiet young man's head. Roman had just assumed Hunter hadn't said a word on the short ride to the hotel because he was still in shock from the episode in the club, but now he was beginning to wonder if it was something else that had had him preoccupied.

"Sit," Roman said again, his eyes pinning Hunter's until he finally shuffled to the bed and sat. He flinched when his ass made contact with the mattress.

Roman shrugged off his suit jacket and used the time it took to hang it up in the small closet to try and get control of his fury. Regret burned liked acid in his belly that he hadn't stepped in the moment he'd walked through that curtain and understood what he was seeing. Since the act of putting his jacket away wasn't cutting it, Roman rolled up his shirt sleeves and then went to the sink that was just outside the bathroom. He could see Hunter's back in the mirror so he didn't need to worry about the young man taking off on him. Not that it looked

6

like that was even on Hunter's mind because he just sat quietly on the bed, his head hung. Roman washed his hands and then splashed some cold water on his face. On the way back towards the bed, he grabbed one of the two chairs sitting by the small table and plopped it down in front of Hunter and sat.

"How old are you?" Roman asked.

Hunter's focus was on Roman's hands and it wasn't until Roman relaxed them and placed them on his thighs that Hunter seemed to jerk out of his daze.

"I'll be twenty in a couple of months."

Jesus fucking Christ.

Roman managed to school his reaction and keep his tone in check when he said, "You were bleeding. I can take you to a hospital to get checked out."

Hunter shook his head. "I'm fine. I just want to get cleaned up."

"If you take a shower, there won't be any evidence if you decide to pursue charges."

Hunter swallowed hard before saying, "It wasn't rape." His voice was so soft that Roman barely heard him.

Roman leaned back in the chair and scrubbed his hands over his face. "Hunter, what I saw in that room...fuck, I don't know what that was but I'm really struggling to accept that it was consensual."

With Hunter's head still hung, Roman didn't see the sheen in his eyes until he dashed at his face with the back of his hand and it came away wet. "It wasn't rape," Hunter repeated. "I...I didn't know there would be that many of them when I said yes."

"Yes to what?"

"The big guy...the one with the long beard."

Cooter. The guy Roman hoped wouldn't be able to take a pain-free breath for a good long while.

"He propositioned you?" Roman suggested.

"Asked if I wanted to play pool. I knew what he meant. His friends were already back there when we got there."

"Did you want it? Did you say no-"

"Look, can we just do this?" Hunter interjected. He finally lifted his eyes and Roman was both surprised and relieved to see that they no longer looked empty. Unfortunately, they were so alive with pain that Roman actually found himself reaching out to touch Hunter before he could think better of it. He managed to catch himself at the last moment and he had to fist his hands on his thighs to keep them from moving. No way in hell could he get more wrapped up in this kid's problems than he already was.

"I'm not going to fuck you, Hunter," he finally said.

More tears filled Hunter's eyes and he shook his head before dropping his gaze once more. "Then can I go?"

"You're not a prisoner," Roman muttered but when Hunter instantly stood to leave, Roman grabbed him gently by the wrist.

"At least get cleaned up before you go. I can give you a ride back to your car when you're ready."

Roman could feel Hunter's pulse thrumming beneath his fingers but he wasn't sure if the young man was afraid of him or something else. The only reason he was even considering the answer being something else was the fact that Hunter wasn't trying to escape his hold, and his pretty lips had parted when he'd sucked in a sharp breath at the contact.

A quick nod was Hunter's answer and when he still didn't move, Roman forced himself to release him. But watching Hunter walk stiffly towards the bathroom brought back the image of him being brutalized and it took all of Roman's self-discipline to stay where he was instead of going back to the club in the hopes of finding the bikers and finishing what he'd started.

≈

Hunter stood quietly as the hot water rained down on his body. Since he was standing directly under the spray, the water hit his head first and then cascaded in clear ribbons down the side of his face and to the bottom of the tub where it pooled and then disappeared down the drain. The sight of blood mixing with the water had Hunter closing his eyes as shame washed through him.

Tonight hadn't gone anything like he'd planned. The stop at *Red's* had been an impulse; a last desperate attempt to stave off the gut-wrenching turmoil of having to go back to the one place in the world he'd hoped to never see again. His initial plan had been to find some liquid courage and then maybe, if he was lucky, a burly cowboy who'd help him forget the shitstorm he was about to walk into. He'd gotten the burly part within a minute of entering the club; it just hadn't come in the package he'd expected. Hunter hadn't even had a chance to order a drink before the biker had propositioned him, so when Hunter had walked into that room, he hadn't even had the benefit of alcohol to dull his senses as he took in the eyes of the hungry men watching him. There'd been a moment when the biker had stepped away from his side to join his friends that Hunter could have used to turn and leave – to walk back to the safety of the crowded dance floor. But as he'd watched the men crudely rubbing themselves in anticipation, a dark, twisted thought had formed in his mind and he'd stepped forward instead of backwards before he could reconsider. And then it was like there was an invisible force guiding him forward.

He'd had no illusions about what the men would do to him so when he was shoved face down on the pool table and felt his pants and underwear being yanked down, he'd bit back the automatic instinct to tell them no and he'd focused on a plaque on the wall near the entrance to the room. It was in the shape of a pool table with two pool sticks crisscrossing over the top of it. Below the racked balls were a dozen gold plates, each with different names on them and what he assumed were years in which the player had won whatever award the plaque represented. He'd just started adding up the individual numbers of the first year listed when biker number one had slammed into him.

Nothing could have prepared him for the excruciating pain that had followed and he'd ended up pressing his mouth down against the stiff green felt so his scream wouldn't be heard throughout the club. He'd had nothing to grip with his hands to act as a counterpoint against the brutal thrusting that had followed but it hadn't mattered because two of the other bikers had grabbed his arms to hold him down. He wasn't sure if they'd done it because he was moving too much or if it had been a preventive measure to keep them from losing their newfound toy but he hadn't really cared either way because the pain had been so intense that he'd been on the verge of passing out. After a while, his body had gone numb and he'd been able to focus on the numbers on the plaque once more and he'd lost track of everything else. At some point his arms had been released but he'd already retreated so far back into his head that he couldn't say for sure when. Time ceased to exist as did the grunts and moans behind him and the ugly words that were hurled at him. There'd been no pain, no men, no pool table.

And then it was over and he was looking into the bluest eyes he'd ever seen – eyes filled with a strange mix of rage and pity.

Hunter forced himself to straighten and reached for the soap. The bikers had been a mistake – he'd been foolish to think they'd somehow be his salvation; that they'd somehow take away the darkness inside of him or miraculously change the part of himself that he'd been trying to deny for nearly a decade. Instead, they'd been another reminder of yet another bad choice. At least he was the only one who had gotten hurt this time.

Hunter made quick work of scrubbing his body clean and then carefully pressed his hand between his cheeks to wash away the little bit of blood that remained. Although he was still hurting, he was hoping what he'd told the mysterious stranger about not needing medical attention would be true. And he absolutely refused to consider what might have happened if the man with the striking blue eyes hadn't intervened. It had been clear that the bikers hadn't cared much about his comfort because they hadn't even bothered to replenish the lube when he'd clearly needed more so they probably wouldn't have even blinked at the idea of tearing him up inside. He could only hope that they'd all used condoms because after the first guy had finished with him, he'd been too far gone to notice and while it seemed like the only thing that had seeped out of his body was his own blood, he couldn't be completely sure.

The temperature of the water began to shift from hot to warm so

Hunter knew his reprieve was over and he shut off the water and climbed out of the shower. He dried himself off with one of the scratchy white towels and reached for his clothes. They smelled of sex and smoke and he decided to forgo the underwear when he saw several small bloodstains on them. He put them in the garbage can next to the toilet and then covered them with several wads of toilet paper. He took a few minutes to towel dry his hair and comb his fingers through it and then steeled himself to face the man in the other room.

He could hear the TV going as he opened the door but when he got to the main part of the room, any words he was about to say died in the back of his throat as his eyes took in the sight of the beautiful stranger. He was leaning against the headboard of the queen bed with a laptop open on his lap. But his eyes were closed and his head was pressed back against the cheap-looking wood. Hunter knew he should just go. It would be easy enough to grab the bus back to the club to get his car. But instead of moving towards the door, he moved closer to the bed and studied his rescuer. He guessed him to be in his early thirties and he had to be at least a couple inches over Hunter's own six-foot frame. He wasn't heavily built like a body builder but he did have wide shoulders and a broad chest that filled out the crisp white dress shirt he was wearing. His black slacks hinted at muscular thighs and were pulled snuggly over his hips. Hunter's whole body drew up tight at the sight of the man's bulge outlined beneath the thin fabric.

Before he could deal with the unwanted bout of lust that burned through him, the guy shifted and his laptop leaned precariously to the right. Hunter managed to catch it before it fell and he carefully put it up on the nightstand next to the bed. He glanced over to see that the man hadn't woken up and then Hunter did something that he knew was a really bad idea. He carefully lowered himself to sit on what little space there was between the man's body and the edge of the mattress. They weren't actually touching but the close proximity gave Hunter the chance to study the man's face in more detail. He had black hair that was shorter on the sides and a bit longer on top. Hunter knew just by looking at it that it would feel like silk between his fingers. A little bit of stubble graced the man's jaw but it was his lips that Hunter kept going back to – they were full and firm looking and there was just the tiniest scar cutting into the upper lip. He was reaching out to touch the scar before he even realized he was doing it and when his fingers made contact with it, the man's eyes slowly opened. But to Hunter's surprise, he didn't move at all. Their eyes met and Hunter's gut clenched at the raw beauty he was seeing. The need to touch, to connect was so overwhelming that his fingers shook with it.

As a tremor of desire went through him, Hunter tried to draw his hand back but the man captured his wrist in a gentle hold and then lowered it to the bed next to his hip. The move forced Hunter forward just the tiniest bit and he knew even as he shifted his weight that he couldn't stop himself from what he was about to do. The man didn't move, didn't even seem to breathe as Hunter leaned in. Their eyes stayed connected until the very last second when Hunter closed them just as he got his first taste of the mysterious man who was quickly turning his world upside down and inside out.

∾

*F*uck, the kid's kiss was like a wet dream. And technically, it was barely even a kiss since all Hunter did was brush their mouths together for the briefest of moments. But when he only drew back a fraction of an inch, Roman's heart seized because he knew it wasn't over.

Roman forced himself to remain completely still as Hunter's lips met his again. He still had a hold of Hunter's wrist and it took every ounce of control he had left to not use it to draw Hunter even closer. The second kiss was as chaste as the first but this time Hunter didn't draw back – instead, he hovered against Roman's lips for just a moment before covering them completely with his. And then one stroke – one fucking stroke of that lush, sweet tongue and Roman snapped. He released Hunter's wrist so he could wrap his hand around the back of Hunter's neck while his other hand settled on Hunter's waist. Hunter gasped at the contact and Roman took advantage and sank his tongue into Hunter's mouth. Hunter's sweet taste exploded against Roman's tongue as he explored Hunter's hot, wet mouth and he swallowed down Hunter's moan as their tongues finally met. Warning bells went off in the back of Roman's head as Hunter's inexperience at kissing quickly became clear but instead of releasing Hunter like he should have, Roman softened his kiss and gently began exploring Hunter's mouth.

Hunter's whole body was stiff but the more Roman kissed him, the more pliant Hunter's muscles became and the younger man began pressing closer and closer. Roman managed to find a shred of sanity still left in his brain and tried to draw back from Hunter's intoxicating mouth but whatever beast he'd awakened in Hunter wouldn't be denied and Hunter's mouth followed his until Roman's head hit the headboard. And suddenly the tables were turned and it was Hunter's tongue searching out every part of his mouth, stroking over every surface. Fire pooled in Roman's gut as Hunter's long fingers brushed over his ear and then clasped the side of his head to hold him still. Insecurity gave way to confidence and Hunter's scorching caresses had Roman's dick standing at full attention.

When they were finally forced to separate so they could grab some much needed air, Hunter drew back and lifted his fingers to his mouth. Roman didn't dare move as he watched a gamut of emotions pass over the other man's features – shock, wonder, dread. The last look said a lot and Roman managed to grab Hunter by the wrist before he could get up and escape like he so clearly wanted to.

"Come lay down for a bit," he murmured when Hunter's gaze finally lifted to meet his. "Just rest – nothing else," Roman said softly.

Hunter looked down at where Roman was still holding on to him and Roman released him so that the young man knew anything he did from that moment forward would be his choice. Hunter looked torn for a moment and then to Roman's surprise, he nodded. But instead of getting up and going around to the other side of the bed, Hunter actually crawled over his body and even though they didn't actually touch, just the sight of Hunter hovering over him even for that split second had Roman stifling a moan. He couldn't ever remember a time when he'd gotten this wound up this fast. Not once. His control in bed was like his calling card but one kiss from a nineteen-year-old kid had tied him up in a haze of desperate need.

Hunter settled on the other side of the bed and put as much space between their bodies as possible. Roman reached for the remote on the nightstand to turn off the TV and then closed his laptop before turning off the light. He didn't bother shifting down to lay flat on the bed because he knew there was no way he was going to fall asleep anytime soon. But at some point he must have because when he woke up the next morning, he was lying on his side in the middle of the bed and there was just an empty space next to him. He ran his fingers over the sheet but it was cold to the touch and he was oddly disappointed that not one shred of evidence of Hunter's presence still remained.

CHAPTER 2

*R*oman drummed his fingers on the steering wheel of his
rental car as he looked to his right. The road didn't look
much different than the one straight ahead but the one to the right
would end up taking him back to his past, to a time in his life he'd
spent years trying to forget. It was a road he'd taken three months
earlier when his fear had overshadowed his need to protect himself
but a part of him had regretted it because all he'd done was open old
wounds that had yet to close. Straight ahead was the safer option –
the option that represented who he was now...a cool, collected busi-
nessman whose only focus was on the deal at hand. Turning right
would be tantamount to granting the half-brother he'd idolized
forgiveness.

He'd been in this exact same spot three months earlier after
learning from his brother's realtor that Gray had bought the mountain cabin a few years earlier. It was information he'd garnered in his
own unique way out of the talkative woman after Gray had seemingly
disappeared from the public eye. As a bestselling author, Gray
Hawthorne had become a fixture in celebrity gossip rags and websites
after he'd sold the rights to three of his well-known detective series
books so they could be made into a movie trilogy. The move had

netted Gray fame and fortune and everything that came with it, including being stalked by the paparazzi who'd ended up snapping a picture of Gray in an intimate embrace with a well-known and supposedly straight actor who was up for the lead role in the films. The picture and rumors behind it had caused endless speculation about Gray and the engaged actor. And while that part wasn't necessarily reason for concern, the fact that Gray hadn't been seen or heard from in the weeks following the scandal had had Roman growing concerned.

Even though he and Gray hadn't spoken in more than three years, Gray's celebrity status had allowed Roman glimpses into his brother's life and when that had all gone dark, Roman had felt a twinge of fear that was entirely unwanted and unexpected. He'd tried ignoring the situation but he'd soon found himself imagining the worst when day after day went by and no one, not even those closest to Gray, had heard from him. So Roman had done some digging and found out that Marina, Gray's realtor, had helped him find him the cabin and, on a whim, Roman had decided to make a stopover in Montana on his way out of the country to see if his wayward relative was there. So when he'd gotten to the intersection that he was currently sitting at, he hadn't hesitated to make the turn and spend the fifteen-minute drive up the mountain to the remote cabin. But nothing had prepared Roman for what he found…nothing.

The day was burned in his brain and likely would be forever. He'd found the cabin without any trouble and had even seen his brother and another man standing outside in the driveway when he'd pulled in. Roman had been so busy mentally preparing himself for what he would say that he hadn't actually taken in Gray's appearance until he was within a few feet of him and when it had finally registered what he was seeing, he'd nearly fallen over.

Cancer.

The one word had played on a seemingly endless loop in his mind as he'd reached out to shake Gray's hand and then the hand of the man he was with. Even though Gray had been wearing a small, knit cap, Roman could still tell that all his hair was gone. If that had been the only change, Roman might have passed it off as a strange style choice but Gray's eyebrows were gone too and he'd lost so much weight that he actually looked smaller than Roman even though they'd been the same size since Roman had been in his twenties. His skin was frighteningly pale and his eyes had looked sunken in their sockets.

Roman had managed to keep his shock in check even once he and Gray were settled in the cabin but when Gray had asked why he was there, Roman had actually felt the lie catch in his throat before he'd spoken. He'd finally managed to tell him that Gray's mother had asked him to check on Gray and he'd been relieved when his brother had accepted the story. He'd kept the visit short but there'd been that final moment when Gray had indirectly invited him to stop by for another visit that Roman had felt his throat close up with emotion and he'd wanted to reach out and touch Gray just to see if the moment was real. How many times as a little boy had he wished for that moment – the one where Gray wanted him around? Where Gray might actually like him? The simple answer was never and that had been what had kept Roman away these past few months with the exception of his one visit to the hospital to check on Gray after he'd been assaulted by a man hunting his lover, Luke.

But his silence hadn't kept Gray from reaching out and every time he did, Roman felt himself wanting to answer the phone when he saw Gray's name flash across the screen or answer his texts with something other than declining his invitation to visit or talk. But he hadn't done either. He'd deleted the voicemails without listening to them and he'd only read the short texts asking him if he had time for a visit or a chat. He didn't watch or read any of the interviews Gray had done to talk about being a cancer survivor, either.

So then why the hell was he having so much trouble deciding which direction to point his rental car in? He could be the bigger man and accept the olive branch Gray was offering. After all, he wasn't the same little boy desperate for someone to tell him things were going to be okay. He didn't need someone to hold his hand while he watched his mother's casket being lowered into the ground or soothe away his fears when he'd walked through the front door of the massive house that would be his new home. So what if Gray was feeling regretful now? Cancer didn't give him a free pass for the disdain he'd shown Roman time and time again. Nor did the fact that Gray had only been seventeen when he'd been introduced to the half-brother he hadn't known existed.

Roman could feel his agitation getting the better of him so he sucked in several deep breaths and focused on the task at hand. He was here for a business opportunity, pure and simple. Whether he pursued it or not had nothing to do with Gray...it was about making money. And even more importantly, it was about making a name for himself which he'd already done a dozen times over. The Hawthorne family had liked pretending he didn't exist but since he'd managed to secure his own position in their social hemisphere, they wouldn't likely be able to forget him any time soon.

He'd already made more money than all of them combined and he would never tire of the look of pure hatred that would pass over his stepmother's features when one of her snooty friends would introduce him as their charitable organization's newest benefactor. But the best part would be that moment when Victoria Hawthorne stood with bated breath as she waited to see if this would be the one time he would reveal their connection to one another; that he was, in fact, more of a Hawthorne than she would ever be. And then there'd be those few seconds when he played dumb and merely shook her icy hand and murmured a polite greeting that Victoria's apprehension would show because she knew she was at his mercy this time around.

Until the day he'd take it all the way and reveal all of the Hawthorne family secrets.

So fixing what had been broken between himself and Gray so long ago served no purpose. He'd needed a brother when he was ten. At thirty-two he didn't need anyone. Not one goddamn soul.

With that thought in mind, Roman wrapped his fingers around the steering wheel and pushed down on the gas. He'd come to Dare for one reason and one reason only and it had nothing to do with re-visiting a part of his past that just didn't matter anymore.

~

*R*oman wasn't particularly surprised to find that the small town of Dare made Missoula look like a gleaming metropolis. It was what he'd expected considering the town's small population and remote location. It was also what would make the resort he was considering building all the more successful. After all, the men and women who made up his clientele would be making the trek to the backwoods of Montana so they could "rough" it and a town like Dare would add authenticity. Of course, "roughing it" to people who had every conceivable luxury money could buy meant only having six bathrooms in their seven bedroom homes. And although Dare was a cute enough little spot with its town center surrounding a small, lush park complete with a flock of ducks, it would positively explode with economic success if he ended up moving forward with the deal. It was a fact that the realtor, who also happened be the mayor of Dare, handling the land buy hadn't missed because he'd been positively drooling ever since Roman's assistant had called him to arrange an examination of the nearly ten-thousand-acre spot that was part of the overall stretch of land he was considering just south of the town.

Stepping away from his car, Roman glanced at his watch and then headed towards the small realty office at the end of the block. There were a few people out and about and every single one sent him a polite greeting of some sort. By the time he reached the single glass door that read *Greene Realty* on it, he was actually missing the rude L.A. commuters who clogged the busy sidewalks.

The first thing he saw when he opened the door was a petite, blonde haired woman at one of three old desks against the side wall. The small space was unbearably hot so the poor woman had a huge fan blowing on her. The rattling fan blades prevented her from hearing his entry so when he reached her desk and cleared his throat to get her attention, she jerked in her chair and let out a startled gasp.

"My apologies," he murmured as she clutched her chest. Her recovery was slow and she actually ended up knocking her ceramic

19

mug to the ground. It shattered and she let out another cry of distress when coffee splashed over his shoes.

"Oh dear Lord, I'm so sorry," she said hurriedly as she began yanking tissues from the dispenser on her desk. She was on the ground before he could even say anything and to his shock, she actually ended up kneeling in the spilled coffee and began dabbing at his shoes before doing anything else.

"Ma'am," he said quickly as he reached for her elbow to help her up.

"Grace, do you have those MLS numbers I asked for!" a heavy voice shouted from a back room somewhere.

The woman at his feet stiffened in his hold and her wide eyes flew from his face to her desk.

"Grace!"

"It's fine," Roman said softly as he pulled the woman to her feet and took the handful of tissues from her.

"I'll be right back, Mr…"

"Blackwell. Roman Blackwell."

The woman's eyes widened even farther and her mouth opened enough for another small gasp to escape her lips. She began wringing her hands as she shook her head and then looked at the mess on the floor. Her distress was clear as day but before he could even say anything, he heard her name bellowed yet again.

"It's okay, go," he said.

The woman he could only assume was Grace snatched a piece of paper from the printer on her desk and then rushed towards the doorway against the far wall. He couldn't hear her voice as he bent down to clean up the remnants of the mug but he did hear a loud curse and then the man seemed to have enough sense to lower his voice because everything was muffled after that. Several long seconds passed and as Roman was in the process of wiping up the last of the coffee, he heard the man say, "Grace, what is this?"

Roman glanced up to see a man in his late fifties leaning heavily on a pair of crutches. Grace was standing just behind him, her face ashen. He saw the man send her a sharp look and then she was rushing across the room and taking over the task of cleaning up the coffee.

"Mr. Blackwell, it is such a pleasure," the man said as he made his way across the room. His tone was bright and cheerful as he added, "I do apologize for my wife. Ironically, grace was never one of her stronger qualities."

Anger went through Roman at the degrading comment but he bit his tongue. He was here for a deal, that was it. Last night had been a reminder of what happened when he was foolish enough to get caught up in someone else's problems. Your whole world got fucked up by one kiss...

"Mr. Greene," Roman said as he forced himself to step past the woman on the floor. He crossed the room to shake the man's extended hand and couldn't help but want to wipe his palm on his pants afterwards.

"Malcom Greene," the man responded brightly, his too white teeth making his thin lips look small. "Welcome to Dare."

Roman didn't respond and was pleased to see Malcom stiffen. Good, he already had the man on edge. Ten seconds to get control...a new personal best.

"Well, as you can see, I've had a bit of an accident," Malcom stuttered as he motioned to his ankle which was wrapped in an Ace bandage. He fell silent, clearly waiting for Roman to inquire about his injury but when Roman said nothing, he shifted his weight on the crutches. He guessed Malcom to be around 6 feet tall with a heavier than average build but he looked fit for his age. His brown hair didn't have even a hint of silver in it so he likely colored it and his clothes were on the higher end in terms of quality. Interestingly enough, his wife's clothes looked a decade out of date and she wore no makeup. Her hair was pulled back into a simple braid.

"I sprained it," Malcom laughed awkwardly. "Stepped off the curb wrong if you can believe it."

Roman ignored the man's attempts to draw him into chit chat and instead said, "You assured me I'd be able to examine the property today."

Malcom froze for a moment and then his face flushed as he nodded frantically.

"Yes, yes, you will. My son-" Malcom's attention shifted to his wife. "Where is he?" he snapped.

"He'll be back any second. He went to the pharmacy to get your aspirin, remember?"

Malcom's face got even redder as he glared at his wife and a chill went through Roman as he wondered what exactly the man would have done if he hadn't been there. Malcom's eyes shifted back to him.

"My son will be able to show you the property – he knows it like the back of his hand," Malcom said quickly.

Before Roman could make the man squirm even more, he heard the door behind him open and when he glanced over his shoulder, his whole body seized up with a mix of excitement and dread when he saw the shock of blond hair.

"Dad, they were out of aspirin so I got you some-"

The young man's words died off as he lifted his head and his surprised green gaze met Roman's. But unlike the night before, this time his eyes were anything but empty. There was only one thing in them as he glanced from Roman to his father and then back to Roman. Fear. Absolute and total fear.

Malcom's voice barely even registered when he said, "Mr. Blackwell, this is my son, Hunter."

~

*N*o. The word kept growing louder and louder in Hunter's mind as he struggled to take in enough air to keep from passing out. His chest actually hurt as he took in the sapphire eyes that refused to release him from their hold.

God, if he'd seen those eyes when he'd woken up this morning, he never would have been able to force himself out of the man's bed. Hell, it had been bad enough that he'd ended up pressed up against the guy's broad chest with his nose buried against his neck. The temptation to swipe his tongue over the corded muscles had been so profound that he'd actually done it before he could stop himself. And he'd gotten hard instantly. Luck had been on his side because the man hadn't woken up then or even when Hunter had disengaged himself from the strong arms that had been wrapped around him. Hunter had let himself have one last look at the guy before he'd left the hotel room, his regret that he would never see him again weighing heavily in his gut.

Hunter was helpless to tear his eyes away from the man and he was actually moving forward towards him as if being pulled by some invisible string when a sharp pain radiating through his hand stopped him. The end of his father's crutch hit his fingers for a second time, knocking the small paper bag in his hand to the ground. He managed to turn his head long enough to see his father's dark scowl and a tremor of fear went through him when he saw his father's mouth moving but couldn't hear what he was saying. God, how long had he been standing there staring at the guy?

And then the man was standing in front of him, his big hand closing over Hunter's. He could feel the callouses that had felt so good against the back of his neck last night when the guy had held him still for his kiss.

"Roman," the man said softly as he gently shook Hunter's hand that was still stinging from his father's attempt to get his attention.

"Hunter," Hunter responded as relief coursed through him. The guy wasn't going to reveal that they knew each other...Roman. His name was Roman. Hunter's relief was short-lived as Roman's finger suddenly stroked over the inside of his wrist. It felt so good that Hunter actually shuddered and he let out a soft sigh. Roman must have noticed because his gaze fell to Hunter's mouth and heat filled his gaze.

"So as I was saying, Mr. Blackwell, Hunter will take you up to the property to have a look around and then you and I can meet back here to go over the specifics."

Hunter was glad when Roman finally released his hand but was surprised when he didn't look at his father when he said, "I intend to do a thorough inspection of the land, Mr. Greene. If and when I'm ready to talk specifics" – Roman finally glanced over his shoulder at Hunter's father but his expression was steely and unflinching – "I'll let you know."

The look of muted outrage on his father's face was both frightening and thrilling at the same time. Few men spoke to Malcom Greene with such blatant disrespect and the ones who did usually ended up regretting it. His father's status as mayor probably didn't seem like much to a man like the one standing before him but Malcom Greene's hard-nose, conservative political views had managed to make him some powerful friends in powerful places.

"We should go," Hunter murmured as he leaned down to grab the discarded bag off the floor. He leaned past Roman to hand the bag to his father and instantly regretted it because his body brushed up against Roman's for the briefest of moments. He noticed his mother standing near her desk, her hands clenched around what looked like a bunch of wadded up tissues and she sent him a quick smile that didn't quite reach her eyes. He ignored the urge to go to her since that would just set his father off even more. And he knew it wouldn't make a bit of difference…it never did.

Hunter didn't miss his father's warning look as he turned and hurried towards the front door. He could feel Roman's presence behind him but didn't turn around. As soon as they reached the sidewalk, Hunter looked up and down the quiet street. It had been pure luck that he hadn't run into anyone he knew on his walk to the pharmacy across the city square and a borderline miracle that the clerk behind the register was an older woman he'd never seen before. But he knew his luck wouldn't hold out for long so he quickly searched out Roman's car and basically ran to the passenger side. He didn't miss the strange look Roman shot him as he found his keys and then pressed the button on the key fob to unlock it. He practically jumped into the car and secured his seatbelt before dropping his head so that anybody walking by wouldn't see his face. The car's tinted side windows were a blessing in disguise.

"You okay?" Roman asked once he'd settled in the driver's seat.

Hunter managed a nod since being closed up in the small space with the man whose presence was playing havoc with all his senses wasn't making it any easier to relax. "Um, if you want to back out and go that way," Hunter said as he pointed in the direction he was talking about. He waited but when the car remained exactly where it was, he looked up and swallowed hard when he saw Roman studying him.

"We need to talk about what happened last night."

CHAPTER 3

"Nothing…nothing happened," Hunter sputtered.

"So that wasn't your tongue shoved down my throat last night?" Roman asked with amusement.

Color flooded Hunter's cheeks and Roman was reminded again by how innocent the younger man seemed to be, the previous night's events at the club notwithstanding.

"I get it," Roman said with a sigh. "You don't want your parents to know you're gay-"

"I'm not," Hunter interrupted. "I'm not…what you said."

"Fine, bi then."

"No!" Hunter nearly yelled and then his eyes shifted back to the door to his father's office. Shit, the kid was as deep in the closet as he could be. "Can we just go?" Hunter asked quietly, his eyes once again on his lap.

Roman started the car but didn't put it into gear. The more he remained silent and unmoving, the more agitated Hunter became. The way the guy's eyes darted up and down the sidewalk had Roman wondering if he was hiding from someone.

"Roman, please," Hunter whispered.

It was the first time Hunter had said his name and it turned

Roman on more than it should. But his need for answers was actually stronger than his lust and he said, "If you're not gay, what were you doing in that club last night?"

Hunter stiffened at the question but didn't answer. But within seconds, his jumpy gaze settled on a young woman walking down the sidewalk in their direction. She had yet to notice Hunter.

"Okay," Hunter said hurriedly. "I'll tell you if we can just go now."

Roman should have felt more of a sense of satisfaction but all he felt like was an ass for using Hunter's need to remain unnoticed against him. He put the car in reverse and then drove in the direction Hunter had told him. Once they had made it to the outskirts of town, he glanced at Hunter expectantly. Hunter wasn't cowering anymore but he still looked tense.

"Why the club, Hunter?" Roman asked.

"I didn't know what kind of place it was," Hunter responded lamely.

"Let's say I'm willing to suspend belief long enough to believe that bullshit - are you telling me the sight of all those men groping each other on the dance floor didn't give you a clue?"

Hunter remained stubbornly silent, his eyes focused on the scenery flying by.

Roman shook his head in agitation and reminded himself it was none of his business. He was here to up his own net worth, not help some confused kid admit he preferred dick to pussy. So he had no idea what possessed him to ask, "Last night with those bikers – was that your first time?"

Still no response but Roman didn't miss the way Hunter dashed at his eyes.

"Look, if it was about needing it rough because you like pain or something, there're places you can go for that...there are guys who can give you what you need without putting you in danger."

Roman felt sick even mentioning the idea to Hunter since the thought of some man – any man – inflicting pain on the young man's body to help him get off had Roman's protective instincts firing on all cylinders.

27

"It wasn't about that," Hunter suddenly whispered so softly that Roman barely heard him.

"Then what-"

"I went there to prove I wasn't...I wasn't what you said."

Jesus, the poor kid couldn't even say the word gay?

"And did it?" Roman asked gently. Hunter still hadn't looked at him even once since they'd left town.

"Watching those men dancing together, kissing, touching..." Hunter's voice dropped off.

"Turned you on," Roman supplied.

Hunter nodded. "And then that biker came up to me and I didn't... I wasn't..." Hunter struggled to find the right words and this time Roman remained quiet. "I thought that if I was with someone like him then maybe it wouldn't be true."

A chill went through Roman as understanding dawned. The realization was so disturbing that he had to pull the car over to the side of the road. His fingers bit into the steering wheel as he forced himself to dispassionately ask, "And when you followed him into the pool room and saw the other men?"

But Hunter didn't answer him and Roman didn't really need him to. Roman started counting in his head in a desperate effort to remain calm as he tried to accept what Hunter had put himself through just to prove to himself that he wasn't attracted to men.

"I didn't know it would be like that..." Hunter choked out and Roman saw silent tears begin to slip down his face. "I knew it would hurt but I didn't expect..."

"Did you tell them to stop?"

Hunter shook his head. "I figured the pain would eventually go away. And it did. I didn't feel anything anymore...didn't hear anything, didn't see anything."

Tears continued to dampen Hunter's skin but Roman was at a loss as to what to do or say so he just reached his hand out and closed it over one of Hunter's where it was resting on his trembling thigh. Hunter shifted his hand but it wasn't to release Roman's – it was to link their fingers together. The move had something loosening and breaking free deep inside of Roman's chest.

"It was a mistake – I knew it as soon as the first guy...but I kept hoping maybe it worked," Hunter admitted as he began wiping at his face with the sleeve of his free arm. His voice kept cracking as he spoke and it was hard for Roman to understand his next words but when he did, he felt his heart clench.

"And then you kissed me."

~

*H*unter missed the warmth of Roman's fingers even though he knew he shouldn't. Roman hadn't said a word after Hunter's admission – he'd just pulled his hand free of Hunter's so he could put the car in gear. Forcing his eyes from where Roman's thick, strong fingers were wrapped around the steering wheel, Hunter clenched his hands together in his lap.

"Take the next right," he murmured.

"Your dad said you're familiar with the property," Roman finally said after he'd taken the turn.

"I practically grew up on it," he answered and a warmth spread through him as the memories started to slowly come back one by one. "It belonged to my grandparents."

Roman seemed surprised by that. "Do they still own it?"

"Gran does. Pops died a few years back."

"You know why your grandmother is selling it?"

"I didn't know she was," Hunter admitted. He'd only found out the news himself this morning and while he'd been stunned to hear that his grandmother was letting go of the land where she and his grandfather had planned to someday live out their golden years, he'd known better than to question his father about it.

"She and Pops started building a little cabin out here but he died before they could finish it." Hunter didn't add that he'd spent more nights than he could count in the small shell of a structure just so he wouldn't have to go home. His parents had always believed his lie that he was hanging out with friends and fortunately they'd never thought to check up on him – probably because it had been the only time in his life he'd ever been brave enough to lie to his father's face.

"This is it," Hunter murmured once Roman's car cleared the small hill. He glanced at Roman to see his reaction to the breathtaking view but other than a slight narrowing of the eyes, Roman didn't react at all. Hunter turned his attention back to the wide swath of rolling land in front of him and drew in a deep breath. Unlike much of the dry, dusty, perpetually brown grassy areas that surrounded Dare, Gran and Pops' meadow was a lush green ocean of grass and was dotted with a rainbow of wildflowers as far as the eye could see. The breeze blowing through the valley made the long grass look like it was dancing and Hunter could almost feel the cool, slightly rough texture of the blades stroking his fingers.

Within minutes, the paved road turned into a dirt one and Roman slowed the car considerably. Hunter lowered his window and drew in the scent of cool air and damp earth and then folded his arms on the window frame and dropped his head down and closed his eyes. He could still remember the first time his grandfather had shown him this place. The memory was almost as clear as the last time he'd been here with Pops.

Hunter didn't notice that the car had stopped at first and when he finally did, he turned and saw that Roman was studying him intently.

"What?" Hunter asked curiously.

Roman just shook his head.

"The lake's still about a mile up," Hunter murmured as he felt that familiar, aching feeling deep in his gut that he was quickly coming to expect around this man.

"When was the last time you were here?" Roman asked softly.

"It's been a while."

"How long?"

"Eighteen months. The day of my graduation."

The day everything had changed…the day *he'd* changed everything by uttering one lie to protect another.

"This place means a lot to you," Roman said softly.

Hunter couldn't help but smile. "You remember that feeling you always got on the last day of school...that excitement knowing that there was just that last single bell standing between you and a whole summer of freedom?" Hunter looked back out the window. "Coming here was like that. Every time."

"But not this time," Roman observed.

Hunter let out a little laugh. Did nothing get past the man? "I guess there are some things not even this place can fix," he whispered. Swallowing hard, Hunter forced himself to say, "We should get going. My dad will be expecting us and there's still a lot left to see."

Roman must've decided to take pity on him because the car started moving again. "What do you plan on doing with the land?" Hunter asked.

"Building a resort."

A sick feeling went through Hunter as he realized what that meant. "So you'd put up a hotel or something?"

"More likely a combination of individual residences and a lodge of some kind."

"Individual residences? Like cabins?"

Roman actually chuckled. "No, actual houses."

"A lot of the property is too rugged for houses," Hunter murmured.

"They'd be constructed down here in the valley. The lake would be the central focus but we'd offer a wide range of amenities and activities."

Disappointment tore through Hunter. "What kind?"

"Cross country and downhill skiing and snowmobile trails in the winter, off-roading, hiking, horseback riding and water sports in the summer."

Everything he loved about this place would be gone – buried underground by a back hoe or driven away by the hustle and bustle of tourists who didn't give a shit about what this land had meant to him.

"You can't-" Hunter heard himself saying but he managed to cut the words off mid-sentence.

"Can't what?" Roman asked as he pulled the car to a stop near the trail head that led to the lake.

31

"Nothing," Hunter whispered. He felt fingers brushing against his arm but he managed to escape the touch by climbing out of the car. Because he knew that if Roman touched him even once, Hunter would end up begging him not to take this last reminder of who he'd once been away too.

≈

*R*oman watched Hunter stride up the small incline towards the trail that disappeared into a line of huge trees. God, he felt like he'd just told the kid he was going to skin his puppy or something. He had no doubt Hunter was horrified by the prospect of what would happen to his grandparents' land in order to turn it into a world class luxury hideaway. To his own surprise, Roman had actually felt a niggle of doubt when they'd crested the small rise and the lush valley in all its glory had come into view. With the mountains as a backdrop, the sight was truly breathtaking and if Roman hadn't been preoccupied with Hunter, he would have stopped the car just to take in the view himself. But he'd still been reeling from Hunter's simple admission about their kiss. And then he'd seen the brief moment of pure bliss on Hunter's face when he'd seen the valley and it had nearly stolen Roman's breath.

God, he needed to get a fucking grip. He was here to figure out if he could pull off another deal that would pad his and his investors' bank accounts, not worry about the tender emotions of some barely legal kid who was clearly dealing with a mess of shit that Roman had zero interest in getting involved in. Besides, maybe Hunter needed to see how the real world worked.

"Yeah, right," Roman muttered as he got out of the car. If the events of last night were anything to go by, Hunter needed a lot more than Roman would ever be able to teach him. Knowing that the young man had actually decided the way to not be gay anymore was by subjecting himself to a brutal gang rape had had Roman wanting to both hold and strangle the kid at the same time. And then he'd wanted to turn around and drive back to town so he could tear Hunter's father a new one because it was clear from the man's domineering behavior that he was likely the one Hunter was hiding his true self from.

It took less than a minute to catch up to Hunter because the younger man was waiting at a fork in the trailhead. He was shifting his weight back and forth but it was the way his hand was stroking over his front pocket that had Roman taking notice. He hadn't noticed before but he could tell there was something in Hunter's pocket by the slight bulge in the loose fabric but he couldn't make out what it was.

"This way leads up the mountain," Hunter murmured as he pointed to the trail heading west. Roman followed him down the trail to the right and within minutes it began to widen and the trees became less dense. The lake was much larger than Roman expected and he could see several small streams emptying into the clear water along the west side – runoff from the mountain he realized. The east side of the lake had a really nice beach that would be perfect for anyone willing to brave the cool, blue water.

"Look," Hunter murmured and Roman felt his dick harden to painful proportions as Hunter brushed his arm to get his attention. He followed the direction Hunter was pointing in and saw a bald eagle sitting high in the branches of a tree just a couple hundred feet away.

"That's Fred," Hunter said.

"Fred?"

The eagle suddenly took flight and then dove towards the water. A few seconds later it was flapping its giant wings as its claws closed over something in the water and then it was airborne again, an enormous fish clutched between its talons. Roman tracked the bird to the other side of the lake where he was able to make out another eagle sitting near a nest.

"And that's Ethel."

Roman chuckled and warmth sifted through him when Hunter did too. "Gran has a thing for *I Love Lucy*."

"What about Lucy and Ricky?"

"Let's hope we don't run into them."

"Why not? Are they bears or something?"

Another laugh.

"No, skunks."

"You're shitting me," Roman muttered.

To his amazement, Hunter laughed even louder. "No. Gran found Lucy when she was just a baby – her mom and brothers and sisters were killed by a coyote so Gran took care of Lucy till she was old enough to make it on her own. Every time Pops and I would come out here, she'd show up and follow us around like a dog which was just fine since she never sprayed us. But then one day there's another skunk with her. Pops didn't realize she wasn't alone until it was too late."

Roman smiled but he wasn't sure if it was because of the story or because of its effect on Hunter. A wide smile split his lip as he said, "I was only twelve so I couldn't drive us back so Gran had to come get us. She showed up in their neighbor's truck and was pulling a horse trailer behind it. She made Pops ride home in it so he wouldn't stink up the car."

Hunter began walking and Roman fell in step next to him. "I could hear him bellowing even from way up front in the truck. He had to shave his beard off to get the stink out. Cursed Lucy and Ricky every time he saw them after that."

"Did you spend a lot of time out here with him?"

Hunter sobered and Roman instantly regretted the question.

"We'd camp out here most weekends. He'd bring me out here after school during the week to go fishing but it was harder to get away as I got older."

"How come?"

Hunter glanced at him, his emerald eyes heavy. "My dad wanted me to focus on other things. School, sports."

"What did you want?"

Hunter stopped walking all together and looked at Roman as if he'd grown two heads. His reaction was answer enough and he wasn't surprised when Hunter said, "I wanted to make him proud."

Roman merely nodded because he couldn't fault Hunter for the admission. How many times had Roman tried his best to impress Victoria and Walt with a stellar report card or some academic award? When that hadn't worked, he'd gone the route of athletics to seek their approval. A cold reality hit him as he realized if his father and Victoria had even shown him the tiniest scrap of attention for all his efforts, he could have easily ended up like the young man before him.

"This is the cabin," Hunter said as he motioned over his shoulder before winding his way through some trees to a small clearing where a weathered looking structure sat. It was just a foundation made of stone and a few logs that had been placed on top of each other to form a large rectangular space. Roman could tell the logs themselves had been taken straight from the land because they looked rustic and natural, not artificial.

"Did you and he work on this together?" Roman asked as he trailed his fingers along the bark free wood.

Hunter nodded. "We started on it about a month before he died."

"What happened to him?"

Hunter came to a stop in the center of the space. "It took us all weekend just to get these logs in place. It was Memorial Day weekend so I didn't have school that Monday so I begged him to stay one more night. I knew my dad would be pissed because he had this barbecue planned in the town square and I was supposed to be there to serve food to people but Pops talked him into it. We spent the rest of the day fishing and Gran came out and we ate the fish we'd caught. Gran didn't like camping so she went home and Pops and I put our sleeping bags here," Hunter said as he motioned to the floor. "He was so excited to be spending the first night in his and Gran's new cabin. He talked for hours about how he was going to build a room for me and maybe when I was older we'd build a place for me and my family to stay in when we came for a visit. Next morning, I couldn't wake him up. I...I had to tell Gran he was gone."

"How old were you?" Roman asked gently.

"Fifteen."

"I'm sorry, Hunter."

Hunter shook his head. "I think he knew."

"Knew what?"

"That I wasn't normal."

Roman wanted to tell Hunter he was normal but he kept his mouth shut so Hunter would continue.

"Pops never used the words girl or wife when he was talking to me about stuff. It was always, 'Hunter, you meet someone special yet?' or 'When you meet someone at school, you be sure to bring them home so your Gran and I can make sure they're good enough for you, okay?' *Someone, they, them*," Hunter said softly.

His eyes finally lifted to meet Roman's and Roman didn't miss the spark of hope he saw there. "You think maybe that was his way of telling me he knew? That he was okay with it?"

"Yeah, Hunter, I do."

Hunter nodded his head slightly and then looked around the cabin once more before he straightened and seemed to shake free of the moment. "If you want, we can keep going around the lake or we can double-back and hike up the mountain a bit. There's a nice hot springs up there."

"Hot springs," Roman said as he followed Hunter back towards the lake. He glanced up to see that Frank the eagle was still sitting protectively near his mate who was picking at the fish. Next time he'd have to remember to bring binoculars so he could see the birds up close.

"Did you keep coming here after you lost your grandfather?" Roman asked as he caught up to Hunter.

"Yeah."

"By yourself?"

Hunter hesitated. "My dad and I would come up here once in a while to go hunting but he gave up on it after a while. Said I took all the fun out of it 'cause I always cried like a girl every time he shot something."

"And after?"

Hunter's eyes shot to him and he could see the indecision there. Finally, he nodded. "I tried working on the cabin at first but I didn't really know what I was doing without Pops."

"What about your grandmother? Friends?"

"Gran hasn't really been back here since Pops died. Maybe that's why she's looking to sell. Friends? I knew they'd turn it into a place to party or get high."

"Wasn't there anyone you wanted to share it with?" Roman hedged.

A small smile tugged at Hunter's lips. "Is that your way of asking if I had a girlfriend?"

Roman chuckled. "I suppose it was."

"There were girls who were friends but nothing ever serious."

Hunter didn't expound on the subject and Roman didn't press because it wasn't any of his business. But if Hunter's inexperienced kiss was anything to go by, he doubted Hunter's situation in the girl-friend department had changed much over the years.

"Why resorts?" Hunter suddenly asked as they reached the spot where the trail split.

It was on the tip of Roman's tongue to brush Hunter off with some flippant response about money but then he remembered the look in Hunter's eyes when he'd asked about whether or not Roman thought his grandfather might have known about his issues with his sexuality.

"My mother," he began.

~

*H*unter felt Roman's arm brush against his as they were forced to walk closer together as the trail narrowed. He supposed it would be just as easy for him to move in front of Roman or behind him but he really wanted to see the man as he spoke.

"Your mother?" Hunter prodded when Roman fell silent.

"She was always flipping through magazines and tearing out the ads for resorts. The really fancy ones, you know? White sand beaches, perfect pools with waterfalls and empty lounge chairs lining the edge. Every month she'd buy a couple travel magazines and she'd show them to me at night instead of reading a bedtime story."

"How old were you?" Hunter asked with a small laugh.

"Seven. But I didn't mind because she'd turn the whole thing into an adventure and make up stories about the things we'd see and do. I knew more about world destinations than I did about Curious George or Marmaduke."

"Who?" Hunter asked.

Roman sent him a 'you've got to be kidding me' look and then gave him a gentle shove when Hunter couldn't prevent the knowing chuckle from escaping his mouth.

"Did you ever get to go on any of your grand adventures?"

Roman shook his head. "My mom was a waitress so there wasn't a lot of extra money lying around."

"How about after you started building them?"

The tension in Roman's frame had Hunter wishing he could take back the question. There was only one thing that put that look of loss in a man's eye.

"How old were you when you lost her?"

"Ten," Roman said quietly.

"Sorry," Hunter whispered and he couldn't stop himself from reaching out to run his hand down Roman's upper arm. The move was supposed to be about comfort but all it did was spike up the dull ache of desire that had been lurking in Hunter's belly since the moment he'd laid eyes on Roman in his father's office this morning. And from the way Roman glanced at his hand and then his mouth, he knew Roman was feeling it too.

Hunter drew his hand back and put as much distance between their bodies that the trail would allow. "Where did you build your first resort?"

"California. I'd already bought a couple of old warehouses and turned them into condos when I saw this old hotel for sale in Big Sur. The two investors I'd brought into the project wanted to tear it down and build something from scratch but there was something about it… it was like it was more than just a building. Like it had a soul."

"Did you tear it down?"

Roman shook his head. "I bought out the investors and fixed it up instead. Rooms sold out before the doors even opened and there's a two year waiting list to stay there."

"Wow, I'll bet it's beautiful."

"It is. Everything's top of the line. Top chefs, state of the art rooms, every amenity you could think of…" Roman said proudly.

"Just think, there's probably some kid and his mom tearing out pictures of your resorts and making up stories about them."

Roman stiffened and all the pride that had been in his gaze disappeared instantly. He stopped in the middle of the trail and just stood there looking…God, he looked devastated.

"Roman, I'm sorry…I didn't mean anything by that."

"It's okay," Roman said woodenly. "You know what, maybe we should head back. I've got some calls I need to return."

"Roman-" Hunter said as he grabbed Roman's hand before he could turn and head back down the trail.

"And you should probably be taking it easy anyway. You're bound to still be sore after last night."

The reminder was like a slap in the face and Hunter felt any lingering warmth inside of him disappear and he dropped Roman's hand.

"Yeah, you're probably right," Hunter managed to get out as he reached into his pocket to run his fingers over the items there. His anxiety eased enough that he was able to keep it together as he stepped back from Roman and then led the way back towards the car.

CHAPTER 4

*H*unter's relief at escaping the uncomfortable silence in Roman's car was short-lived because his father was on him the second he walked through the door to his parents' office.

"Where is he?" his father snapped as he craned his neck to try and see the front door. "Is he coming in?"

"Um, no, he said he had some calls to make," Hunter murmured as he hurried past the reach of his father's crutches and went to drop a kiss on his mother's cheek.

"Hi," he murmured.

His mother paused only briefly in her typing but whatever she might have said was drowned out by his father's bellow.

"Boy, get over here and tell me what happened!"

Hunter saw his mother flinch at the outburst and her eyes quickly dropped back to the computer screen. A tug of disappointment went through Hunter at the move but he pushed it away and forced himself to walk back to the desk his father was sitting at.

"Well?" his father shouted.

"He didn't say much," Hunter admitted which was mostly the truth since the brief conversations he'd had with Roman hadn't been about what he actually thought about the land.

"God, I knew you'd fuck this up," his father snorted. "You were gone less than two hours – no way you showed him everything!"

"His calls-"

"Were a fucking ploy! Probably to get away from you and your sniveling."

Sadly, Hunter suspected his father was right. Roman's excuse had sounded pretty lame and then he'd thrown in that last remark about the night before...

A stapler bouncing off his chest ripped Hunter from his thoughts and he automatically stepped back when he saw his father reach for his crutches to pull himself upright. "You better pray he calls me!" his father snarled as he got in Hunter's space.

Hunter managed to stand his ground and nod but he dropped his eyes since he knew it was the fastest way to diffuse his father's anger. Well, one of the fastest ways. "He will, Dad. He did...he did mention something about how refreshing it was to be working with a realtor who knew what he was doing for a change."

The trick worked because his father's chest puffed out somewhat. His father finally eased back a bit and Hunter murmured, "I thought I'd head back to school tonight. I've got a paper due on Monday."

"No," his father interjected. "You're not going anywhere. If Blackwell wants to see the property again, you'll need to show him. Dr. Meyers says I'm out of commission for another week at least."

The idea of spending even another day in Dare had Hunter saying, "I can't afford to miss any classes-"

His father's palm cracked against his cheek before he could even finish the statement. "You will do as I fucking say, you hear me?" Another slap followed and Hunter bit back the tears that threatened and nodded quickly.

"Now get in back and finish cleaning out that storeroom."

Hunter stepped back from his father and turned to head towards the back room. A glance at his mother showed that she was still focused on the computer screen, her thin fingers moving tirelessly over the keyboard. He wasn't surprised that she didn't even look at him once as he passed.

41

~

*H*unter enjoyed the soothing sound of an owl hooting somewhere nearby as he tossed another piece of wood onto the fire before laying back down on his sleeping bag. Even with the temperature dropping into the mid-forties, he didn't regret his decision to spend the night at the lake for even a second. The cloudless sky meant he'd sleep under a blanket of stars tonight and the sound of the forest coming alive as the nocturnal wildlife went about their lives was a hundred times better than listening to his father rant and rave about whatever trivial thing he'd decided was unacceptable in the world that he thought only revolved around himself.

It hadn't taken much to convince his father to let him leave the house to hang out with "friends." For some reason it had always been some kind of badge of honor for his father that Hunter had managed to become one of the more popular kids in his high school. As long as Hunter hung out with the kids his father deemed "the cool ones," Hunter was golden. But if he'd dared gravitate towards the wrong ones, his father had never hesitated to let him know it in the only way he knew how. And for the most part, Hunter had managed to follow the unspoken rule…until the one day when his inner need had overshadowed his fear. One weak moment when he'd given in to the desperate craving he couldn't ignore.

It took Hunter a moment to realize the owl and all the other inhabitants of the forest around him had gone silent and he automatically sat up and reached for the rifle sitting next to his sleeping bag. It wasn't unheard of for bears to show up at the lake in search of food but he would have expected his fire to keep them at bay for tonight. A light off in the distance flashed through the trees and fear tripped through Hunter at the thought that his father had finally discovered his sanctuary. Fuck, there'd be hell to pay if he had.

"Hunter?"

The sound of Roman's deep voice had Hunter climbing to his feet with a mixture of excitement and trepidation.

"Over here," he called as he began walking towards the flash of light. It suddenly went out completely and he heard a muffled curse. "Just stay put, I'm coming to you," Hunter said as he picked his way through the trees. It took just minutes to reach Roman who was stuffing what looked like his phone into his pocket.

"Forgot to charge it," he muttered as he lifted his hand to keep the light from the flashlight Hunter was holding from hitting him square in the eyes.

"Sorry," Hunter murmured as he dropped the light so it was pointing at their feet. "What are you doing here?" He could see Roman was holding something bundled in his arms.

"You mind if we talk by the fire," Roman responded.

Hunter could tell Roman's coat wasn't heavy enough for the elements so he led him back to the fire and pointed to his sleeping bag. He sat down next to Roman and bit back a groan when their bodies brushed as he reached for another log to toss on the fire.

"You expecting company?" Roman asked as he glanced at the gun Hunter didn't realize he was still holding.

"Bears come down here every once in a while," he answered as he put the gun down. "What are you doing here, Roman?"

"Hell if I know," Roman muttered as he began unfolding the blankets that had been bunched up in his arms. Hunter helped him spread the blankets over both their laps. He could tell from the material that they were the kind of blankets you'd find in a cheap motel.

"Are these from your hotel?"

"I don't know if the *Dusty Spur* qualifies as a hotel but the owner was quick to reassure me it was Dare's finest accommodations," Roman answered.

"It's Dare's only accommodations," Hunter interjected. "That still doesn't explain what you're doing here," Hunter reminded him.

Roman was quiet for a long time. "I didn't like how we left things this afternoon…how I left them. And then I realized that I didn't even have your number so I couldn't call or text you. I didn't know how long you'd be in town for and I remembered you saying how much you liked coming out here so I took a chance…"

When Roman didn't say anything else, Hunter pulled out his phone and handed it to Roman. "Put in your number."

Roman glanced at him and then took the phone and did just that. When he gave it back, their fingers briefly brushed and Hunter nearly shook his head. How the hell could one innocent touch make his whole body feel like it was on fire? He forced himself to concentrate on the phone and typed out a quick text message to Roman's number and hit send.

"I owe you an apology," he heard Roman say softly.

Hunter wanted to laugh. "You don't owe me anything. What you did for me last night…"

"I wish I'd gotten there sooner…" Roman suddenly whispered and Hunter turned his head and saw that Roman was staring at him. Even with the little light that the fire offered, Hunter could see the other man really meant it and he felt his insides do a crazy flip-flop.

"I wish I'd met you first," Hunter heard himself admitting and for once, the truth didn't feel so wrong.

~

*R*oman knew that if he leaned down just a little, he could get another taste of Hunter. Maybe if he did, he'd discover that last night was some anomaly – that whatever emotion had twisted and rolled through his body last night as Hunter had sealed their mouths together was the result of a waning adrenaline rush and nothing else. But then again, if it were that simple, would he really have spent the whole afternoon feeling like a complete and utter asshole for the callous retort he'd thrown at Hunter before calling off the hike? Would he have spent most of the evening pacing the floor of his crappy motel room before trekking off into the dark Montana night to find Hunter so he could apologize for his behavior?

And Christ, that fucking admission that Hunter wished he'd met him first!

There was no doubt in his mind that if he'd met Hunter last night in the club, he would have done anything and everything to get him back to his hotel room, his youth and inexperience be damned.

Roman forced himself to tear his eyes from Hunter. One more kiss would just fuck everything up. For him, for Hunter. He needed to get things back on track.

"That thing you said about some kid and his mom tearing out pictures of my resorts-"

"I didn't mean anything by it, Roman. I swear."

"I know. It's just...I never even realized it until you said it."

"What?"

Roman felt sick even voicing it. He'd spent the whole day obsessing over how he'd become so sidetracked by money and prestige that he hadn't ever made the connection himself.

"I was so proud of myself for building these beautiful places that my mom always dreamed of visiting that I never even realized she wouldn't have been able to. I made them completely unattainable to people like my mom – every single resort I've built would have been just another dream for her."

"You wanted to be successful," Hunter offered.

"No," Roman said, shaking his head. "I wanted to rub people's noses in it. I wanted to show them that I could be someone despite my last name...despite where I came from."

"Any people in particular?" Hunter asked cautiously.

Roman chuckled. The kid was too damn smart.

"My father and his wife."

"Is that who you went to live with after your mom died?"

Roman nodded. "My older half-brother, too."

Hunter was quiet for a moment before saying, "Your brother was older than you? Your dad was married before he met your mom?"

"Nope. I'm what they used to call a bastard back in the olden days," Roman muttered. "My father was having an affair with my mother while he was still married to Gray's mother. Gray is my half-brother."

"Fuck," Hunter whispered. "Wait, so you had to go live with your dad and the woman he was cheating on?"

Pain radiated through Roman's chest and for a brief moment an

45

irrational fear went through him that he was having a heart attack. But as he struggled to draw in breath, he realized that for all the times he'd remembered his shitty childhood with Victoria and Walt, it was a hell of a lot different to be talking about it out loud.

"Hey," Hunter whispered as his hand settled between Roman's shoulder blades. "We don't have to talk about this, okay?"

Roman managed a nod and tried to focus on catching his breath as he felt Hunter's fingers begin massaging the back of his neck. His cold skin instantly heated at the touch and when Hunter urged him to lay down on his side and then settled along his back after covering them with the blankets, Roman felt the tension start to ease from his body.

"What's in Missoula?" Roman asked as Hunter's body heat began to seep into him. His unruly body began to betray him as his anxiety switched over to desire.

"I go to school at the University of Montana."

Right. Hunter was still a teenager for God's sake. That fact should have settled Roman's ardor but it didn't – not one fucking little bit.

"What are you studying?"

"Political science."

"Are you hoping to get into politics?" Roman asked.

At Hunter's silence, Roman rolled over so they were facing. "You're not the one who wants the degree, are you?"

"Public service is a noble profession," Hunter murmured.

"Is that your argument or his?" Roman asked gently.

"Veto," Hunter whispered, his eyes down cast.

Roman reached out to stroke his fingers over Hunter's cheek. "Fair enough," he whispered. He gently tipped Hunter's chin up so that he was forced to look at Roman. "Can I stay here tonight?" His hand was resting on Hunter's neck and he felt him swallow hard.

"What? The *Dusty Spur* not to your liking?" Hunter asked.

Roman ignored the nervous attempt at humor and let his thumb stroke over Hunter's frantic pulse. "I like these accommodations much better," he murmured.

He heard Hunter inhale sharply before he finally nodded. Since staying face to face was a supremely bad idea, Roman flipped onto his back and tucked his arm beneath his head. He felt Hunter shift next to him, his warm body barely touching Roman's. Strangely enough, the lack of contact bothered Roman even more so he extended his free arm and worked it beneath Hunter until he finally got the silent message and used Roman's arm as a pillow. And then it got better because Hunter shifted just enough to get more comfortable and ended up pressed against his side.

Neither spoke as they stared at the inky sky above them. Roman had been to the most glorious spots the world had to offer and he could honestly say nothing compared to the sight of the canopy of stars above him. And there sure as hell had never been anyone who even came close to making him feel what Hunter did...not that he knew what that was exactly; he just knew it felt fucking perfect.

~

*H*unter came awake slowly and knew right away he was alone because there was no warm arm keeping his head off the ground anymore. And while he wasn't exactly cold beneath the blanket, he missed the warm, hard body that had been pressed against him all night. Sunlight was just starting to seep over the lake and he could see a flock of Ring-necked ducks diving for their breakfast. Disappointment went through Hunter in knowing that Roman had left without even letting him know but he supposed it would have been too much to expect otherwise. He'd read too much into last night. And even if by some miracle he hadn't, would it really matter what Roman's motivations for staying were? It didn't change the fundamental truth that Hunter was beyond fucked up. His actions at the club were proof of that and that wasn't even the tip of the iceberg. Not to mention what Roman would think of him when he found out the devastation Hunter had heaped on an innocent person because of his own cowardice.

"Hunter."

Roman's voice was loud enough to carry but he wasn't shouting. But Hunter didn't miss the tremor of concern in his voice so he snatched up the gun and ran in the direction he'd heard Roman calling from.

"I'm coming."

Fear rattled through Hunter at the thought of Roman having come face to face with a bear and he quickly double-checked the rifle to make sure a round was chambered. He already had the gun raised to his shoulder as he spotted Roman standing near a cluster of bushes just a few dozen yards beyond the campsite.

"What? What is it?" Hunter asked quickly as he scanned the area.

"Please tell me that's Lucy," Roman said softly, his eyes at a spot near his feet.

Hunter's relief was so prominent that his knees actually felt wobbly but he managed to close the distance between him and Roman who was standing perfectly still. A skunk was just feet from him, its dark eyes staring at him as its nose sniffed the air.

"It is," Hunter said with a chuckle.

"How can you be so sure?"

"See that scar on her face? Gran thinks the coyote that killed her family almost got her too."

"Thank fuck," Roman muttered but when he started to move, Hunter snagged his arm.

"Just a second, let me distract her. It'd be a shame if we had to shave all your pretty hair off," Hunter said with a smile.

"Asshole," Roman bit out.

Hunter reached into his pocket and pulled out what was left of the granola bar he'd been snacking on last night before Roman's arrival. Lucy instantly went on alert at the sound of the cellophane and she didn't hesitate to waddle her way over to him. He broke the granola bar up into a couple of pieces and scattered them around the ground and then slowly stood and reached for Roman's hand.

Once they were well out of spraying range, Hunter began to laugh. A glance at Roman's irritated features just had him laughing harder and a second later he found himself being pressed up against a tree, Roman's big body pinning him in place. All his humor quickly fled and he stifled a moan when Roman restrained his hands by holding them against the tree next to his head. Being at Roman's mercy should have scared him but it didn't. Not even a little bit.

Roman didn't speak or move as he held him in place. His cobalt eyes just held Hunter's as if he was looking for something. Finally, he whispered, "Morning."

Hunter's mouth felt dry as he said "morning" back. His eyes dropped to Roman's mouth and he wondered what Roman would do if he closed what little distance there was between them and ran his tongue over the seam. Would Roman open to him instantly or would he make him work for it?

It took a second for Hunter to realize Roman was speaking to him because it felt like his heart was pounding so hard that it was all he could hear in his head. "What?" he asked dumbly.

"Would you show me the hot springs this morning?"

Hunter managed a nod. Spending even another second in Roman's company was an incredibly bad idea but he knew there was pretty much nothing at this point that would drag him away from this man even a moment earlier than he had to.

"And then maybe you can show me some more of the land?"

Right. Because last night hadn't changed the reason Roman was here.

Hunter tugged his hands free of Roman's hold. "Sure. Um, can you call my dad to let him know you want to see it? He thinks I spent the night at a friend's house."

If Roman thought the request was strange, he didn't say so. "I have a charger for my phone in my rental. How about we check out the hot springs and then we can head back to my car and I'll call him from there? Maybe we can head back to town to get some breakfast?"

"There are some fast food places about twenty minutes from here. They have drive-thrus."

Again, if Roman thought his behavior was odd, he didn't call him on it. He simply said, "Sounds like a plan" and began walking back towards the campsite.

~

*R*oman pulled his car into the spot next to Hunter's car. Hunter got out of his own little beat up Escort and fidgeted on the curb as he waited for Roman to get out. Once he did, Hunter extended his hand and murmured, "It was nice to meet you. Have a safe trip home."

The impersonal gesture irritated Roman and just served as icing on what had turned out to be a disappointing day. And it had all started as soon as he'd grabbed Hunter and pinned him to that tree. It had been an impulsive move on his part. One second Hunter had been laughing at him and the next second Roman had needed to feel Hunter…needed to drink down the vibrancy that was written all over his beautiful features as his shallow chuckles had to turned to a full-on laugh that had pervaded his entire body. In that moment Roman had finally seen his first glimpse of the real Hunter – the one who wasn't terrified of being outed or facing a future that wasn't of his choosing. So he'd grabbed Hunter and as soon as he'd felt Hunter's lithe body lined up with his, Roman had gotten lost in himself, in Hunter, in what he wanted and what he was doing. And when he should have been trying to find a way to distance himself from Hunter, he'd found himself voicing an excuse for them to spend another day together.

Roman had no need to see any more of the property outside Dare. There was no doubt that it and the additional, adjoining acreage the state of Montana was selling would be perfect for what he had in mind. And he had no concerns that his investors wouldn't feel exactly the same way when he flew them out to take a look at the place. There'd been no reason for him to spend another day in Dare – in fact, he could have left yesterday afternoon and put the past two days out of his mind. But instead, he'd woken up this morning with Hunter wrapped around him and he'd lain there for nearly two hours enjoying the feel of the other man's body clutching his like it was some kind of lifeline. He would have been content to lay there all day like that but his body had had other ideas and he'd gone off to find some privacy to take a piss. Then Lucy showed up along with Hunter with his infectious laugh and his plan to distance himself from Hunter had been shot to hell. But just like that, Hunter retreated into himself and turned into the consummate tour guide as he showed Roman the hot springs. By the time they reached the fast food joint to grab some breakfast, Roman had given up on trying to draw Hunter out of his funk.

But being dismissed like he was just some stranger off the street was just too fucking much so instead of taking Hunter's hand and wishing him well, Roman coolly said, "I'd like a quick tour of the town if you don't mind."

Hunter's look of surprise and then downright horror had Roman felling a twinge of guilt but he steeled himself to remain silent. Hunter glanced over his shoulder at his father's realty office and then back at Roman. Then he scanned the town's city center and finally nodded. There were only a couple of people near the park in the center of the square and Roman guessed that was the biggest driving factor in Hunter's acquiescence. Roman fell into step next to Hunter as they began walking along the sidewalk. Hunter nervously scanned their surroundings as he rattled off details about each little store and office they passed and when a person either walked past them or exited one of the shops, Hunter hung his head. By the time they reached the opposite side of the square, Roman was fed up and was about to ask Hunter what the hell was going on when Hunter stopped so suddenly that Roman actually continued several steps before he realized Hunter wasn't next to him anymore. He turned to glance at Hunter and saw that all the blood had rushed from his face and when Roman turned to see what he was looking at, all he saw were two men walking out of one of the buildings.

One of the men was close to his age and dressed in a police officer's uniform while the other man was considerably younger, Hunter's age probably. The two men were holding hands and talking to each other in low voices.

"Do you know them?" Roman asked.

"Hunter?"

Roman snapped his attention back to the two men and saw that the younger one was now looking just as stunned as Hunter.

"Hunter?" the cop asked, his voice going cold as his eyes settled on Hunter.

"Rhys, don't!"

The young guy shouted and grabbed for his boyfriend but the older man shook him off.

"Hey, buddy…" Roman said calmly as he tried to step in the man's path but he was shoved out of the way. He managed to catch himself before he fell but it gave the guy several seconds to reach Hunter who hadn't moved at all. The guy punched Hunter in the face without any kind of warning and then grabbed him by the throat and shoved him back against the brick wall of one of the shops.

"You worthless piece of shit!" the man screamed at him. He pulled his arm back to hit Hunter again but Roman managed to reach them in time and he shoved the cop off and placed himself between the two men. Not once had Hunter even lifted a finger to defend himself. Even now, he only had eyes for the young man who'd managed to grab his boyfriend by the arm and hold him back.

"Don't!" the young man said as he got into his lover's face. His voice seemed to penetrate the rage the other man was in because he finally stopped trying to get past his boyfriend.

"Rhys, what the hell?" came another voice and Roman saw a second cop trotting down the sidewalk towards them.

"Finn, what's going on?" the second cop asked the young man. He was a big guy with dark hair. Roman used the temporary distraction to turn and check on Hunter who was standing pressed up against the wall exactly where the cop had left him. Blood trickled from a small gash on his cheek.

"You okay?" Roman asked as he gently tipped Hunter's face to the side to examine the injury. Hunter didn't answer him – he just stood there shaking violently.

"You have any idea what you did you little prick?" Rhys suddenly shouted.

"Rhys!" Finn shouted.

"What the fuck is wrong with you?" the second cop asked as he got in Rhys' space.

"It's that little fucker, Hunter Greene!" Rhys snapped.

The second cop stiffened and then glanced over his shoulder at Hunter. Luckily he stayed where he was because while Roman had no doubt he could take on Rhys, two armed guys were another matter entirely. The cop turned his attention back to Rhys and said something in a low voice that Roman couldn't make out. When he seemed satisfied that Rhys was staying quiet for the moment, he turned on his heel and walked towards him and Hunter.

"I'm Deputy Jax Reid," he said quietly. He didn't bother asking Roman to move which was good since Roman wasn't about to let anyone get to Hunter again. Instead he studied Hunter's face and softly said, "Hunter, do you want to press charges?"

"Yes," Roman instantly said.

"No," Hunter whispered. "No," he repeated more firmly and shook his head.

Jax studied him for a long moment. "Are you sure?"

Hunter nodded vehemently and Roman could tell he was barely holding it together.

"Deputy Tellar won't bother you again," Jax said as he turned and went back to Rhys and Finn.

"Take Finn home, Rhys," he said firmly.

Rhys was still seething but appeared to be more in control of himself. He reached down and wrapped his hand around Finn's but his frigid eyes were still on Hunter when he said, "Stay the fuck away from Finn, do you hear me?"

"Rhys, now!" Jax bit out.

Rhys turned and led Finn to an old pickup truck sitting at the curb and it wasn't until the truck peeled out of the spot and headed out of town that Roman finally relaxed. Jax gave him a brief nod before striding back to the police station.

Roman turned to check on Hunter and saw that he was still in a state of shock from the attack.

"Hunter, talk to me. Tell me what that was about."

Hunter just shook his head again and when Roman reached for him, he dodged his touch and then hurried across the street. Roman managed to catch up to him when he reached his car but he was so agitated that he yanked himself free of Roman the second he touched him. The distress was written all over his face but he had yet to utter a sound or shed a single tear. He simply climbed into his car, started the engine and calmly pulled out of the parking spot as if nothing had happened.

Roman got into his car and followed him. The house Hunter pulled up to was a stately white colonial with a white picket fence surrounding the large property. It looked very out of place on the quiet street that was lined with older ranch and cape cod style homes. Hunter left his car parked in the driveway and disappeared into a side door. By the time Roman got inside, he didn't see any sign of Hunter and a quick search of the house showed that Hunter's parents weren't at home. He found what he could only assume was Hunter's room if the trophies lined up on the dresser and the academic award certificates covering one wall were anything to go by. There was a twin bed in the center of the small room and a desk pushed up against the only window. Nothing about the room gave any additional insight into Hunter because there were no pictures or posters or knickknacks that he would have expected to find in someone's childhood space.

Roman went to what he assumed was an attached bathroom and tried the door only to find it locked. He knocked and called Hunter's name but there was no answer. A tremor of fear went through him as he knocked again.

"Hunter, can you open up please? I just want to make sure you're okay."

Silence.

Roman pounded on the door hard enough to make it rattle but Hunter didn't respond in any way. So there was absolutely no hesitation on Roman's part when he stepped back just enough so he could put his shoulder forward and throw his weight against the door. It gave on the first try and just as it flew open, he heard a rattle as something hit the floor and his eyes immediately went to a spoon laying on the tile floor between Hunter's feet. Hunter was sitting on the edge of the bathtub and was busily jerking his shirt sleeve down as he tried to palm the lighter that was in his left hand.

Rage tore through Roman as he yanked Hunter to his feet and pushed him against the wall by the door.

"Where is it?"

Hunter opened his mouth to say something but when nothing came out, Roman lost it and began searching the bathroom. He snatched the spoon off the floor and then ripped the lighter that Hunter was still trying to hide from his hand.

"What is it? Meth? Heroin? You think that shit is going to fix you? To make you not want dick anymore?" Roman snarled as he flung the spoon and lighter into the sink. "You think shooting up's going to make whatever the hell just happened out there go away?"

"I'm not an addict," Hunter whispered feebly.

Roman knew he was just as close to losing it at as the cop who'd lashed out at Hunter. Grabbing Hunter's left arm, he yanked it forward and reached for the sleeve.

"No!" Hunter suddenly screamed and began fighting him.

"Not an addict, huh?" Roman snapped as he pinned Hunter with his body and forced the sleeve up.

"No, Roman, don't! Please don't!"

But Roman ignored Hunter's desperate pleas and the tears that were now flowing freely down his face and pushed the sleeve up past the elbow. His eyes began searching for the track marks he knew were there but he froze at what he found instead. Round red marks, at least a dozen of them, littered the inside of Hunter's forearm. Some of the injuries looked fresher than the others and from the different severity levels of the scarring, some were older and had likely been severe at some point.

"What is this?" Roman asked in confusion as he turned Hunter's arm over and saw even more scars on his outer arm.

When he looked up, he saw that Hunter had closed his eyes at some point but tears were still streaking down his skin. Hoarse, choking sobs were rattling deep in his throat.

Roman turned to examine the injuries again and then felt a chill go through him as he started to see the shape of each wound. He shook his head in disbelief as he finally began to understand what he was looking at. It was so unbelievable that he found himself searching out the discarded spoon. The fact that the metal was still warm to the touch should have been answer enough but he took the spoon and held it just above the freshest looking injury that was just now starting to blister. Horror went through him as the outline of the spoon matched up to the injury and in his shock, he dropped the spoon.

"Oh God," he whispered and as soon as he did, a mournful cry left Hunter's lips and he pulled his arm free of Roman's now lax grip and then slowly sank to the floor. Hunter crossed his arms over the top of his head, his forearms hiding his face from view. His sleeve was still pushed up and Roman fleetingly wondered if Hunter had inflicted the same kind of injuries on his other arm.

Roman backed up until he hit the sink. "Why?" he stuttered as took in the sight of Hunter folded in on himself. "Why would you do this?"

Hunter didn't answer him, didn't even look at him. Instead he lurched to his feet and rushed out of the bathroom. Roman hurried after him and managed to catch up to him just as Hunter was opening his car door. Sobs were still erupting from his throat and he began fighting Roman the second he touched him.

"Don't!" Hunter screamed. "Don't touch me!"

The young man's pain was so palpable that Roman felt tears filling his own eyes.

"Hunter, please," he whispered brokenly as he wrapped his arms around the younger man. He could feel Hunter frantically trying to push him away but after several long seconds, Hunter's whole body gave out and he buried his face against Roman's neck. Roman could feel hot tears sliding down his throat.

"I've got you," he murmured against Hunter's head. "I'm here, okay?"

Hunter didn't answer him but he did feel Hunter's arms finally close around him. He had no idea how long they stood there for but when Hunter's crying finally slowed, Roman leaned down and put his lips against Hunter's ear.

"Come with me, okay?"

Hunter nodded against his chest and wiped at his face when he finally pulled back. The young man was a complete mess and blood continued to drip from the wound on his cheek. Hunter pulled his sleeve down to cover the burns and then swiped his arm over his face again, smearing the blood in the process. Roman took his hand and led him to his rental and got him settled in the passenger seat. As he walked around the car to the driver's side, his mind began firing through his options. The clear solution was to take Hunter to a hospital where they'd have experts who could help him deal with his obviously scarred psyche but even the thought of Hunter locked away in some psych ward had him mentally shaking his head. No way. He just couldn't do it.

Roman settled into the driver's seat and cast a look at Hunter who sat quietly in the passenger seat. He reached out and gently turned Hunter's face so he could see his eyes. The pain was gone and so was Hunter. All that was left was the same shell of a young man he'd seen being brutalized on that fucking pool table less than forty-eight hours ago. And in that instant, Roman knew exactly what he needed to do.

CHAPTER 5

"Roman?"

Roman watched his brother's face go from shocked to thrilled in the space of two seconds and then he was being dragged into Gray's arms. Under any other circumstances, he would have extricated himself from his brother's hold as quickly as possible but for some reason he didn't want to think too much about, he wrapped his arms around Gray and held on as tightly as he could. He felt Gray stiffen slightly and then he was fiercely returning the embrace.

"I need your help," Roman whispered.

Gray must have heard something in his voice because he put just enough distance between them to make sure their eyes met. "Anything," he answered.

Relief flooded Roman as he nodded and then stepped back. Hunter was standing quietly at the bottom of the porch stairs, ignoring the large German Shepherd that had darted outside as soon as Gray had opened the door and was now eagerly sniffing Hunter's lax hands. Roman went down the stairs and took Hunter's hand. The contact seemed to snap Hunter out of his daze because his hand tightened around Roman's when he looked up and saw Gray watching them both with concern.

Roman didn't bother with introductions as he led Hunter inside. "Everything okay?"

Roman looked up and saw Gray's boyfriend, Luke Monroe, watching them from the entrance to the kitchen. His eyes swept over Hunter and then shot to Gray. He didn't say anything as he disappeared towards the back hallway.

"Here," Gray said as he motioned to the living room couch. By the time Roman got Hunter settled, Luke was back with a small black bag that looked like a shaving kit. He sat down on the coffee table so he was facing Hunter.

"Can I take a look?" Luke said gently to Hunter as he motioned to his face.

"Luke's training to be a paramedic," Gray said quietly.

Hunter nodded stiffly. His grip on Roman's hand hadn't eased at all and when Luke began cleaning the injury with some kind of antiseptic wipe, he flinched but remained quiet. Luke's movements were quick and efficient as he added a couple of butterfly bandages to close the small gash.

As Luke started to clean up his supplies, Roman put out his hand to stop him and then forced Hunter to look at him. "We need to show him," he said gently.

Agony filled Hunter's eyes. "No, Roman, please…"

Roman ignored Luke and his brother and put his palm over Hunter's uninjured cheek to hold him steady as he pinned him with his eyes. "You can trust them, I swear it. They won't judge you."

Hunter stared at him for a long time and then finally closed his eyes and gave a little nod. But when he made no move to pull up the sleeve on his left arm, Roman released his hand long enough so he could do it himself. To both Gray and Luke's credit, neither man made a sound as the burn wounds were exposed. Luke took Hunter's arm in his hands so he could get a closer look and then said to Gray, "Can you get me a washcloth – run it under cool water?"

Gray nodded and left the room. He was back within a minute. Luke took the washcloth and pressed it over the freshest wound.

Roman could tell that the blister had broken at some point, likely during his tussle with Hunter.

"I'm going to put some antibiotic cream on this and wrap it for now so it doesn't get infected but you'll want to let the air get at it a little later, okay?"

Hunter managed a nod.

Roman looked up to find Gray and saw his brother watching him with concern. "Do you have a place he can lay down for a bit?"

"Yeah, sure."

As soon as Luke was done bandaging Hunter's arm, Roman helped Hunter to his feet and led him to the guest room that Gray showed them to. Gray left them alone as Roman pulled back the covers and sat Hunter down on the bed and removed his shoes. "Just get some rest, okay?"

Hunter didn't respond. He just rolled onto his side so that his back was to Roman. Roman covered him with the blanket and then started for the door. But he slowed his step and then went to the bathroom instead. He was glad when he came back out and saw that Hunter was still turned away from him because no way in hell did he want Hunter to see the things he was carrying in his arms.

~

He knew. Roman fucking knew.

Humiliation coursed through Hunter as he heard the bedroom door click shut. His body felt too hot so he pushed the blanket off and sat up. God, how had he let this happen? He'd always been so careful in the past but today it was like everything around him had been put on pause the second he'd recognized Finn Stewart. And as the man who'd been with Finn had descended on him, all Hunter could think was that he was finally going to get what he deserved... what he'd earned when he'd ruined Finn's life eighteen months ago. But one punch hadn't been enough – sure, it had hurt like hell but he'd wanted...needed more. Because the punishment he'd inflicted upon himself hadn't been enough.

The whole thing had ended before it had really begun and instead of getting on his knees to beg Finn to forgive him or find a way to get the punishment he deserved, he'd run...again. Like the fucking coward he was. The darkness had begun to consume him before he even reached his car and it was only the familiar feel of his spoon and lighter in his pocket that made it possible for him to even get home. Relief, no matter how temporary it was, had been only minutes away as he entered his thankfully empty house. His whole body had danced with energy and need as he waited for the lighter to do its job and he held it in place longer than he usually did because he knew he was too far gone for anything but a major hit. There'd been no pleasure when he pressed the scalding metal to his skin...there never was. Pain had shot through his entire body a split second later and it wiped away every other emotion as if they'd never existed. It was like someone had hit reset on his life and for that brief moment he was the old Hunter Greene...the one whose cowardice had only ever hurt himself.

His moment of clarity had also allowed him to finally hear the pounding on the bathroom door but before he could even respond, it was crashing open and all the relief he'd felt shattered and his world imploded as he realized his most shameful secret had been found out...and by the one man he would have done anything to keep it from.

Hunter could already feel the anxiety building again. He couldn't deal with this. Not now...not ever. But he could go back to the way things were. Get good grades, pretend he liked girls, do what he was told. He'd been doing it long before Roman came into his life and he could easily go back to it. After all, he'd had a lifetime to practice. He just needed to get away...that simple.

Hunter put his shoes on and climbed to his feet. Between the pain in his arm and his face, he felt off balance so he took his time heading towards the bedroom door. He had no clue how the hell he was going to get past Roman or his friends but he'd figure something out. Something that didn't involve ever having to hear that mix of pity and disgust in Roman's voice ever again.

～

*R*oman was glad when Gray and Luke didn't say anything as he piled the few items he'd taken from the bathroom in the guest room on the kitchen table. He suspected he was overreacting by removing the two bottles of cleaning supplies, razor and bottle of aspirin but he wasn't taking any chances. He knew from experience what happened when you underestimated the pain someone was in.

"Sit," his brother said as he pulled out one of the kitchen chairs and placed a cup of coffee on the table.

Since his body felt shaky and weak, Roman did as he was told and settled into the chair. Gray sat next to him and Luke took the third chair across from him. He didn't miss the way Gray's hand immediately sought out Luke's. The affectionate gesture had something breaking apart in Roman and he dropped his eyes to study the coffee.

The dog appeared and pushed her nose against his leg. "What's her name again?" he asked as he settled his hand on the big dog's head.

"Ripley," Gray answered.

Roman smiled. "I love those movies," he said softly. His eyes shifted to Luke. "Since Gray was never big on movies, I can only assume you gave her the name?"

Luke chuckled and nodded.

Roman felt Gray's hand settle briefly on his shoulder. "What happened, Roman? Who is he?"

Incredibly, Roman felt more tears threatening to fall. He forced them back and said, "His name is Hunter. His father is the realtor handling the sale of some property I was looking at. Hunter's been showing me the land for the past couple days."

Roman was glad when Gray didn't jump on the fact that he'd come to town without telling Gray.

"He was showing me around town and we ran into these two guys. I guess Hunter knew one of them. The other guy went crazy and started calling Hunter names and then he fucking hit him. Asked him if he had any idea what he'd done. Another cop showed up-"

"Wait, the guy who hit Hunter was a cop?" Luke interjected.

"Yeah…he was wearing a uniform. The second cop called him Rhys I think. The younger man's name was Finn."

Luke and Gray looked at each other.

"What?" Roman asked. "Do you know them?"

It was Gray who answered. "Rhys is Luke's foster brother. They grew up together in Chicago. He's the reason Luke came to Montana a few months ago."

Roman didn't know all the details of Luke's past other than the few he'd gained from news stories. At some point Luke had been framed for murder by one of his Commanding Officers in the army and after several attempts on his life, Luke had arrived in Montana where he'd ended up meeting Gray by pure chance.

"So wait, do you know what Rhys was talking about?"

Luke and Gray shared another look and he could tell by the expression on their faces that neither wanted to be the bearer of bad news. Like it could get any fucking worse at this point.

"Rhys told me the story of how he and Finn and Callan met," Luke finally said.

"Callan?"

"Callan Bale. He's the owner of the CB Bar Ranch. Finn has worked for him for years but they didn't get together until Rhys arrived in town earlier this summer."

"So what, they're together? The three of them?"

Luke nodded. "Callan was in the closet but Finn was out."

"What does any of that have to do with Hunter?"

"Hunter outed him, Roman," Gray said softly.

Roman couldn't believe what he was hearing. He began shaking his head but couldn't find any words.

"Hunter and Finn were in school together. Apparently there was some kind of party at Hunter's house on the day they graduated. He and Finn were caught making out by Hunter's father."

A sick feeling twisted inside of Roman.

"Hunter told his father that Finn assaulted him."

"No," Roman whispered.

Luke took over the story. "Hunter's father had Finn arrested for assault. Callan managed to get the charges against Finn dismissed but Hunter's father made sure the story got out. Nearly the entire town turned against Finn."

Roman felt like he was going to be sick. He couldn't reconcile the act with the Hunter he knew.

"It gets worse," Gray said.

How the hell could it get worse?

"Finn's father beat him so badly that night when he got home that he ended up in the hospital. Callan kicked his father off the ranch and Finn hasn't seen or spoken to him since."

"Did Hunter…did he know what happened to Finn?"

"According to Rhys, Hunter left town the next day," Luke explained.

"It has to be some kind of mistake," Roman said.

Gray and Luke remained silent at that.

"Is that it? Or is there more?"

"Roman, Dare isn't exactly a mecca of gay-friendly people," Gray said. "I mean, it's getting better but back then the majority of people just saw Finn as some kind of deviant and with Hunter's father fanning the flames…well, they didn't make it easy for Finn, or for Callan for that matter."

"What happened?"

"It started small…the stores would refuse Finn service, people called him names, that sort of thing. Then they started going after Callan because he refused to fire Finn. He couldn't get fair prices for his cattle, he and Finn had to go to other towns to buy supplies." Gray glanced at Luke before continuing. "At one point, a couple of guys poisoned the water supply on Callan's land. It killed half his stock. They also kept cutting the fences and a few months ago they burned down his barn. Finn got shot in the process."

Roman pushed back his chair and stood. "Jesus," he muttered as he began pacing back and forth in the small kitchen. His first instinct was to go into the bedroom and make Hunter explain what he'd been thinking when he'd spouted that terrible lie. And why the hell hadn't he come forward and told the truth?

And then an image of Hunter bent over that pool table flashed in his mind and his anger gave way to pity. Hunter may have made a foolish, unthinking choice but he hadn't walked away completely unscathed. Roman returned to the chair and dropped his head into his hands.

"He's punishing himself for it," he said quietly.

"His arm?" Luke asked.

Roman nodded. "That and other stuff," he said, unwilling to share the details of what the bikers had done to Hunter...what he'd allowed them to do in some sick attempt to make sure he'd paid for what he'd done to Finn.

"It's called self-harming," Luke said. "They taught us about it in the army so we'd be able to recognize the signs in other soldiers."

"Is it related to PTSD?" Gray asked.

"It can be. It's a coping mechanism," Luke explained. "I met a guy in basic training who used to do it when he was a teenager. His parents thought he just doing it to get attention and his shrink was convinced he was just doing it for the rush."

"The rush?" Roman asked.

"Yeah, I guess for some people, the act actually causes them to feel pleasure but for most it's about finding relief or feeling in control."

"I'm scared to death he's going to do it again," Roman whispered. "Or worse..."

Roman's thoughts were interrupted by Ripley's excited barking. Gray looked around the kitchen. "She must be by the back door," he murmured as he stood to check on her.

But Roman was already up and hurrying to the guest bedroom. Panic went through him when he saw the empty bed and he quickly ducked into the bathroom to make sure it was empty. It was so he left the room.

"Mud room's back there," Gray said from just behind him.

Roman followed the sound of the barking dog. There was a small room at the end of the hallway with a door leading out the back of the cabin. When he didn't see Hunter anywhere, fear curdled in his gut.

"Ripley will find him," Gray said as he pushed the door open. "Go," he nodded to Roman.

Roman trotted after the dog. Although he quickly lost sight of her, she kept up her excited barking and it took him just minutes to catch up to Hunter who was striding through a heavily wooded area.

"Hunter," he called as he got closer but Hunter ignored him. It wasn't until he actually grabbed Hunter's arm that the young man rounded on him and hit Roman in the chest with his closed fists.

"Why couldn't you just leave it alone?" he shouted.

Roman caught Hunter's wrists before he could strike out at him again but then released them just as quickly. The move seemed to catch Hunter off guard.

"Do it," Roman said.

When Hunter didn't respond, Roman grabbed his hands and forced them into fists. "Fucking do it!" he shouted as he put Hunter's fisted hands against his chest.

Hunter pushed away from him and kept walking.

"You lied to me," Roman said softly. Hunter stopped but didn't turn so Roman closed the distance between them and then stepped around Hunter so that they were once again facing each other. "About the men in the club," he added.

"I told you why I let them…"

"Yes, but that wasn't the only reason, was it?" When Hunter didn't answer him, he continued. "When will it be enough, Hunter? How much pain do you need to feel before you start forgiving yourself?"

Hunter laughed harshly. "Forgive myself? Didn't you hear what they said in there?"

Roman had already figured that Hunter had likely overheard his conversation with Gray and Luke.

"What I heard was a story about a kid who made one really bad decision…a decision with terrible consequences. But this isn't the fucking answer!" Roman said as he carefully grabbed a hold of Hunter's injured arm. "Letting men brutalize you won't undo that night, Hunter! Hurting yourself won't give that young man the last eighteen months of his life back!"

"You think I don't know that? You think I haven't tried a thousand times to find the courage to tell Finn how sorry I am? How I wish I could take it all back? You think I don't wish I was strong enough even now to admit to my fag hating dad that I was the one who kissed Finn first?"

Hunter suddenly slammed his fist into the nearest tree. Roman managed to grab him before he did it again.

"Tell me what words to use to explain to Finn why I did what I did? Because I sure as shit don't know what they are. How do I ask him to forgive me for taking his only family away from him just so I could keep my fucked up one? How do I tell him I'm sorry he got beat up by his dad just so that I wouldn't get beat up by mine?" Hunter was nearly screaming now.

"So yeah, when I saw those guys in the club, I knew they'd mess me up and a part of me welcomed it! That's why I didn't say no. That's why I didn't fight when they held me down. Why I didn't cry when they kept telling me I deserved it. You can't deny something that's true, can you?"

Some of the ire seemed to go out of Hunter because he dropped his eyes and then shook his head slowly. "I'm letting you off the hook here, okay, Roman? I'm fine – everything's fine. You don't need to save me again. Go home, forget you ever met me."

"That simple, huh?" Roman said as anger coursed through him.

"What do you want from me, Roman?" Hunter finally asked, his anger and frustration draining away.

"I want the real you back...the you I saw this morning when you were lying in my arms. The you I saw when you came running to my rescue before you realized it was Lucy who had me cornered. The you who couldn't stop laughing his ass off at me afterwards." Roman moved forward as he spoke and was thrilled when Hunter took matching step backwards because within a couple of seconds he backed into a tree and Roman moved into position before Hunter could escape.

"I want the you whose only thought this morning when I had you pressed up against that tree was whether or not I wanted you to kiss me." Hunter squirmed against him and the move set off fireworks in Roman's abdomen. He leaned down so that his lips hovered just above Hunter's. "The answer to that question is yes…it will always be yes."

The last syllable hadn't even cleared his lips when Hunter reached up and seized his mouth.

~

*H*unter didn't give a shit what Roman's motivation was for the stunning words he'd said and he didn't care if Roman had meant them or not. All he cared about was Roman's hungry mouth moving over his, searching, plundering, owning. Unlike their kiss in the hotel, Roman showed him no mercy this time around. His control over Hunter's mouth and body were absolute and Hunter could only hang on for the ride. Roman's hands sought out his and then dragged them up and over his head. He used one hand to hold both his wrists in place as his other hand skimmed up and down Hunter's side. The tree scratched against his back as he writhed in Roman's hold in an effort to get closer but Roman's grip on him was unyielding and nothing he did offered any kind of relief as Roman kissed him hard and deep. Fingers bit into his waist to keep his hips from seeking out Roman's but before he could protest, Roman pressed hard against him and Hunter cried out at the feel of their shafts brushing against each other.

Roman's lips nipped and sucked at his jaw and throat as his hand slipped behind Hunter to palm his ass. Heat shot out to all his limbs as Roman began grinding against him just as his thick, rough fingers drifted under the waistband of his jeans to graze over his heated flesh. It wasn't until a second hand reached down to rub over his aching cock that Hunter realized his hands were free. He quickly dropped them down to wrap around Roman's neck and fisted one hand in Roman's hair so that he could force him back up for another bone melting kiss.

The hand that had been palming his ass disappeared and Hunter gasped when he felt his jeans being loosened, then opened. His underwear was brushed aside just as quickly and Roman swallowed Hunter's cry of pleasure as Roman's fist closed around Hunter's cock. He knew it was too much too fast but there was no stopping the tingling that started at the base of his spine. Roman gave him just a couple of tugs before he pulled back from Hunter entirely. Hunter wanted to cry out at the loss but the sight of Roman releasing his dick from his pants had him snapping his mouth shut. He had no idea if Roman was expecting him to jerk him off or take him into his mouth but he didn't have to wonder for long because Roman pressed forward again so that their leaking cocks brushed against one another and then he was taking them both in his big hand.

The sensation was almost too much to bear but Hunter couldn't tear his eyes away from the sight of Roman's hand working their shafts over at the same time. The contrast of Roman's rough hand and the soft skin of his cock brushing against Hunter's aching flesh was so powerful that Hunter began shoving his hips forward in an effort to increase the sensation. Roman's response was to press him back against the tree and seize his mouth as he began fisting their dicks in earnest. The orgasm wrenched through Hunter with such force that he had to tear his lips from Roman's so that he wouldn't inadvertently bite into the tender flesh. His body jerked uncontrollably as jet after jet of come spurted from his body.

Roman's face was plastered against his neck and his roar of satisfaction ripped through Hunter causing more come to spill from his body. He managed to look down just as Roman's seed shot from his reddened cock and the sensation of the hot come dripping over the head of his own cock left Hunter shaking. Lips closed over his as a hot, greedy tongue surged into his mouth. The hold on his dick eased and then disappeared entirely but before Hunter could register the loss, he felt Roman's fingers plunging into his mouth. The taste of his and Roman's come should have freaked him out but the dark, hungry look in Roman's gaze as he fed Hunter the evidence of their release had him sucking down every last drop he could find. And then

Roman's mouth was on his again and Hunter gave up on all rational thought and threw himself into returning the kiss.

~

"*I* can't be gay."

Roman wasn't sure if the fact that Hunter used the word "can't" instead of "not" was a good thing. He supposed he should just be glad Hunter was even speaking at all. After what had happened in the woods behind Gray and Luke's cabin, Hunter hadn't said a single thing. He hadn't fought Roman when Roman took his hand and led him back to the cabin and when he'd introduced Hunter to Gray and Luke, Hunter had merely nodded his head. But only after he'd removed his hand from Roman's. They'd both passed on Gray's offer of dinner and had gone to the guest bedroom to try and get some sleep even though it wasn't even eight o'clock at night yet. Hunter had managed a call to his father saying he was staying with a friend again but if he'd been accepting the night before, he wasn't tonight and Roman had clearly heard him yelling at Hunter to get his ass home. At that point, Roman had picked up his own phone and dialed Malcom Greene's number. Malcom had put his son on hold instantly and answered on the first ring and as Roman watched Hunter hang up his phone and crawl under the covers fully dressed, Roman had distracted Malcom with discussion about the next steps concerning the property. Once he'd hung up, he waited to see if Hunter's phone would ring again but it remained blessedly silent.

Roman had stripped down to his underwear and climbed into bed with Hunter but didn't reach for him. While he had no idea if Hunter was regretting the encounter by the tree, Roman was wrestling with the impact of it. The whole thing had been quick and dirty and barely counted as sex but it had been fucking perfect and Roman couldn't remember ever coming as hard as he had in that moment when Hunter's hot come had slid over his hand. There were so many things about his relationship with Hunter that should have had him running for the hills – their 12-year age difference, Hunter's virginity which

70

he considered just that since he refused to call what those bikers had done to him a sexual act, Hunter's need to punish himself for a past he didn't know how to escape and now this...the young man who'd just blown everything he'd ever known about sex out of the water didn't want to be gay.

Roman didn't respond to Hunter so he was surprised a couple of minutes later when Hunter whispered, "Is it always like that?"

A small huff left Roman's throat. "No," he said. "It's never fucking like that."

He felt Hunter shift slightly so he turned his head and saw Hunter was looking at him. Since he hadn't yet turned off the light on the nightstand, Roman could see the confusion on Hunter's face. "It's never been like that for me," he said firmly and he saw a flush of color settle over Hunter's face as he realized what Roman was saying. Roman couldn't stop from reaching across the bed and running his fingers through Hunter's hair. Hunter closed his eyes at the contact but instead of turning away again like Roman expected him to, Hunter rolled towards him and settled against his side, his head cushioned by Roman's arm. Roman's whole body relaxed as if it had been waiting for that exact moment.

"How old were you when you knew?" Hunter asked as his fingers stroked over Roman's skin.

Roman ignored his twitching dick and said, "Twelve."

"Were you scared?"

"No, just confused because I liked girls too."

That got Hunter's attention and he levered up on one elbow so he could look Roman in the face. "You're bi?"

"I never really put a label on it but I guess you could say that. I dated one woman exclusively in college for a few months and I've been with a handful of others but I find myself more strongly attracted to men for the most part."

"So you could be normal if you wanted to," Hunter said, the shock clear in his voice.

Roman knew Hunter hadn't meant any offense by the statement so he said, "I'm not a big believer in the argument that someone's sexuality is a choice."

Hunter was silent for a moment and then sat up. Roman pushed himself upright enough so he could lean back against the headboard. The confusion on Hunter's face was heartbreaking.

"Hunter," Roman said softly as he leaned forward to put his hand on Hunter's uninjured cheek. "I know people have probably been telling you your whole life that two men being together is wrong, that it's a sin and it goes against nature…I suspect a lot of people have been telling you a lot about how you should live your life, haven't they?"

Hunter dropped his eyes but didn't respond otherwise.

"I don't want to be one of those people, Hunter. I don't want to tell you how you should or shouldn't feel."

That seemed to get Hunter's attention because he lifted his eyes.

"When we came into the cabin, did you see my brother and Luke?"

Hunter had been behind Roman when they'd entered the cabin through the back door so he hadn't been sure if Hunter had seen the way Gray and Luke were holding onto each other as they spoke softly in the kitchen.

"What did you see?"

"They were touching, talking," Hunter said softly.

"Did you see anything else?"

"They…they reminded me of Gran and Pops. They used to do that – get so lost in each other that it was like nothing else existed."

"So you didn't see two men doing something wrong?"

Hunter shook his head. "I saw two people in love," he said quietly as he slowly lowered himself back down to the bed. Roman was pleased when Hunter rested his head on Roman's stomach and Roman used the opportunity to brush his fingers over Hunter's soft hair.

"I wish I could take this from you, Hunter," Roman whispered.

Hunter turned over so that he was facing Roman. His eyes were heavy with a mix of pain and confusion as they settled on his left arm which was completely covered save for the little bit of white bandaging peeking beneath the cuff. "It was an accident…the first time it happened." His eyes lifted to meet Roman's. "I got really sick the week of my mid-terms during my freshman year. I ended up getting a C on one of them and my dad lost it. He accused me of getting the bad grade on purpose. I told him I'd be able to get my grade back up before the semester ended but I don't know if he even heard me. When I hung up the phone it was like something inside of me just snapped. In that moment I hated everyone and everything and I just…" Hunter shook his head slowly, clearly unable to continue with whatever he'd been about to say.

He took a deep breath and finally said, "I just started grabbing things and throwing them - I was completely out of control. I'd been cooking something on the stove and when I grabbed the pan, the grease spilled onto my arm. The pain was so intense that it just took everything else away. Everything that had been swirling around inside of me just disappeared – like someone popping a balloon. I cleaned up the mess I'd made, fixed myself something to eat and went on like it never happened. Every time those thoughts started to come back, I just looked at the burn on my arm and I felt better. But then it started to heal…"

"And the pain inside started to build again," Roman offered gently.

Hunter nodded. "I knew it was wrong and I tried for a really long time not to do it again but then I'd start to think about Finn and the way he looked at me when I said what I said about him…" Hunter swallowed hard.

"Did you ever try to talk to him after that night?"

Shaking his head, Hunter said, "I left town the next morning. My dad…he sent me to stay with this pastor friend of his who ran a youth group. I didn't realize what it was at first…"

Roman tensed as he realized the direction Hunter was headed in.

"Most of the first day was just about studying all these bible passages. Then the pastor brought in all these guys and girls who were supposed success stories and they started telling us how they'd found their way back to the light after being tempted to sin by the devil."

"It was one of those 'pray the gay away' places," Roman said softly.

Hunter nodded.

"I don't understand. Why did your dad send you there if he

believed your lie about Finn assaulting you?"

"I thought my dad would just kick Finn out of the party and tell him to stay away from me. But then he called the cops. While they were questioning Finn, I pulled my dad aside and tried to tell him that maybe it had all just been a misunderstanding…that maybe I'd accidentally sent Finn some kind of signal or something. I thought he'd just let it go. But he just told me to go in the house. Once everyone was gone, he came into my room and started yelling at me about sending out gay signals. Then he started asking me if it was because I was a queer. He got in my face and started asking me that over and over again so I told him I'd said that stuff about it being a misunderstanding because I was embarrassed for people to know a fag had touched me. That seemed to calm him down but he sent me to that place anyway. I was only there about a week because my dad pulled me out early so I could spend the rest of the summer interning for a friend of his who worked for the governor."

"Did you come home at all after that?"

Hunter shook his head. "I was too ashamed. I cut myself off from everyone so I wouldn't have to be reminded of what I'd done, especially because so many of them believed my lie." Hunter's eyes lifted to meet his. "I didn't…I didn't know things had gotten so bad for Finn or his boss. I figured it would all just blow over." Hunter dashed at his eyes. "Luke said…he said Finn was with that guy and his boss, right?"

Roman nodded.

"You think he's happy?" Hunter asked quietly. "I mean, he looked really happy talking to that guy…Rhys…before he saw me, didn't he?"

"Yeah, I think he is. And if this is anything to go by," – Roman gently brushed his thumb beneath the wound on Hunter's cheek – "I think Rhys really cares about him."

Hunter nodded and then closed his eyes. "I'm sorry, Roman."

"Sorry for what?" Roman asked.

"That I wasn't more…" Hunter murmured as sleep began to claim him.

"More what?" Roman whispered.

"Just more."

CHAPTER 6

"*W*here is he?" Roman nearly yelled as he hurried past Gray who was clearing dishes off the kitchen table.

"Relax," Gray said. "He's out in the shed with Luke," Gray explained as he came up behind Roman in the living room and handed him a full cup of coffee. Relieved, Roman took the mug and set it down on the table next to the couch so he could finish buttoning up his shirt which he'd barely remembered to yank on shortly after waking up in the guest room by himself.

"What are they doing out there?" he asked as he tried to settle his nerves enough to work the buttons through holes that suddenly seemed too small. His first thought was that Hunter had taken off on foot down the mountain and images of his broken body laying bloodied and battered after being mauled by some wild animal or falling down a ravine had tormented him in the few long seconds it had taken him to climb out of bed and drag on his pants. Then he'd seen the closed bathroom door and he'd panicked at the thought of opening it to find Hunter lying in a pool of bloody water.

"Hunter was asking about the bookshelf," Gray said as he motioned to the custom bookshelf Luke had made for Gray. It was a truly beautiful piece of furniture with several white birch trees making up the back and sides of the bookcase. "Luke's been playing around with the idea of trying to make more furniture so he took Hunter out there to show him some of his tools and stuff."

"Did he seem okay this morning?" Roman asked as he grabbed his coffee and followed Gray back to the kitchen.

"Little tired…nervous at first but he opened up once he and Luke started talking about the bookshelf. He's a nice kid. Sit, I'll make you some breakfast."

"Um, just the coffee, thanks," Roman said as he dropped down in one of the kitchen chairs.

Gray settled in the chair across from him. "Rough night?"

Roman nodded. Throughout the night, Hunter had had several nightmares. The first one had just had him bolting upright in bed, his breath coming in heavy drags. Roman had asked him about the dream but Hunter had merely shaken his head and lain back down. He hadn't been fully awake during the second and third and both had started with him begging his unknown attacker to stop. Roman had managed to pin his arms to keep him from lashing out at him and after a few soft words, Hunter had settled and then drifted back off to sleep. He'd had the same nightmare once the previous night when they'd spent the night at the lake but Roman had figured it was a normal, one-time thing. Now he wasn't so sure. Although Hunter refused to call what the bikers had done to him rape, it was unlikely he'd walked away from the encounter with only a battered body.

"I'm sorry, Gray," Roman said softly as his eyes met his brother's across the table.

"For what?" Gray asked gently.

"For not telling you I was in town. For not having any intention of telling you," Roman admitted.

"I kind of figured that was the way of things," Gray said.

"Yet you kept calling, texting. Why?"

"Same reason you came out here to check on me three months ago, I suppose," Gray answered. "You actually had me with that story about Mom – Victoria – being worried about me. I called her right after you left. Apparently I interrupted one of her sessions with clients because she only had enough time to ask me what I wanted and to scold me for my behavior embarrassing her."

"Sorry," Roman muttered. He hadn't given much thought to the validity of his lie or that Victoria would be so dismissive of Gray even after weeks of him seemingly dropping off the face of the earth.

"Don't be. That was one of the best days of my life."

That got Roman's attention and he whipped his head up. "What?"

"It was the day I realized I might actually have another chance with you...to be the big brother I should have been all along."

A strange mix of excitement and anger went through Roman. He wanted to yell that it was too fucking late – that he didn't need Gray. But it was complete and utter bullshit. Maybe he didn't want to need Gray but he'd been exactly the first person Roman had thought of when he'd understood the truth about what Hunter was doing himself.

"Don't worry Roman, I'm not looking for miracles," Gray said gently. "I already got more than my fair share of those."

Roman had no doubt who Gray was talking about, at least for the first miracle. He suspected beating cancer was a very close second to finding the love of his life.

"I saw those burns on his arm and I just...I just went right back to that night..."

"To the night you lost your mom you mean?" Gray asked.

Roman swallowed hard. "You know about that?"

"Not the details," Gray responded. "I heard Mo-Victoria say how your mom died when she was fighting with Dad one night when I was home from college. I'm sorry, Roman. No one ever told me when you first came to live with us."

"I'm sure it was hard enough to hear your dad had been cheating on your mom all those years. It probably wouldn't have mattered much that his mistress killed herself," Roman said. After a moment, he continued. "She never did what Hunter does but she always had that same empty look in her eyes that I sometimes see in his. When I saw what he'd done to himself, I just panicked. I knew I had to get him out of there but it was like I couldn't think, couldn't breathe. What if I did or said something to make things worse? What if I missed some sign and he…"

The thought was too disturbing to even contemplate so Roman snapped his mouth shut. He was surprised when he felt Gray's hand close over his where it was resting on the table.

"Roman, even if you spend the rest of your life hating me, I will always be here if you need me."

"I don't hate you," Roman murmured. "I just…"

"You can't forgive me," Gray finished for him.

God, Roman felt like such a fucking hypocrite. Hadn't he been urging Hunter to forgive himself for the mistakes he'd made and yet he couldn't find it in himself to let go of the pain Gray's indifference had caused him all those years ago?

He must have been quiet too long because Gray said, "Can I ask you something?"

Roman nodded.

"Is there something between the two of you?"

Roman smiled. "Just going to go right to it, huh?"

A small smile graced Gray's lips. "It's just…he's so young and you guys are so different. I didn't even know you were interested in men."

Roman's first instinct was to say Gray hadn't been around enough to know about his preferences but he bit back the automatic response and said, "It's not something I announce to everyone I meet but I don't hide it either. I suppose I've never been in a relationship long enough with either a man or a woman to even make it necessary to "come out." And Hunter…he's so messed up about being attracted to men that it wouldn't matter either way if there was something there or not."

"Is there anyone he can turn to?"

"He mentioned a grandmother but I'm not sure if they're still in touch."

"I've met her. She takes care of our friends' daughter while they're working. Dane is a vet and Jax is the town's other deputy besides Rhys."

Roman remembered the big cop who'd intervened yesterday.

Interesting that both of the small town's law enforcement officers were gay.

"She ever mention Hunter?" Roman asked.

"Not to me but I've only spoken to her briefly in passing. She was the one who spearheaded the rebuilding of Callan Bale's barn after the two fuckers who were vandalizing his property burned it down so she seems supportive of our cause."

So Hunter's grandmother was open to the idea of homosexuals while Hunter's own father clearly wasn't. And from what Hunter had said about his grandfather, he hadn't appeared to have had an issue with his grandson's sexual preference either.

Roman heard the back door open but when he saw only Luke round the corner, he immediately stood. "Where is he?"

"He's making a phone call," Luke said as he leaned down to brush his lips over Gray's. "Don't worry, I made him promise he wouldn't take off again. Ripley's out there with him so even if he does, he'll be easy to find. I showed him our spot," Luke said to Gray and they shared a quick smile between them.

"Straight out the back door about 200 hundred yards. You can't miss it," Luke said before Roman could even ask.

Roman nodded and hurried out the back of the cabin. He was relieved to find Hunter sitting on a large fallen log just past where the backyard turned into dense woods. He was tossing a stick into a small stream for Ripley.

"Morning," Roman said as he sat down next to Hunter.

"Hi," Hunter said just as Roman's phone began to ring. "That's my dad," Hunter said. "I told him I was planning to head back to school today unless his new client needed me to stick around a little longer to show him around some more."

Roman felt a prickle of disappointment go through him as he realized he was about to end the only valid reason he had to keep Hunter around for a while. But knowing just how toxic this town and his own family were to Hunter, Roman had no issue with answering the phone and telling Malcom Greene he'd be leaving town this afternoon and wouldn't need Hunter's services anymore. He ignored Malcolm's efforts to try and draw more information out of him regarding his plans to pursue the purchase of the property and hung up the phone without saying goodbye.

"Thank you," Hunter said softly.

"What will you do now?" Roman asked.

Hunter took the stick that Ripley dropped in his lap and studied it for a moment before tossing it into the water. "Go back to the way things were," Hunter said. "Minus the gay clubs," he added with a small smile and while Roman knew he'd meant it as a roundabout way to reassure him that there wouldn't be a repeat of the episode with the bikers, the comment did nothing to ease the aching in Roman's gut.

"I need you to promise me something," Roman whispered.

Hunter shook his head. "Roman, please don't ask me to make a promise you know I can't keep."

Frustration went through Roman because that was exactly what he'd been about to do. Roman turned and swung one leg over the log so that he was straddling it. The move had him facing Hunter and a surge of pleasure went through him when Hunter did the same thing and then went a step further and moved close enough so that their legs were touching. Hunter met him halfway when he leaned down to kiss him and while the kiss was tame compared to the one they'd shared yesterday, it still left him burning inside.

"You could come with me," Roman whispered against Hunter's mouth. "I could set you up somewhere, help you start fresh. You could do and be anything you wanted to be."

Hunter smiled and then kissed him hard. "You are an amazing man, Roman Blackwell. Wherever your mom is, I'll bet you've made her proud more times than you can count."

It was just too fucking much. Roman dragged Hunter up against him and kissed him over and over until they were both shaking from the emotion of it all. He buried his face against Hunter's neck and said, "I don't know if I can let you go." He felt Hunter's fingers stroking through his hair.

"You won't have to," Hunter said against his ear. "Because for once, I'm going to be the strong one." He felt lips skim his cheek and then

Hunter was pushing the stick he'd been throwing for Ripley in his hand. "Play with Ripley for a while, okay?"

Roman managed a nod and kept his eyes on the big dog sitting at his feet. He stayed there long after he heard the footsteps move away from him and he didn't move when he heard the sound of a car's engine start. It wasn't until he felt his brother's hand settle on his shoulder that he finally dropped the stick on the ground and forced himself to get up. Life was calling and it was time he got back to it.

~

Hunter gave Luke a last wave as he watched the pickup truck back out of the driveway and head back down the street. It wasn't until the truck was out of sight that he felt his knees give out and he had to lean against his car so he could catch his breath. Walking away from Roman had been so much harder than he'd thought it would be which made no sense since he'd known the man less than 48 hours. Saying no to Roman's offer to help him start over had been even harder because his first thought when Roman had suggested it was that it would be a way to stay connected to Roman. And while he knew Roman had only done it out of pity, a part of him hadn't cared because he would have given anything to know there was still some link to the man who'd changed so much for him. There'd even been a little shard of hope that maybe someday Roman would see him as something other than a pathetic mental case who couldn't even admit what his body had been telling him for years. Luckily, he'd had just the tiniest amount of pride left and he'd made himself let go of Roman. Because as much as he wanted, needed Roman, Roman didn't need him.

Forcing himself to straighten, Hunter went into the house to get his stuff but stopped when he saw his mother standing at her ironing board in the kitchen.

"Good morning, darling," she said flatly as she kept her focus on the shirt collar she was pressing. "Did you have fun with your friends?"

The question was the right one but the way she asked it was all wrong as usual. He could have answered that the party he'd lied about going to last night had turned into one huge fuckfest and she would have responded by asking him if he wanted her to make him some breakfast.

"Can I make you some breakfast?" she asked, her voice hollow and dull.

God, would this be what he would look like when he was her age? Like he'd lived a thousand lifetimes and hadn't enjoyed any of them?

The easy thing to do - the expected thing – would be to give her a quick kiss on the cheek, tell her he loved her, get his things and go. It was what she wanted and truth be told, a part of him wanted that too. Because doing anything else would likely mean he'd have to hear things he didn't want to hear. If he just kept his mouth shut like he was supposed to, the two of them would go on being what they'd always been – props in someone else's life.

Hunter went to his mother's side but instead of leaning in to kiss her, he reached for the iron's power cord and pulled it free of the outlet. His mother actually kept ironing until he put his hand over hers. Her lackluster eyes finally lifted to meet his and he carefully took the iron and set it aside.

"Your father has a lunch meeting and he needs his blue shirt because he's wearing his pin stripe blazer and white takes away from-"

"Mom," he said gently and took her hand in his. The contact finally seemed to snap her out of her daze and her fingers lifted to brush over the wound on his cheek. She stopped just short of actually touching it though.

"Hunter, you have to remember your father knows what's best…"

Disappointment went through Hunter as he realized his mother assumed the injury on his face had come from his father…and that he'd somehow done something to warrant it.

"Mom, why didn't you tell me the truth about what happened after I left?"

Her eyes dropped instantly and another streak of hurt hit him. She knew exactly what he was referring to but he voiced it anyway. "You told me the stuff with Finn Stewart blew over – that everything went back to normal after I left."

"You always had a soft spot for boys like him…troublemakers," she said firmly as she smoothed her hands over the collar of the shirt. "He got what he deserved for doing what he did."

Hunter reared back as if she'd struck him. "I told you the truth about that night, Mom. I told you it wasn't his fault. That I started it. You said…you said if I stayed away, that if I left things alone it would all go away."

His mother shook her head. "No, that boy, he tricked you into saying that stuff. I knew he'd do it again if you came back."

Hunter actually felt bile creeping up the back of his throat. All this time he'd thought he had a secret ally in his mother. That if and when he really needed her, she'd be there for him. He'd been terrified that she'd hate him when he'd admitted that the encounter with Finn had been because he'd instigated it but when she'd said she understood, he'd taken that to mean she was okay with it…with him. But she'd done the same thing as his father – used his lie to hide a truth she didn't want to accept.

"Why?" Hunter asked.

His mother reached up to plug the iron back in. "Your father needs this shirt because the white one isn't right for the pin striped blazer."

Hunter just stood there waiting and hoping that she'd look up and say something, anything that would explain everything away. That some miracle words would fall from her lips and his world would right itself once more. But she kept ironing away and when she asked him if he wanted her to make breakfast, he left the kitchen and ran up the stairs to his room. The familiar ache in his gut kept churning and twisting until his skin itched. He tried shaking the feeling loose but it just kept building and building. He ran his hand over his pocket and bit down on his lip hard when he felt nothing. He hurried to the bathroom and actually let out a cry of relief when he saw the spoon lying on the floor and the lighter sitting in the sink. He slammed the bathroom door shut but it didn't latch into place since the housing in the door frame was bent.

Because Roman had been desperate to get to him. To make sure he was okay.

Hunter snatched up the spoon and grabbed the lighter and sat down on the floor. He yanked his sleeve up and then got the lighter going and held the spoon over it. He watched the flames lick at the metal and felt his whole body draw up tight in anticipation. Long after he knew he should pull the lighter away, he kept it there. And then he looked down at his arm to find the perfect spot. He released the button on the lighter and let it fall to the floor, the sound ricocheting through the room. He lowered the spoon to just above the delicate skin on the inside of his wrist. The burn would be harder to hide but maybe the pain would stick around long enough this time to…

To what?

When will it be enough, Hunter? How much pain do you need to feel before you start forgiving yourself?

Roman's words clung to every corner of his brain as the intense heat from the spoon drifted over his skin. He wanted it so bad he could taste it. But how long until he would need it again? The pain from yesterday's burn still radiated up and down his arm but it hadn't even made a dent in the turmoil coursing through him. Would the next one be any different? Would it change any of the million things that were wrong in his fucking little life?

I wish I could take this from you, Hunter.

Hunter opened his eyes and wasn't surprised to find his vision blurred by tears. He climbed to his feet and went to the sink to turn on the cold water. He held the spoon beneath the running water for several long seconds and then tested the bottom of it carefully to make sure it was cool to the touch. Then he tossed it into the garbage can. He did the same with the lighter and then scrubbed his face. The churning in his belly had eased by the time he grabbed his backpack off the chair by his desk. He knew he didn't have the strength to face his mother so he exited the house through the front door and went to his car. A glance at the clock in the dash showed that if he left now, he could still make it to his *Intro to Political Science* class. He backed his car out of the driveway and headed towards the road that would take him north to Missoula. But by the time he reached the last intersection on the way out of town, he knew there was a stop he needed to make.

∾

*H*unter's hands were shaking so bad that he ended up folding his arms in an effort to keep from reaching for his empty pocket. He hadn't seen any cars outside the barn when he pulled in but he knew they could just be up at the main house at the top of the hill. Since it was the middle of the day, it was highly likely that the inhabitants of the CB Bar Ranch were out in the fields checking on the cattle that were the ranch's lifeblood. If that were the case, he'd have to find some place to settle in and wait them out because he wasn't going to chicken out now. He just hoped like hell that if the big cop who'd slugged him yesterday was the first person he encountered, he'd somehow last long enough to still be able to verbalize his apology if and when Finn showed up.

The brand new barn looked like it had just recently been painted. It had been little comfort to learn that no animals had been killed when the old barn had been torched. He'd managed to glean a little bit of information about what had happened that day as he'd been talking to Luke but he hadn't pressed the other man for details because he hadn't wanted to hear the disdain in Luke's voice that he knew would be there since they both knew whose fault it was that Finn and the men he loved had had to endure so much unjustified hatred. He'd been horrified when he'd overheard Gray telling Roman about the barn yesterday but he'd nearly lost it when Gray had said Finn had gotten shot. Luke had reassured him this morning that Finn had made a complete recovery but it didn't change the fact that it never should have happened in the first place.

The barn was empty when Hunter entered so he walked all the

way through it to the other side which led to some pastures. He could see several horses grazing in the larger pasture on the hill behind the barn but there was one horse standing nervously in the center of a round corral just beyond the barn. It shifted uneasily at his approach and then moved as far away from him as it could when he folded his arms across the top of the fence. Even from a distance, he could see scars covering the animal's nearly all white coat. He took a few steps around the edge of the corral to get a closer look and began humming the tune of one of his favorite songs to try to soothe the animal as he neared it. To his amazement, the horse didn't move. It shifted back and forth and tossed its head several times but stayed where it was. Hunter once again folded his arms over the top of the fence and began singing the words to the song. By the time he was done, the horse had actually taken a few steps toward him.

The animal watched him warily and although it didn't come any closer, it didn't move away either. "I get it," Hunter whispered to the animal and he watched its ears flick forward. They watched each other for a while until the horse's ears began to twitch and then it started shaking its head again and striking the ground with its massive hoof. It let out a sharp whinny and then backed up until it was as far away from him as it could get. It wasn't until a voice spoke from off to his right that he realized he was no longer alone.

"Can I help you?"

The man watching him from near the barn door was huge – bigger than Roman or even the cop who'd tried to kick his ass yesterday. His black hair was partially hidden by a brown cowboy hat and he was wearing a long sleeved work shirt and faded blue jeans. Hunter had no doubt he was looking at Callan Bale, the owner of the CB Bar Ranch and Finn's other lover. He swallowed hard and tried to speak but found that the words wouldn't come out. So much for not letting his cowardice show.

The man began walking towards him and Hunter was ridiculously proud of himself for standing his ground.

"His name's King."

"What?" Hunter asked stupidly.

The man nodded towards the horse. "His name's King. The rescue group that saved him named him that because of what he had to go through to get here. They figured a strong horse deserved a strong name." He draped his arms over the corral and studied the horse who had settled down somewhat but still seemed agitated.

"This is as close as he lets me get to him," the guy said quietly. "It's been four months. We have to use those" – the man motioned over his shoulder to a bunch of metal gates leaning up against the fence – "to move him back and forth from his stall and we have to sedate him for the vet to look at him or for the farrier to work on his feet."

"I'm sorry," Hunter murmured as he looked back at the horse.

"What were you saying to him?"

"What? Nothing," Hunter blurted. But when the guy just pinned him with a hard stare, Hunter said, "I wasn't talking – I was singing."

The man didn't respond at first. "You told him you get it," he finally said.

Damn, the man had good ears.

"Get what?" he asked as he turned his back on the horse and stared at Hunter.

"Nothing," Hunter answered quickly.

"I'm Callan Bale," the man finally said and when he extended his hand, Hunter wanted to throw up. God, a few more seconds and this man was going to tear him limb from limb.

Steeling himself, Hunter didn't reach out his hand. Instead he said, "Mr. Bale, I'm Hunter Greene."

The blow he was waiting for never came. There were no words of hatred or damning him to hell. Instead Callan just said, "I know" and continued to hold his hand out expectantly.

Hunter shook his hand briefly, half expecting the man to sucker punch him as soon as he took it but Callan merely gave him a quick shake and then released him. When his big hand reached for his face, Hunter took a step back before he could stop himself. His move only caused Callan to hesitate for a moment and then he was gently tilting Hunter's face to the side.

"Rhys shouldn't have done this," he murmured. "I'm sorry."

Something inside of Hunter shattered into a million pieces. "What?"

"I said I'm sor-"

"Oh my God," Hunter said as he wrapped an arm around his stomach to staunch the pain he felt. If he hadn't known better, he'd have thought there was a mortal wound that had ripped him open and all his life's blood was spilling from his body and pooling on the dusty ground beneath his feet. "Please, Mr. Bale…please don't ever say that to me again."

"Why not?" Callan asked gently…too gently.

"You know why not," Hunter whispered. "Is he…Is he here?" Hunter managed to ask.

"No," Callan said. "He and Rhys went to Bozeman to look at a bull. Finn's got some ideas about how to improve the quality of our herd," Callan added. "He's taken over the ranch so I can focus on doing what I love," he said as he nodded at the big horse who was still watching them from a safe distance.

Hunter had no clue what to say to that since he had no idea why Callan was sharing so much information with him. Hell, the man should have kicked him off the property the second he laid eyes on him.

"He's okay, Hunter," Callan suddenly said and Hunter realized his thoughts must have been written all over his face.

Tears threatened to fall as he realized how much he'd needed to hear those words.

Hunter nodded quickly. "I'm sorry for everything, Mr. Bale. I truly am," he said in a rush. "I'll fix things – I'll make sure people know it was me."

Hunter began walking before he even finished speaking because the tears were already falling down his face. He'd steeled himself for hatred, derision, rage. He'd done nothing to prepare himself for kindness.

"Hunter, wait," Callan said as he gently grabbed him by the arm and held him in place. Hunter couldn't force himself to look up at Callan so he just hung there and waited.

"I saw you there that night. At the hospital."

The statement was so unexpected that Hunter snapped his eyes up to meet Callan's. "No," he said with a shake of his head.

"I was coming back from the cafeteria. I'd gone to get some coffee. They'd given Finn something to help him sleep so I knew he'd be out for a bit. When I came back, I saw someone coming out of his room. He was wearing a hoodie but I could see his hair. It was so light that it almost looked white."

Hunter sucked in a breath. "I...I heard about what happened from a guy whose mom was a nurse in the ER."

"I didn't know it was you till just now," Callan said as he glanced at Hunter's hair. "So I never told Finn. I saw your face, Hunter. Even from as far away as I was, I saw your face."

Hunter tried to shake Callan off but the big man wouldn't release him. "It was nothing," he muttered as a brief image of the beating he'd gotten for trying to suggest to his father that he'd sent Finn a mixed signal went through his mind. "It wasn't even half of what I deserved."

"Look, I don't know what your situation is these days but I know Finn would be okay with me telling you to make sure you're safe first and foremost. Too many people in this town went after Finn because of who he was, not what you said. Those people won't suddenly stop hating him or me or Rhys just because you admit what really happened that night. All you'll do is make yourself a target."

"I don't think I can keep living this lie," Hunter admitted. "I need to tell the truth, not just for Finn but for me too."

He was surprised when Callan clasped the back of his neck with his big hand and looked him square in the eye. "I'm not asking you to hide who you are, Hunter. In fact, I'm flat out telling you right now not to. I denied who I was for so long that it nearly cost me one of the most important people in my entire life. But knowing what I know about your father – having seen the hatred he has for people like us – I need you to think of your safety first. Go to your grandmother or someone else you trust."

"Gran...Gran and I don't talk anymore. She knew I lied about Finn and told me I should tell the truth. I've been too ashamed..."

"Your grandmother loves you, Hunter. Don't doubt that."

Hunter shook his head. This was too much. It was all just too much.

"Then come stay with us. We have an extra room you can use till you figure something out."

An obscene laugh bubbled up deep inside Hunter's throat. He'd destroyed this man's life, ruined his livelihood and nearly cost his lover his life and he wanted Hunter to move in? So he could fucking protect him?

Shaking free of Callan, Hunter took several steps away from him. "Tell Finn I'm sorry, okay? Tell him I'll figure out how to fix things and I won't come back to Dare - he'll never have to see me again."

"Hunter-"

Hunter put out his hand when it looked like Callan was going to try to grab him again. "I'll be okay, Mr. Bale. I'm going back to school. I'll…I'll do what you said and make sure I'm safe before I tell everyone what really happened."

He didn't give Callan a chance to answer him as he turned and basically ran for his car. He automatically checked his pocket for his spoon and then cursed himself. Because the reality was that it wasn't his spoon and his lighter that he wanted. The only thing he wanted was on a plane somewhere getting as far away from Hunter as he could.

CHAPTER 7

*R*oman knew he was driving much too fast for the road conditions but the closer he got to his destination, the more he needed to know if this trip would be any different than the last two. It was the third weekend in a row he'd made the drive out to Hunter's valley and he was terrified that it would be the third weekend in a row he'd be disappointed. With the last two weekends, he'd had the benefit of having enough daylight left to make it to the lake but weather in L.A. had delayed his plane so by the time he'd picked up his rental car, darkness had already fallen. And while it was only nine o'clock, it was pitch dark outside. He was lucky enough to have a full moon to guide him though and if he hadn't been so preoccupied, he would have enjoyed the way the moon lit up the land around him.

Leaving Hunter had been one of the hardest things he'd ever had to do. But that had lasted only until he tried to call Hunter the first time and got a message saying the phone had been disconnected. Because at least when he'd left Hunter, he'd known he was safe for the moment – had known he could reach out to him if he needed to or that Hunter could get in touch with him if things got bad. But when he'd lost that last link to Hunter, he'd nearly gone insane. He'd even called Malcom Greene on the pretense of wanting to see the property again. A casual question about if his son would be available to show him and his investors the property had been brushed off with a blanket statement about Hunter being busy with school but that Malcom was ready and able to answer any and all questions he had.

He'd called Gray on more than one occasion to see if he'd heard anything and his brother had promised to let him know if he had any news but there still hadn't been any sign of Hunter. He'd learned of Hunter's visit to the CB Bar Ranch from Luke but hadn't gotten any details other than Hunter had gone there to talk to Finn who'd been out of town along with the hot-headed Rhys. Luke had reassured him that Hunter had left the ranch in the same condition he'd arrived in but the information didn't bring him any closer to figuring out where Hunter was. His desperation had even led him to stalking the various buildings on the University of Montana campus where the political science classes were held. And it all had been an epic waste of time.

Roman's jaw rattled as he hit a particularly deep rut but it didn't slow him down. And when he finally saw his headlights bounce off of the dark green Escort parked at the end of the road, Roman let out a deep breath. And then he hit the gas. He was going so fast that he narrowly avoided slamming into the back of Hunter's car. He jammed it into park and then snatched the flashlight off the passenger seat.

It took him just minutes to find the fork in the trailhead and he began winding his way around and over the fallen trees in his path. He smelled the campfire before he saw it and then a flash of light cut across his path as he heard Hunter call out, "Who's there?"

Roman was close enough to see Hunter's outline along with the rifle he held in his right hand. "It's me," he called just as he cleared the trees and began striding across the small clearing just above the shoreline.

"Roman?" Hunter's dazed voice said but he didn't move at Roman's approach. He didn't speak either. He simply waited and when he realized Roman wasn't slowing down, he dropped both his gun and his flashlight.

Roman wasn't sure if it was his arms dragging Hunter against his body or if Hunter had come to him willingly but either way he didn't care as he crushed his mouth down on Hunter's. And since Hunter was trying to crawl up his body so he could get even closer to him, Roman realized it didn't matter either way. Lust shot through Roman as Hunter began grinding their hips together. Every kiss he gave Hunter was returned with fervor and any doubt he had that Hunter might not want him fled when he felt his jacket being pushed off his shoulders and long fingers tugging his shirt free of his pants and searching out the skin at his lower back.

"More," Roman said hoarsely as he fisted his hands in Hunter's hair to hold him still for his kiss. "I need more."

"Yes," Hunter breathed against his mouth.

That one word released the floodgates and Roman reached down to wrap his hands around the backs of Hunter's thighs. Hunter must have known what he was going to do because his arms instantly went around Roman's neck. Since Hunter refused to release his mouth, Roman had to use the fire as his guide to get Hunter to the sleeping bag he knew would be there. By the time his feet hit the fabric, Hunter had wrapped his legs around Roman's waist and locked them in place so instead of lowering Hunter to his feet, Roman let himself sink to his knees and then he was pushing Hunter onto his back and covering him with his body. On any other day he would have been happy just to lay there and explore Hunter's sweet mouth but he was too raw and needy from the weeks of not knowing if Hunter was okay to linger so he ripped his mouth free of Hunter's and closed them over Hunter's neck and sucked hard. Hunter moaned and bucked his hips up against Roman. Using his greater weight, Roman forced Hunter's hips flat again and then rubbed their erections together as his hands sought out the hem of Hunter's shirt.

Instead of removing the shirt, Roman slid down Hunter's body and then shoved the shirt up just enough to reveal Hunter's lightly muscled chest. He felt Hunter stiffen when Roman's lips skimmed over a patch of jagged skin and he didn't need to look to know what he was feeling. Instead of ignoring the scar, Roman kissed it softly and then gave the next one a little farther down the same treatment. With each caress, the tension eased from Hunter's body and by the time Roman's fingers began working his jeans open, Hunter was writhing beneath him once more.

Roman managed to get the button and zipper open but when he went to pull the jeans down, he hesitated and then looked up. His breath caught when he saw Hunter watching him, his hungry eyes filled with so much emotion that Roman felt his heart constrict painfully in his chest.

"Is this okay?" he asked.

The sight of Hunter catching his lower lip between his teeth as he nodded had Roman's dick swelling even more and he quickly worked Hunter's jeans just low enough to release Hunter's cock. His mouth watered at sight of the long, curved shaft and leaking crown and he didn't hesitate even for a second to suck as much of the velvety flesh into his mouth as he could.

"Roman!" Hunter shouted in wonderment. Roman managed to look up to see that Hunter was leaning up on his elbows so he could watch but his head was thrown back. He didn't need to see Hunter's face to know the pleasure he was experiencing because Roman could feel Hunter's whole body jerking beneath his hands with every drag of his mouth up and down Hunter's dick. As soon as Hunter lifted his hips to try to get deeper into Roman's mouth, Roman spread his palms over the smooth globes of Hunter's ass and then held him tight so he could control Hunter's thrusts into his mouth. But he didn't last as long as he would have liked because Hunter's moans were driving him insane and he could feel his own orgasm threatening to crest whether he was ready for it to or not. And as much as he was enjoying the feel of Hunter's hot flesh kissing the back of his throat, it wasn't enough. Not even close.

With that in mind, Roman released Hunter and then dragged him upright and kissed him hard. "I need you," he said in a guttural voice as he searched out his wallet and fumbled around for the condom and pack of lube he kept there. Even though he had to take his gaze off of Hunter long enough to find the supplies, Hunter's fingers never stopped touching his neck and face as he pressed sweet kisses along his jaw and cheek. The show of trust was humbling and managed to cool Roman's ardor enough to allow him to kiss Hunter long and deep. As he did, he wrapped his arm around Hunter's waist and then lifted him enough so he could maneuver them so that Roman was lying on his back on the sleeping bag. Hunter seemed surprised by the change in position but when Roman handed the condom to Hunter and then began working his own pants off his body, Hunter just looked at him in confusion.

"Have you put one of these on before?" Roman asked when Hunter didn't move.

"Um…in health class we had to put them on bananas but I've never put them on someone else before…" he said and then his whole countenance froze as Roman slid his underwear off. Roman's cock was so heavy with need that it bounced against his abdomen for only a second before bobbing upright again.

"Did you ever put one on yourself?" Roman asked.

Hunter was still too focused on his dick to respond so Roman fell silent as he waited. And the second Hunter's questioning gaze lifted to meet his, Roman nodded in silent permission. Hunter licked his lips and then reached out a shaky hand. His fingers barely touched Roman's cock on their first pass but his dick did its own version of a happy dance and twitched hungrily. Fascinated, Hunter ran his thumb over the slit and Roman bit back a curse. With each hesitant touch, Hunter grew a little bit more emboldened and within a minute he was eagerly closing his hand around Roman and giving him little tugs.

"I can't," Roman muttered as he sat up and kissed Hunter hard. "I'm not going to fucking last if you keep doing that," he ground out. "And I've needed this since the first time I felt these beautiful lips on mine." He kissed Hunter again, more softly this time and said, "I promise you can touch me as much as you want after, okay?"

Hunter nodded and then a shy smile spread across his lips. He searched out the condom which he'd dropped at some point and then tore the wrapper open. He carefully removed it from the packaging but when he reached for Roman's dick, Roman grabbed his wrist.

"I want you inside of me, Hunter."

~

*H*unter was sure he'd heard Roman wrong. No way would a big, strong, experienced guy like Roman let someone like him…

"Stop it," Roman whispered and he felt Roman release his wrist long enough to reach up and sift through his hair and then gently hold him still for another bone melting kiss. "Stop thinking it."

"Sorry," he said softly. "It's just that you're more experienced, older, stronger…"

"Truth?" Roman said. "Yes, I almost always top because sex was never just about pleasure for me…it was about power and control. For me, bottoming means trusting the person you're with to take care of you. It means making yourself vulnerable. I've never wanted that with anyone else – I never wanted anyone to see that part of me. I want you to see it. Don't ask me why because I'm too scared to ask myself that same question. Just…just know that I need this and if I'm lucky enough for you to show me the same trust someday, then you'll know what it feels like to be so deep inside of someone that you don't know where they end and you begin. Because I know without a shadow of a doubt that that's what it will feel like when we're together."

Hunter was so overwhelmed that he felt like he couldn't breathe. He slammed his lips down on Roman's and forced him on his back as he thrust his tongue into Roman's mouth. Roman's tongue was there to welcome him and as they played, Hunter reveled in the feel of their cocks sliding against each other. It took everything in him to release Roman's mouth and rear back to his knees so he could fumble with the condom. He got distracted when he saw Roman rip open the pack of lube and spread some on his fingers and he knew his mouth was hanging wide open as he watched those same slickened fingers disappear between the globes of Roman's ass. Some unnamed force of courage went through him and he lowered one hand to pull Roman's hot flesh back just enough to watch two of Roman's fingers buried deep within his own body. Every twisting and thrusting motion of Roman's fingers had Hunter's dick bobbing in anticipation and he felt more moisture well up from the tip when Roman's digits popped free of his hole.

"I've never...I've never done this with anyone," Hunter said lamely as he forced his eyes back to his dick and tried desperately to get the condom on. Big hands settled over his and gently took the small piece of latex from him. Lips coasted over his briefly as the condom was rolled down his length.

"Just do whatever feels good. I guarantee I'm going to like everything you do to me."

He got another kiss and then Roman asked, "What position do you want me in?"

Fuck, he had no idea. He had no idea about any of this. But one look at Roman's dark eyes and he realized he did know. "I want to see you," Hunter whispered.

The look that passed through Roman's gaze left Hunter reeling but before he could think on it too much, Roman was laying back down and pulling his legs up and opening them wide. His big fingers closed over his own ass cheeks and spread them and Hunter nearly choked on the sight of the small hole that greeted him. Jesus, how would he ever fit into something so small without hurting Roman?

Hunter moved forward on his knees which was awkward since he hadn't thought to take his jeans all the way off. His fingers shook as he guided his cock to the entrance to Roman's body and he looked up just to make sure Roman was okay. Roman nodded and then exhaled just as Hunter pressed forward. Logically he knew there would be resistance but a jolt of fear that he would end up hurting Roman if he went too fast had Hunter hanging there, the tip of his cock still mostly visible.

"Hunter..."

Roman's broken whisper caught his attention and he glanced up to see Roman's desperate eyes on his – desperate, not pained. Desperate, not scared. Desperate...for him.

Hunter applied enough pressure so that his crown finally pierced Roman's body and sank inside. The heat and pressure were terrifyingly good so he maintained his forward motion until another couple inches of his cock disappeared. Instinct had him pulling those same inches back out and then sliding back in again. He repeated the move over and over until his balls were flush with Roman's sensitive skin. Roman had released his grip on his own ass at some point and Hunter saw that he was fisting the sleeping bag. Uncertainty went through him as he tried to read Roman's face but he couldn't tell if he was in agony or ecstasy so he gently leaned forward and brushed his lips over Roman's.

"Okay?" he whispered.

Roman nodded and then swallowed hard. "It feels so good...I didn't know..." Roman shook his head and then lifted just enough to seal their mouths together. Reluctant to break the connection, Hunter kept kissing Roman as he began moving his hips. He swallowed Roman's gasp as he pulled almost all the way out and then sank back in to the hilt.

"Fuck!" Roman cried.

Hunter did it again but faster, harder. Roman's eyes slid shut as Hunter let his body settle into a powerful rhythm and when he twisted his hips every few strokes, he felt Roman's big hands settle on his ass. Roman made no effort to guide Hunter's hips with his strong hold – his hands just followed Hunter's motions and his fingers pressed firmly into Hunter's hot skin. It was such a turn on knowing that Roman had the power to control their encounter but chose not to that Hunter actually began to lose it and he started ramming into Roman as hard as he could. He muttered a broken apology against Roman's mouth but couldn't slow himself down and from the way Roman began moaning as his hips lifted to meet every one of Hunter's thrusts, Hunter knew Roman wasn't feeling anything but pleasure.

The pressure and friction proved to be too much. "I'm really close," Hunter whispered and he had enough sense to reach between their bodies to start jacking Roman off. He had no idea if the pressure he was applying was enough but he had his answer a moment later when Roman screamed his name and began jerking uncontrollably beneath him. The muscles in his ass clamped down on Hunter, triggering his release. Heat shot through his entire body followed by a wave of electricity that fired along every nerve ending. Hunter's balls drew up tight as he shot his load into the condom and he let out a harsh sob as the climax consumed him. His body kept jerking long after Roman's body had milked all the seed from his body and he felt tears slipping down his cheeks as Roman's arms wrapped around him. Firm lips sought his out and he used every last bit of his energy to turn his head enough so that Roman's mouth could seal over his.

~

*R*oman was on the verge of calling the whole thing off when Hunter finally reached for the hem of his shirt. As good as the hot water felt, seeing how distressed Hunter was about having to expose his body made Roman's heart ache. It hadn't taken more than a few languid kisses to convince Hunter to take a walk with him up to the hot springs but he'd seen the wariness seep into Hunter's gaze as soon as Roman had started peeling off his own clothes.

It took Hunter a couple of stops and starts to finally lift the shirt over his head. Roman already knew there were at least half a dozen scars on Hunter's chest, because he'd kissed at least that many the night before. So while he wasn't at all unaffected by the sight of the red welts, he was pretty sure he managed to keep his expression neutral as he lifted his hand up to help Hunter in the water. Hunter quickly stripped off his underwear and then took Roman's hand. The pool of water wasn't particularly large or deep, but it was enough to cover Roman up to the middle of his chest once he sat on the natural rock formations that served as a bench of sorts. But since he pulled Hunter down to straddle his lap, more of Hunter's upper body was exposed. With the early morning air around them as cold as it was, Roman asked, "Too cold?"

Hunter had been strangely quiet since they'd woken up about thirty minutes ago but he hadn't withdrawn himself from Roman in any other way so Roman hadn't called him on it. So when Hunter just shook his head and then leaned down to kiss him, Roman guessed that Hunter was still trying to absorb what had happened the night before. And even though it hadn't been Roman's first time, it might as well have been because he was just as overwhelmed by all the emotions that being with Hunter had called forth. He'd been honest with Hunter when he'd told him that he didn't have an answer for why it was so important to him that Hunter see a part of him that no one else ever had. But by the time Hunter had slid into him, Roman already knew the answer. And it only served to scare him even more because it was an emotion that had always taken more from him than it had given. But unlike with his mother and Gray, Roman didn't just love Hunter – he was completely and utterly in love with him. He'd barely survived losing his mother and he'd pushed Gray away in a desperate attempt to protect himself from further loss. What would he do if Hunter didn't feel the same way? Hell, what would he do if Hunter did?

"How did you know I was here?" Hunter asked as his fingertips began rubbing back and forth over Roman's cheek. He liked how Hunter seemed to like touching him in such small ways.

"I didn't," Roman admitted. "I was hopeful but since you weren't here last weekend or the one before-"

"You've been coming here for two weeks looking for me?" Hunter interrupted, his shock evident.

"Your phone was fucking disconnected!" Roman bit out, unable to hide his frustration.

Hunter stilled and then his features softened. "Roman, God, I'm sorry," he whispered as he leaned down to brush a conciliatory kiss over Roman's lips. "The phone was under my dad's name so I got rid of it. He must have had it disconnected."

"Why didn't you send me your new number?"

Hunter dropped his eyes. "I didn't think you'd want to hear from me again."

Hurt lanced through Roman. "Did I do something to make you think that?"

"No-"

"Because I've been going fucking insane thinking something

happened to you," Roman snapped. He knew his anger was too much and just further proof of how deep he was into whatever this thing with Hunter was, so he tried to push Hunter off of him so he could get out of the water.

"No, Roman, please don't," Hunter said as he grabbed onto Roman's upper arms to keep from being dislodged.

"I just need some space right now," Roman muttered.

"Please, Roman, just wait," Hunter begged as he tried to reach past Roman to where his jeans were lying near the edge of the pool. He had to release Roman to actually get them and he kept glancing back at Roman as if afraid he'd move away and that was the only thing that kept Roman from following through with his need to escape.

Hunter fumbled with something in his pants pocket. He finally managed to pull his phone free and he carefully held it above the water as he began tapping the screen. "Here," he said as he handed the phone to Roman. Since his hands were wet, Roman reached behind him to snag his shirt so he could dry his hands and then he took the phone. He stilled when he saw his name in the header of the text message and the two words underneath.

Miss you.

He used his finger to go back a screen and saw more than a dozen messages listed, all in draft format, all with his name on them.

I heard your voice today, Roman. I was so close to hurting myself again and then you were there. I could feel you next to me, whispering to me that everything was okay...that I was okay.

Tears stung Roman's eyes. "Why didn't you send these?"

"Two days, Roman. We were together for two days and all you saw of me was me at my worst. These" – he pointed to the phone – "are just more of the same," he murmured. "I wanted to wait until I could show you there was another side of me...a side you might want to get to know better someday."

Roman couldn't move or speak. Hell, he could barely fucking breathe. He could feel Hunter getting tense and when he subtly shifted his weight, Roman said, "Don't you dare fucking move."

Hunter froze and Roman turned his attention back to the phone and began hitting the send button on each and every message. He stopped counting after twenty and he guessed it took him a full three minutes to get them all sent and then he put the phone down on top of Hunter's jeans. He pinned Hunter with his gaze and said, "You need to make a decision right now because I fucking refuse to go through the hell of not knowing if you're okay or not ever again. I want every part of you, good or bad. And just so you know, the only bad part of you I've seen is whatever part it was that convinced you that you're somehow not good enough for me. I want a shot at figuring out whatever this thing between us is but if you don't want that then tell me now because I-"

Hunter cut off his tirade with a hard kiss that effectively shut down all his remaining frustration. "Yes," was all Hunter said as he reached over Roman's shoulders to brace his hands against the edge of the pool. Roman had no trouble feeling the apology in Hunter's next kiss. When Hunter finally drew back, Roman felt the constriction in his lungs ease.

"Thank you for looking for me all these weeks," Hunter whispered as he kissed the corner of Roman's mouth. "And for finally finding me." Another kiss on the other side of his mouth. "And for letting me in so I could see you." A quick brush over his entire mouth. "And for seeing the real me."

Roman groaned and swept his tongue over the seam of Hunter's lips on his next pass. Hunter instantly opened to him and as they kissed, Hunter began rocking his hips back and forth so that their cocks rubbed deliciously against each other over and over. Roman allowed the contact for several seconds before dragging Hunter's hips forward so that there was no space between Hunter's cock and his abdomen. He urged Hunter to resume his grinding by using his hand to press Hunter's lower body against him and then he guided his own cock to Hunter's crease. Hunter tensed up for a brief moment when he felt Roman's flesh brush his hole but then he frantically resumed his pace. The water began to slosh all around them as Hunter's lower body worked them both into a frenzy. Hunter's shout of pleasure was enough for Roman's own body to give it up and as he came, his only regret was that he couldn't see the proof of his orgasm coating Hunter's perfect skin.

Once they'd both caught their breath, Roman forced himself to ask, "What happened at the CB Bar?"

Hunter didn't seem surprised by the question and Roman was strangely glad when Hunter remained plastered to his chest, his thumb playing with some spot on Roman's collarbone. "He apologized to me," Hunter whispered.

"Who did?"

"Mr. Bale...Callan. He apologized for Rhys hitting me," Hunter murmured. "When he said those words, I wanted to die."

"Why?"

"You know why," was all Hunter said.

He did know why and he knew it was something that Hunter would likely struggle with for the rest of his life.

"What happened after that?"

"I told him I was going to tell the truth. He wanted...he wanted me to make sure I was safe first."

Roman tensed at that. He forced Hunter to straighten and said, "Why would he say that?"

"Good and bad, right, Roman?" Hunter asked softly.

Roman forced himself to take in a deep breath. "Good and bad," he agreed.

"The night I accused Finn of assault, I told you that I tried to tell my dad it was just a misunderstanding."

"Yeah, you said he freaked out and kept asking if you were a queer."

"He did more than just freak out. He started hitting me and I could tell he wasn't going to stop this time so I took it back and said I was just trying to make up an excuse so I wouldn't have to admit that a fag had touched me."

"This time?" Roman repeated with barely concealed rage.

"It wasn't the first time, or the last. But I've gotten pretty good over the years at reading him, at knowing what sets him off."

"And you knew that if he even suspected you were gay..."

Hunter nodded. "That night after my parents went to bed, I snuck out of the house and went to see Finn after a friend told me his dad had beat him up badly enough to put him in the hospital. He was asleep when I got there," Hunter said but then had to choke back a sob before he could continue.

"He looked so bad, Roman...If I'd known that his father was like mine, I never would have done it. But the few times I saw them together, they were always laughing and happy. I figured if Finn's dad didn't already know, he wouldn't care because I could see just by the way he looked at Finn that he loved him."

Roman reached up to brush a stray tear from Hunter's face. "I believe you."

Hunter nodded shakily and then said, "I didn't get to talk to Finn because he was asleep so I left. I guess Callan saw me as I was leaving. We'd never met so he didn't know who I was at the time but when I talked to him at the ranch, I guess he recognized my hair. He saw the bruises on my face that night. When I told him I was going to tell everyone the truth, he said I had to make sure I was safe before I did it. He said something about seeing the hatred my dad has for people like him." Hunter hesitated for a moment and then said, "Like us."

Roman guessed it was the first time Hunter was truly accepting that he was gay but he was too preoccupied with Hunter's admission about his father's abuse to acknowledge it. "Why didn't you tell me?"

"Would you have left if I had?"

"Fuck no!"

Hunter tipped his head and Roman grudgingly said, "Continue."

"I knew he was right so I went back to school and started trying to figure out what my next steps would be. I figured the first thing my dad would do when he realized what was going on would be to try and get back the money he spent for tuition so I went to the financial aid department to see if I had any options."

Roman opened his mouth to speak but Hunter clapped his hand over it. "Roman, I swear to God, if you offer me money right now, you're going to see a really bad side of me and since you said you'd take both the good and the bad, I'm not going to hold back, do you understand me?"

Roman smiled against Hunter's hand and nodded. Hunter's hand hovered over his mouth for several seconds before he dropped it and continued. "It turns out my dad never paid this semester's tuition and I missed all the deadlines for financial aid. The counselor was able to set me up with a payment plan and get me into work study. I had some money saved up from mowing lawns and doing odd jobs over the past few years so I was able to make the first payment and I think I'll be able to sell my car for enough to make the second payment. I got all the applications submitted for the loans and scholarships I qualify for so I think I'll be okay for next semester."

"What else?" Roman asked even though it was killing him not to be able to say what he really wanted to say. Hunter looked so pleased with himself that it took the sting out of not being able to just jump in and fix things like he wanted.

"I changed my major to Engineering. I was always pretty good at math and science and I really like the idea of building things or figuring out how something works..."

"Sounds perfect," Roman said gently.

Hunter smiled and leaned down to give him a kiss but when he sat back up, his eyes darkened somewhat. "Um, I also went to the school's health clinic so I could get tested because I can't be sure if all the guys at the club...if they all wore condoms. I'm tested negative," he added hastily. "But I need to get tested again in three months and then again in six months."

"Okay," Roman responded.

"I also got a referral to see someone about...about this," Hunter said as he fingered one of the burns on his chest. "My appointment is next week. I'm gonna talk to the guy about the men in the club too."

"Are you still having nightmares?" Roman asked as he stroked his fingers over Hunter's cheek.

Hunter nodded. He was quiet for a moment before lifting his eyes to meet Roman's. "The message you read," Hunter said quietly as he jerked his head towards the phone. "That was one of the times I was able to stop myself but there were other times that I couldn't."

Roman hated the tremor of fear he heard in Hunter's voice. "I'm not going to make you promise you'll never do it again, Hunter. I just need to know that if you get to that point where you can't take what's happening inside of you, that you'll find me or call me, no matter where I am or what I'm doing or what time it is. I need to be able to try and help you work through it." Roman let his fingers trail over the wounds on Hunter's arm. "You never have to hide them from me – ever," he said firmly.

"They're part of you and I understand that they helped you get through some pretty shitty things. But I need that to fall on me now, no matter what happens with us, okay? Even if I'm the one who inadvertently ends up hurting you."

"God, Roman, you're really going to do it, aren't you?"

"Do what?"

Hunter leaned down so that their lips were almost touching. "Make me fall in love with you," Hunter whispered.

~

"Would you come with me tonight?"

"Yes," Hunter said.

Roman's chest lifted slightly beneath his ear as Roman chuckled and the fingers that were caressing the skin of his lower back stilled for a moment. "Don't you want to know where first?"

Hunter shifted enough so that he was lying more fully on Roman's body and then folded his arms under his chin. Roman adjusted the sleeping bag so it was covering him again.

"No," Hunter responded. Roman smiled and then resumed his petting. His gaze turned to focus on the lake and Hunter used the time to study him. As strong and confident as Roman always seemed to be, Hunter couldn't help but think he always looked just a little bit broken too. "Talk to me, Roman."

"About what?" Roman asked though his eyes stayed fixed on

the lake.

"About whatever it is that keeps your smile from reaching your eyes."

Roman's eyes finally shifted back to his. He didn't speak right away. In fact, it took him so long that Hunter started to feel a niggle of self-doubt. As exciting as the idea of pursuing a relationship with Roman was, he didn't know if he could do it if they weren't equals in it…if it would always be about him needing Roman just a little bit more than Roman needing him.

"Gray asked to see me."

"Is that where we're going tonight?"

Roman nodded. "I haven't seen him since the day you…"

"Walked away from you," Hunter finished for him.

Another nod.

"Why didn't you go see him when you came out here looking for me?"

Roman turned his attention back to the lake. "It was different that day I found you in your bathroom. I was so scared for you and I didn't know what to do. And then I just knew…Gray. Just get to Gray and everything will be okay."

"You needed your big brother," Hunter said gently.

"That's just it…he was never my big brother. Yeah, he was older than me and we shared some DNA but he was never a brother to me."

"Never?"

Roman hesitated. "I guess there were a couple of times where I thought maybe he cared about me just a little."

"Like when?" Hunter asked. Roman still hadn't looked at him so Hunter reached his fingers up to trail them back and forth over Roman's throat. At the contact, Roman swallowed hard but he didn't pull away.

"The first night I spent in my father's house, I freaked out because I was afraid my mom wouldn't be able to find me there. The reverend had kept saying she was with God so I had convinced myself she was an angel and she'd come down to visit me in my dreams but then I panicked because I didn't know how she'd find me."

"You were ten, right?"

Roman nodded. "I went to Gray's room to ask him how my mom was going to know where I was. I was crying so hard that he had to ask me a couple times what was wrong. When I finally got it out, he gave me this nightlight – it was in the shape of a stack of books – and he plugged it in the wall right next to my bed and told me that as long as I had it, my mom would always be able to find me. Then he stayed with me until I fell asleep."

"How old was Gray?"

"Seventeen," Roman said. "After that night I just latched on to him, you know? I was terrified to let him out of my sight. He was…he was nice about it at first, me following him around. But after a while he started shutting me out. He wasn't cruel about it or anything – he just acted like…"

"Like what?" Hunter prodded.

"Like I wasn't there. Then he went to college and I only saw him a handful of times after that."

"You said there were a couple times where you thought he cared."

"I didn't really realize it until I was older. My dad's wife never let me forget that I wasn't really a part of the family. I had to call her by her first name. My dad too. They didn't include me in any events if any of their friends were going to be around because Victoria didn't want people to know who I was. At Christmas, Gray was the only one who ever got me something and I never got to eat dinner with them except when Gray was home from school. I always thought it was because it was a special occasion but now…"

"You think Gray had something to do with it." Hunter said.

Roman's pain filled eyes finally shifted to his. "Sometimes I think I'm remembering things a certain way because I want so badly to believe the lie instead of the truth."

Hunter moved farther up Roman's body so he could cradle his face in his hands. "I know I was pretty out of it the day you took me to see him and Luke but I saw the way Gray looked at you. It wasn't me who put that worried look on his face."

Roman closed his eyes. "This is so fucked up," he muttered. "I was fine with the way things were…I was fucking fine and then it was like he just disappeared off the face of the earth and I was that little kid again."

"You were scared you'd lost him for good," Hunter whispered.

Roman nodded and then said, "And when I found him I was so relieved and that just pissed me off even more. Then I saw him…"

"What?" Hunter asked gently.

Roman squeezed his eyes shut as tears slipped from them. "He had fucking cancer." Roman finally opened his eyes but covered them with his hand. "He looked so bad, Hunter. Like he'd died a thousand deaths. And all I could think was that I was going to lose my big brother. I promised myself when I left that I'd let go of the past - that I'd…"

"Forgive him," Hunter supplied.

"Yeah. But when he called me after he went into remission, I couldn't do it. He kept asking me to come visit; he'd leave me these long messages that I couldn't bring myself to listen to, he sent me texts asking how I was…and I just couldn't fucking do it."

Hunter's heart broke for Roman and he leaned down to brush his lips over Roman's now damp ones. "Baby, look at me, please."

Roman sucked in several deep breaths before dropping his arm. The vulnerability in Roman's eyes nearly killed Hunter. He lifted his thumbs to wipe away the tears that continued to fall.

"Maybe it's so hard to forgive him because you're afraid he'll hurt you again. Maybe the real question isn't whether or not you can forgive him…maybe you need to ask yourself if you can ever trust him again. Maybe you need to put all the rest of the shit – cancer, your childhood – in a corner somewhere and find out if the man he is today is the one you need him to be."

Hunter felt Roman's arms wrap around him and then Roman was sitting up, taking Hunter with him. When he pressed his cheek against Hunter's chest, Hunter closed his arms around Roman and rested his chin on his head.

"I can't go back to being that kid anymore, Hunter. I can't be invisible again."

"You won't, Roman. I promise."

CHAPTER 8

*R*oman let out a string of curses the second Hunter's tongue made contact with the head of his dick. When Hunter had tentatively asked him if he could touch him, Roman had managed to keep his desire in check as Hunter's fingers tested the weight of his balls and then traced every ridge and vein on his cock. But he hadn't been expecting Hunter's next move and even as he watched Hunter lower his head, Roman's brain still hadn't managed to process what was about to happen.

Since the exquisite caress had stopped the second he'd shouted the few choice curse words, Roman looked down expecting to see a nervous Hunter trying to figure out what he'd done wrong. What he found was a young man who looked like he'd just been handed the keys to the magic kingdom. And it made Roman even fucking harder which he didn't think was physically possible.

Hunter, still fully dressed, sat back on his heels and slowly peeled off his shirt. But instead of reaching for his pants, his molten gaze swept over Roman's naked body and then settled once more on his dick which was almost a beet red color. When Hunter's hand coasted down his own chest and then settled on the bulge behind his jeans, Roman wasn't surprised to see a bead of pre-cum form at the tip of his cock and hang there. Hunter's gaze settled on the drop of moisture and then he licked his lips. Roman started to sit up so he could grab Hunter but Hunter scooted farther down the bed and shook his head.

"Uh-huh, remember your promise," Hunter murmured.

"Fuck," Roman muttered as he dropped back down on the bed. He hadn't had any issue with Hunter's insistence that he be allowed to explore Roman's body as much as he wanted since it was something Roman had promised him the previous night just before Hunter had fucked him. But of course, when he'd agreed to this whole thing, he'd been expecting the innocent touches of a man still trying to find his confidence when it came to sex. But a couple of insanely intense orgasms had somehow turned Hunter into a dominant, sexy as hell top who appeared to be bent on tormenting Roman.

Roman forced himself to take deep breaths as Hunter's torture started all over again. He wasn't sure he could stand another round of Hunter kissing and sucking his way over every inch of Roman's body – except his raging cock of course – but he figured if he came too soon like some horny teenage boy, then Hunter would just have to get him all worked up again. But no sooner had the thought entered his head when a hot mouth suddenly covered the tip of his cock. And when Hunter's tongue tentatively licked his slit, Roman couldn't stop from slamming his hips upward. He instantly felt bad when Hunter started gagging but before he could apologize, Hunter was pushing his hips back down and sucking on him hard. A hand wrapped around his base and began dragging up and down as Hunter's tongue rimmed the ridge of his crown.

"Jesus fucking Christ!" Roman shouted as he desperately fisted his hands into the bedspread. While Roman knew he should have been feeling all the little things that showed Hunter's inexperience with giving blowjobs, all he knew was that it felt like the top of his head was going to explode and he was reaching down to try and pull Hunter off of him within less than a minute. But Hunter's sucking only intensified when Roman grabbed his shoulder and instead of trying to warn Hunter of his impending orgasm, Roman actually tightened his grip on Hunter and began fucking his mouth in earnest.

Hunter maintained his hold on Roman's base to keep him from shoving in as deep as he wanted to go but he made up for it by hollowing out his cheeks. And then his sharp green eyes lifted to meet Roman's and that was it – Roman came hot and hard and he watched in fascination as Hunter tried to swallow rope after rope of come. But he couldn't keep up and when lines of white began dripping from his lips, Roman snarled and dragged Hunter up and slammed their mouths together.

He kissed Hunter soundly and then ran his tongue along the skin around Hunter's mouth and sucked up the remaining fluid. Hunter moaned against his mouth and then took over the kiss. Roman used the distraction to work the button and zipper on Hunter's jeans free and then he was plunging one hand into Hunter's underwear. His sharp, twisting tugs had Hunter ripping his mouth free and looking down to see Roman's hand snaking around in his pants.

"Oh God," Hunter groaned as he began meeting Roman's drags with the sliding of his hips. Within minutes Hunter was reaching for the condom and lube that Roman had placed on the nightstand. His moves were jerky and desperate but he was a quick study because he managed to get his jeans pushed down and the condom rolled down his cock in record time. And then, to Roman's surprise, Hunter was pushing Roman down on his stomach. Slick fingers pressed between his cheeks but before they reached his hole he heard Hunter ask, "Is this okay?"

Roman had no idea if Hunter was asking about the position or him being the one to prep Roman this time around and since the answer was the same for both questions, he roughly said, "Do it." Hunter didn't need any more urging because a second later he felt a fingertip brush over his hole while one hand split him open. Roman could tell Hunter was already struggling with his own lust because one finger began breaching him almost instantly.

"Tell me if I'm hurting you," Hunter grated out as he began sliding his finger in and out.

"More," Roman said. He had no idea how Hunter had managed to only make him capable of speaking in one and two word statements or how he'd driven Roman to such a desperate level of need again so quickly but he didn't dwell on it as another finger entered him. Roman had only bottomed on a couple of occasions early on when he'd first explored his sexuality as a teenager so the sensation of being filled was still an oddity. And like last night, the strange, burning sensation quickly gave over to something else that had Roman needing more.

"Hunter," he whispered, his strangled voice sounding strange even to his own ears. But thankfully, Hunter got the message because he pulled his fingers free and replaced them with his cock. Hunter's forward motion was more insistent this time around than last night and Roman let out a harsh cry when his hole collapsed under the pressure and Hunter sank all the way inside of him. Since Roman was lying flat on his stomach, his hips flush with the bed, he couldn't reach his dick to stroke it but when Hunter set an almost punishing pace of fucking right from the get go, Roman didn't care because the slapping of Hunter's hips against his ass had him sliding forward hard enough to give him the friction he needed. And then it got fucking better because Hunter's fingers dug into his hips and yanked him back to meet his thrusts. The rough treatment had Roman breaking out into a sweat as his body quickly overheated and he had to bite into his own arm to keep from shouting out his pleasure. But even with the brutal force of his pounding, Hunter seemed incapable of letting what was happening between them only be about two bodies finding relief because he leaned over Roman's back and fisted his hand in Roman's hair to drag him up for a long, needy kiss that was the exact opposite of the pummeling that Roman's ass was taking.

"It's just like you said, Roman," Hunter whispered against his ear. "I can't tell where I end and you begin."

Roman groaned at the words and let his eyes slide closed as Hunter's arm wrapped around his neck from behind so Roman couldn't drop his head to the bed...so he couldn't escape Hunter's searing kiss. Not that he wanted to.

The orgasm slammed into Roman and sent him hurtling over a cliff into darkness that was dotted with brief flashes of light. He screamed as he shoved his hips into the bed over and over again and then let out another shout when he felt his tortured ass try to draw Hunter in even deeper. Hunter called out his name as he shoved into Roman as far as he could go and began convulsing deep inside his body. Fire burned Roman's insides as the heat of Hunter's release burned through the condom and heated him from the inside out. Every spasm of Hunter's body on and in him had Roman's cock answering with another aftershock. He wasn't sure how long he lay there for before Hunter carefully withdrew from him and then rolled him onto his back. He waited expectantly for Hunter's kiss but it never came. Because Hunter's lips closed over his cock instead and as he gently licked Roman clean, Roman let the darkness of sleep claim him.

~

"Roman," Gray said in surprise. "Come on in."

Roman shifted uncomfortably on the porch and said, "Um, you mind if we go for a walk or something?"

He could tell that Gray had already gone on alert and Roman had no doubt it was because of the tone in his own voice. And after the disaster of a dinner on Saturday night, he couldn't blame Gray for being confused.

"Sure, I'll get my jacket."

Roman waited on the porch and automatically began running his hand over Ripley's head as she pushed against his leg. He wondered if someday he and Hunter would have a dog together and then immediately regretted the thought because all it did was make him think of how hard it had been to leave Hunter this morning.

After dinner with Gray and Luke on Saturday night, there hadn't been any question as to whether or not Hunter would be spending the night with him again – it was just a question of where. They'd talked about going back to the lake but with the nights getting cooler, they'd agreed that a warm, soft bed was in order. They'd barely made it inside of Roman's hotel room when Hunter began tugging Roman's clothes off as he reminded him of the promise he'd made to let Hunter have free roam of his body. A marathon session of lovemaking had followed and had lasted well into Sunday morning and they'd ended up sleeping till almost noon. At that point they'd eaten a quick lunch at the hotel restaurant and then Roman had taken Hunter back to his dorm room so he could get some homework done. Roman had gone back to the hotel to try and focus on some of the work he'd been neglecting in the weeks since he'd met Hunter but it had ended up being a monumental waste of time and he'd spent much of the afternoon reading and re-reading the texts Hunter had written but never sent him. Some had made him laugh while others had ripped him open. All of them had had him wishing there was some easy answer as to how he could build a life with Hunter.

When he heard the door open and close behind him, Roman steeled himself for what was to come. He'd taken everything Hunter had said to him about needing to figure out if he still trusted Gray to heart but as Saturday night had rolled around and he and Hunter had arrived at the cabin for dinner, it was like something inside of him had shut down and he couldn't bring himself to even be alone with Gray. Roman had ended up dumping the responsibility of carrying a conversation with Gray and Luke entirely on Hunter.

"All set," Gray said and Roman followed him down the porch stairs and around the back of the cabin. They followed the same trail that Roman had confronted Hunter on several weeks earlier and when they walked past the tree he'd pinned Hunter up against as he jerked them both off, Roman felt his skin heat. He glanced at Gray to see if he noticed but luckily his brother was focused on the overgrown path beneath their feet.

"How are you feeling?" Roman asked. While Gray looked a thousand times better than he had when Roman had first seen him, he still seemed off somehow. Physically he looked fit and healthy but something in his eyes looked...haunted.

"Pretty good," Gray responded. "Had another CT last week – still all clear."

Relief went through Roman. While Gray's initial diagnosis of testicular cancer should have been highly curable with just radiation, he'd run into complications when the disease had spread to his liver. Chemo had taken care of the tumors but even Roman knew that the risk of reoccurrence was high.

"You look tired. Are you getting enough sleep?"

Gray shook his head. "Not as much as I probably should," he admitted.

"Are you trying to figure out how to get Nick Archer out of that trunk?" Roman asked.

Gray laughed. "You read it?"

Roman bit back a smile. He'd picked up the first book in Gray's *Detective Archer* series by chance when he'd been walking through the airport in London several years ago. There'd been a total of six books so far but the main character's fate was unknown since the guy had been stuffed in the trunk of a car that went over the edge of a cliff in the very last scene of the most recent release. Fans of Gray's work had lit up social media with arguments over whether the series was over or not and Gray had been decidedly quiet on the issue.

"Every word," Roman admitted.

Gray fell silent for a moment before saying, "I haven't been sleeping well because I keep trying to imagine what things would be like if I hadn't been such a selfish prick when you were a kid."

Roman stopped walking and swallowed hard. God, wasn't it supposed to feel good to hear Gray admit it?

"Gray…"

"I keep trying to use the excuse that I wasn't much older than you but that doesn't really change things, does it? You needed me and I wasn't there."

"Gray, stop," Roman said softly. "I don't want this…I thought I did but I don't." He looked up to find Gray watching him with pained eyes.

"Roman, I swear to God, I'd change it if I could."

"I know," Roman responded. And he did. He finally fucking got it. "I don't want to try to go back and fix the past." At Gray's crestfallen look, he hurried on. "Gray, I've been punishing you for months now but instead of walking away, you took it. All the unanswered texts, the deleted voicemails, not telling you I was in town…and then I show up on your doorstep because I had no place else to go and you were right there, no questions asked. If that doesn't make you one hell of a good brother, I don't know what does. But the part I need to figure out now is how to be a good brother to you because so far all I've done is condemn you for failing me."

"You didn't-"

"Cancer, Gray. You had fucking cancer and you never came to me for help. Because you weren't sure I'd give it to you, right?"

Gray dropped his eyes and Roman had his answer.

"Can we just start over, Roman?" Gray asked. "We don't have to pretend none of that shit happened but can we wipe the slate clean or something? Can we figure out how to be a family?"

"On one condition," Roman said seriously.

Gray's wary response was a quick nod of his head.

"You have to tell me if Nick Archer really was in the trunk of that car."

Several long seconds passed before his words finally seemed to register for Gray because all of a sudden he let out a choked laugh/sob and then he was striding forward and dragging Roman into his arms.

~

"You're in love with him, aren't you?"

Roman didn't bother trying to sidestep Gray's question. A clean slate meant no more lies. "Yes."

"How does he feel?"

Roman took a sip of his coffee and scanned the front yard of the cabin. "Don't know," Roman said softly as he glanced at Gray who was sitting on the porch step next to him. "We're so different, Gray." Roman turned his attention back to his cup and quietly said, "I don't know how to make it work."

"What's the problem?" Gray asked gently. Roman knew he'd hesitated too long because Gray said, "His age?"

"That's part of it," Roman admitted.

"The self-injuring?"

"No," Roman said adamantly and he absolutely meant it. "I mean, it hurts like hell knowing that he carries that much pain around inside of him but I can figure out how to deal with it…and he's getting help for it."

"Then what is it? Because from what I saw the other night, he's got it bad for you."

"I'm the first guy he's ever been with…first person, actually."

"And you think whatever he's feeling might just be because of the newness of it all," Gray observed.

"How could it not be? That piece of shit father of his controlled every part of his life and he's just now starting to try and figure out who he is and who he wants to be. What if he figures out at some point that he wants someone his own age or someone with the same interests? My work has me traveling every week and he's looking at another three years of college at a minimum. How do we make being apart more than we're together work?"

"It'll be tough but not impossible."

Roman laughed and then ran his fingers through his hair in agitation. "A month ago my life was exactly the way I wanted it. I spent two days with him, Gray. Two days and I knew I was fucked – how is that even possible?" He turned to look at his brother. "It hasn't even been two hours since I said goodbye to him and I feel like I can't fucking breathe."

"Fuck, Roman, you couldn't just ease me into the whole big brother role with something simple, could you?" Gray groused.

The attempt at levity worked and Roman smiled. "No, I guess not."

"Okay, you want the big brother speech, here it is. Don't wait even one second longer than you have to tell him how you feel because that next second isn't guaranteed. Will it hurt like hell if he doesn't feel the same way? Yeah, it absolutely will. And if that happens…well, you just let me know and I'll go and kick his ass for you."

Gray's accompanying gentle shove had Roman chuckling. Before he could say anything, Ripley jumped up from where she'd been lying at the bottom of the stairs and took off running towards the driveway. A second later, Luke pulled up in his truck. Roman looked over at Gray whose eyes were locked on Luke as he strode toward them.

"Hi," Luke whispered to Gray before he stole a quick but endearing kiss that spoke volumes.

"Hi," Gray returned and as they held each other's gazes for a moment, even in the silence it was like Roman could feel what they were feeling. A month ago he doubted he would have even noticed.

"Hey, Roman," Luke said as he held out his hand. "Thought you were headed out this morning."

"I am," Roman said as he shook Luke's hand. "Had something I needed to fix first," he said as he glanced at Gray. "I'll call you when I land at Heathrow."

Gray nodded. "Stay safe."

Roman handed his cup to Gray and then stood. "Oh, and I'll make sure to keep that little tidbit about Nick Archer to myself."

Roman caught Gray's murderous look just before he turned away. "What the hell, Gray? You told him what happens next but when I ask, you tell me I have to wait to find out along with everyone else?" he heard Luke ask.

"Thanks for that!" Gray called out in obvious irritation. Roman laughed and waved a hand over his head.

~

"Catch you later," Hunter said, forcing a smile to his lips as he bumped fists with his classmate. As nice and funny as the guy was, Hunter had struggled to stay tuned in to the conversation, just like he'd struggled to keep his attention on the professor. Three hours – three hours since Roman had kissed him goodbye and Hunter felt like he was dying inside. How the hell was he going to make it four more days? Yeah, they'd agreed to video chat every night but it wouldn't be the same as feeling all the words Roman spoke through his touches. And he didn't even want to think about how hard it would be to have to sleep without Roman's arms wrapped around him.

Hunter forced himself to take a deep breath as the familiar itch began under his skin. His first appointment with his new therapist wasn't for four more days and he was starting to regret that he hadn't said yes when the receptionist asked if his need to see someone was urgent.

The three weeks since he'd been to the CB Bar Ranch had been some of the most stressful of his entire life because he'd gone from having every aspect of his life decided for him to suddenly having no one but himself to rely on. And to his own secret shame, there'd been a couple of times where his freedom seemed to come at too high a price and he'd considered admitting defeat and calling his father. But there'd been high points too. Like when the student advisor had asked him what kind of career he wanted, he hadn't immediately blurted out the stock answer of politics that had been hammered into his brain for as long as he could remember. He'd just sat there in stupefied silence until the kind-hearted woman began asking him probing questions about what kinds of things he liked. And even when he'd finally settled on an engineering track, she'd made sure he understood that he could change his mind if he wanted to.

After that, he'd thrown himself full force into breaking free of his former life. And while he hadn't actually told his parents he was done with them, he'd ignored all their calls and had ultimately gotten rid of the phone they were paying for. He'd also moved to a different dorm and worked with the university to make sure his information wasn't shared with anyone. There was always still the stress of knowing his father could show up on the campus one day but it was something he'd just have to deal with if and when the time came.

But for all the progress he'd made coming to terms with breaking free from his parents, Roman had been the one part of his life he couldn't find the strength to pursue like he wanted. His mind just couldn't wrap itself around the possibility that someone like Roman could possibly want to explore a relationship with someone as fucked up as he was. Roman was successful, confident, driven, focused – he needed someone who could complement those qualities, someone who could challenge him...not someone who was struggling to accept who he was and what he'd done. So he'd written those texts as a way to stay connected to Roman, even if it was only one-sided. He'd told himself over and over to delete them...to delete Roman's number entirely - but he hadn't been able to bring himself to do it.

And then by some miracle Roman had been there.

Hunter's plan to go to the lake had been last minute but he'd decided he needed a chance to say goodbye...to Pops, to Roman. But it had turned out to be too painful and he'd been about to pack up his things when he'd seen the flash of light coming from the trail. And in the seconds it had taken for Roman to reach him, to feel his lips covering his own, Hunter had known that what he felt for Roman wasn't going to go away...it wasn't going to be ignored. And if Roman's words and actions were anything to go by, hopefully those feelings weren't one-sided.

Grabbing his phone from his pocket, Hunter glanced up to make sure no one was in his immediate path and then began typing out a text to Roman.

Miss you.

He was in the process of putting the phone away when it vibrated in his hand. When he saw Roman's name, he automatically smiled but as he read the text he couldn't help but frown in confusion.

Miss you too. Look up.

Hunter was about to start typing another message when a new text popped up.

Look up.

Exasperated, Hunter finally looked up and then stopped in his tracks when he saw Roman standing near the stairs that led up to his dorm. Not caring who was watching, Hunter hurried across the space separating them and threw his arms around Roman without hesitation.

"What are you doing here? Did you miss your flight?"

Roman gently pushed him back and said, "I can't really miss my flight since it's my plane."

Under any other circumstances, Hunter would have remarked on that interesting tidbit that Roman had failed to mention but something in the way Roman was holding himself had Hunter going on immediate alert. "What? What is it? Are you okay? Did something happen?"

"I'm fine," Roman quickly said though he actually stepped back when Hunter tried to touch him. "Who's the guy?"

"What?" Hunter asked in confusion. "What guy?"

"The guy back there," Roman said, motioning to the corner behind him where he'd said his goodbyes to his classmate.

"Oh, um, just this guy I met in my physics class. I'm a couple weeks behind everyone else since I transferred into the class and he was offering to help me get caught up."

Roman nodded slightly but didn't say anything and Hunter's fear went up another notch. Why wouldn't Roman touch him? Look at him the way he always did...like he was exactly where he wanted to be?

"Roman, what's going on?"

Roman's eyes dropped to the cement sidewalk and his hands disappeared into the pockets of his long coat. "Can we talk in your room?"

Hunter managed a nod but nothing else because it felt like he'd swallowed a beach ball. This was it...this was the moment he'd been secretly fearing since he'd woken up in Roman's arms after making love to him by the lake. Roman had finally come to his senses.

By the time they reached his dorm room, Hunter was already mentally trying to figure out where his nearest lighter was because he could already feel the black swirl of pain churning deep in his body and spiraling out to his limbs. He tried shaking the sensation away by subtly clenching and unclenching his fists but it wasn't working.

"Where's your roommate?" Roman asked as he closed the door.

Right, because Roman wouldn't want an audience for what he was about to do. "Um, he's gone for the week...some kind of family vacation I think," he answered dully.

"Hunter..."

"Roman, I need you to do this quick, okay?" Hunter interrupted. "Just say what you need to say and then go."

Roman was still near the door so Hunter forced himself to look up. Roman was fidgeting like crazy and as heartbroken as Hunter was, he couldn't stand to see Roman struggling so he said, "It's okay, Roman. I get it. I mean, it was just a few days, right?"

"What?"

"You felt a responsibility for me after that night in the club and when you didn't hear from me, you felt obligated to make sure I was okay…"

Hunter ignored the way Roman stilled and his jaw hardened.

"You want a clean break-"

Roman was striding towards him before he could even finish his sentence and when Roman's forward motion continued, Hunter had no choice but to back up until he hit the wall just beyond the kitchen cabinets.

"You need to stop talking right now," Roman growled. "Because I didn't just spend the last hour and a half trying to figure out how to tell you I love you only to have you ruin it with some bullshit about responsibility and obligation."

What?

Hunter opened his mouth to ask that very question when Roman pinned him with a hard stare and he snapped it shut again.

"What you saw downstairs and here just now was me trying to find the courage to tell you how completely in love with you I am. And yeah, I know it's too fast and I know you're probably better off with some guy like that twat down there who couldn't keep his eyes off your ass-"

Hunter was about to interject but Roman cut him off with a hard kiss.

"He was totally checking out your ass," Roman said. "Little bastard is lucky I didn't rip-"

This time it was Hunter's turn to yank Roman down for a kiss but where Roman's was brief, Hunter made sure his wasn't and by the time he released Roman, all of Roman's insecurity seemed to have returned because he couldn't hide the tremor in his voice as he said, "I don't need you to say it back but I need you to know I've never said those words to another living soul before and no matter what happens between us, you're it for me."

When Roman fell silent, Hunter gently asked, "Is it my turn?"

When Roman reluctantly nodded, Hunter reached up to cup his face in both his hands. "I've never said those words either, Roman. And while I'm not afraid to say them to you, I am afraid you won't believe me…that you'll think I'm saying them to spare your feelings or to keep from losing you. So I'm going to wait until I know beyond a shadow of a doubt that you'll believe me…that you won't doubt for even a second how I feel about you."

To Hunter's relief, Roman actually relaxed and then his arms were folding around Hunter, drawing him in. Hunter wrapped his arms around Roman's neck and just held on to him as his insides exploded with joy. Roman loved him. *Him.*

"Can you stay for a while?" Hunter asked, his lips skimming over the skin just below Roman's ear.

Roman's only response was a nod and since neither of them seemed in a hurry to move, they just stood there in his tiny kitchen holding each other.

CHAPTER 9

*R*oman cursed as he inadvertently knocked the empty glass off the nightstand next to his bed as he fumbled for his ringing cell phone. A glance at the clock showed it was just past three in the morning, London time. He couldn't make his eyes focus enough to see the caller ID just before he answered.

"Roman?"

Roman's heart nearly stopped at the sound of Hunter's broken voice.

"Hunter, what is it? What's wrong?" he asked gently even as he jolted upright and searched out the button that would turn on the light next to the hotel room bed.

"Um, I know it's late...I'm sorry-"

"Baby, it's fine, just tell me what's wrong."

Hunter didn't respond at first and Roman's panic went up another notch. He'd video chatted with Hunter earlier in the evening just before he'd gone to sleep and he'd been fine. Roman had been in London for four days and was scheduled to fly back to Missoula in two. He'd been in regular contact with Hunter the entire time via calls and texts and although he could tell Hunter was missing him, he'd still seemed upbeat.

"Hunter, I'm going to switch the call to video, okay?"

"No-" Hunter cried. "I don't want you to see me."

"Hunter, you're really scaring me."

Hunter sniffed and then said, "You said I should call you if…if I felt like I was going to…"

Anxiety coursed through Roman as he realized what Hunter was trying to tell him. "I'm so glad you did, baby…I'm really proud of you," Roman said gently as he swung his legs over the side of the bed and got up so he could move around as he talked. "Take a few deep breaths for me, okay?"

But instead of doing as he asked, he heard Hunter start to cry. "I didn't want you to ever see this part of me again," he managed to get out between shaky breaths.

"Hunter, remember what I told you that day at the hot springs?"

Hunter was quiet for a moment before saying, "Good and bad."

"Good and bad," Roman repeated softly. "Now can you take a few deep breaths for me?"

"Yeah," Hunter said and there was a long silence as Roman waited impatiently and cursed the distance between them. Even if he called Gray and Luke, it would take them an hour to get to Hunter. And if he called the police, Hunter could very well end up locked away in some mental hospital on a psychiatric hold until he was no longer deemed a danger to himself.

"That's good, now do three more."

Hunter's voice sounded a little bit steadier as he said, "Okay."

"Can you tell me what happened?"

"Um…I was thinking about tomorrow and I started getting nervous about what the doctor was going to ask me."

Hunter's first appointment with his new therapist was scheduled for the next day and although he'd expressed some anxiety about it when he and Roman had talked earlier, he also seemed eager to get it behind him.

"I started worrying that if I told him about hurting myself that he was going to say I was crazy and that maybe he'd have to put me in a hospital or something. What if he calls my parents, Roman? Can he… can he make it so they get to say what happens to me again?"

"No, baby, he's not going to do that," Roman said, though in truth, he had no clue. "I won't let it happen, no matter what, okay?"

"My dad…he knows lots of people…"

"Hunter, I guarantee you, I know more. No one's going to lock you up and your father is never getting near you again, do you hear me?"

"Yeah," Hunter whispered.

Roman's insides clenched as the helplessness snaked throughout his entire body. He could feel tears stinging his eyes and so it was more for himself than for Hunter when he said, "Baby, please let me see you."

Hunter was silent for a long time and then his phone beeped and switched over to the video screen. He hit the button and smiled when Hunter's tear-stained face came into view. "Hi," he said softly.

"Hi," Hunter responded, his eyes still watery as he wiped at his flushed face. Roman could tell by the tile at Hunter's back that he was likely sitting in the bathroom, somewhere near the shower.

"What time's your appointment?" Roman asked.

"Nine."

"I'm coming home, okay," Roman said as he began to run through the list of things he would need to do to get back in time. It would be tight but he knew enough people to get his plane readied, have a flight plan filed and deal with customs quickly enough so that he could get back to Missoula by morning.

"No, Roman, don't," Hunter said, his voice a little bit more even. "I need to be able to do this on my own."

Roman sighed and went to sit down on the edge of the bed. "I could ask Luke or Gray to meet you…drive you there and back."

Hunter smiled and shook his head. "It's on campus in the health center – I'll probably walk there." Hunter wiped at his face again and then said, "Thank you, Roman. I feel better. I should let you get back to sleep."

"Actually, I have to be up in an hour anyway so I'm thinking maybe you should keep me company for a bit," Roman said as he settled back against the headboard.

"Okay," Hunter murmured as he got up. The phone tilted a bit as Hunter moved but then settled again and Roman could tell Hunter had moved to his bed. That in itself was a relief. "What should we talk about?" Hunter asked.

Roman thought for a moment and then said, "What are you wearing?"

Hunter laughed. "You can't be serious," he said. "Phone sex? Really?" Hunter said, his voice dropping to a near whisper even though he was obviously alone in his dorm since his roommate was gone for the whole week.

"It's either that or I read you the presentation I have to give in a few hours."

Hunter seemed to think on it for a while and then finally said, "What's the presentation on?"

"Running costs and revenue streams." When Hunter remained quiet, Roman said, "Well?"

"I'm thinking," Hunter quipped.

"Well, while you're thinking, I'm going to get started," Roman said huskily and then switched the view on his phone to reverse the screen. He let his hand slip into his boxers and then laughed when there was an audible indrawn breath followed by a curse as Hunter began fumbling with his phone in a desperate effort to get caught up.

～

*H*unter felt completely wrung out as he left the therapist's office but he was beyond relieved that he was doing it on his own two feet and not being carted out by two guys in white coats. Although he'd believed that Roman would move heaven and earth to get him out of any psych ward he could have potentially ended up in, the idea of having the freedom he'd worked so hard to finally gain taken away from him was overwhelming and had kept him up most of the night after he'd hung up with Roman. Of course, there'd been the brief time in between when he'd been nearly comatose after the orgasm Roman had wrung out of him with some incredibly filthy suggestions about what he was going to do to Hunter when they saw each other again tomorrow.

Calling Roman as he'd sat on his bathroom floor and stared at the lighter and spoon he'd rested on the edge of the sink had been one of the hardest things he'd ever had to do. But there'd been no condemnation in Roman's voice and when they'd finally hung up, Roman had told him he loved him and nothing in his tone or body language made Hunter think it was anything but the truth. When Roman had said he was coming home, the weakest part of Hunter had wanted to cry in relief but the little voice inside his head that had slowly started to grow louder these past few weeks had reminded him that he needed to able to stand on his own two feet...not because he didn't want Roman's support but because he needed to know that there was a part of him that hadn't been completely lost to his fear.

The therapist hadn't been anything like Hunter had expected. For starters, the man was built like a tank and both arms had been covered in tattoos. He'd had piercings in both ears and the only hair on his head was actually on his face. The Mr. Clean lookalike hadn't even bothered to take notes as he casually asked Hunter about himself and when Hunter had balked at telling the man about his self-destructive behavior, the guy hadn't pressured him in any way. In fact, it hadn't been until the last ten minutes of the session that Hunter admitted to burning himself. There'd been no look of horror when he'd said it and the guy hadn't reached for the phone to call someone to come take him away. And to Hunter's complete and utter shock, he hadn't even asked to see the burns. He'd simply asked Hunter if he was interested in learning about some alternative ways to cope with his stress. And then he'd been allowed to leave. No guys in white coats, no recrimination, no lectures.

Hunter grabbed his phone from his backpack and wasn't surprised to see several messages from Roman waiting for him. He'd gotten several before the appointment reassuring him that he was going to do great and that everything would be okay. The most recent messages were more of the same and when he dialed Roman's number, Roman picked up on the first ring.

"Hey," Hunter said softly. God, how did even the prospect of just talking to Roman turn his insides to mush?

"Hey yourself, how was it?"

"Better than I expected," Hunter admitted. "I'll tell you all about it when I see you tomorrow."

"How about you tell me on the plane?"

Hunter stopped walking. "What?"

"I thought we could go away for the weekend. You don't start your work study till next week, right?"

"Right."

"Do you have any classes today?"

"No, it's my free day."

"So what do you think?"

The husky tone in Roman's voice had Hunter shivering. "When do I need to be at the airport by?"

"You've got time," Roman said. "I've arranged a car for you."

Hunter began walking again as excitement flared in his belly. "When will it pick me up?"

"Now," was all Roman said.

Hunter stilled and then turned around. A black Town Car rolled to a stop at the curb and Hunter held his breath as he watched Roman get out, phone to his ear. Hunter lowered his phone and then walked towards Roman. It was surprisingly hard to swallow so when Roman whispered "hi" to him, Hunter couldn't do anything except nod and then wrap his arms around Roman.

"I let you go to the appointment by yourself because I knew it was important to you but please don't be mad at me for not being able to stay away like you wanted. I just needed to see for myself that you were okay."

Hunter shook his head against Roman's chest. "Not mad," he muttered. "Definitely not mad." He felt Roman's fingers close over the back of his neck and gently massage him.

"What do you say we get out of here?"

"I say yes," Hunter murmured. "Always yes."

He felt Roman chuckle against him and he knew it was because he was remembering using the same words to tell Hunter about wanting him to kiss him that day in the woods behind Luke and Gray's cabin.

"Welcome home, Roman," Hunter whispered.

Roman's grip on him tightened just the tiniest bit as he said, "God, I like the way that sounds."

❧

*R*oman could tell Hunter was nervous as they entered the restaurant but he didn't reach out to take his hand like he wanted because he suspected that would just make him more tense. It wasn't something Roman had noticed until after they'd landed at the airport in Monterey and picked up their rental car. Although Hunter had been excited and interested as they'd explored Fisherman's Wharf, he'd seemed slightly off too but Roman hadn't been able to put his finger on what it was that wasn't quite right. At first he'd attributed Hunter's behavior as a response to what he knew was an extremely nerve-wracking first session with his new therapist. But as the day went on, Roman had finally started to realize what the problem was as Hunter would continuously watch the people around them. And once he figured it out, he had no idea how to deal with it.

"Mr. Blackwell, welcome back."

"Alphonse," Roman said with a nod as the well-dressed older man hurried past the hostess stand and greeted him, hand extended.

The restaurant was as busy as it always was but Roman wasn't surprised when Alphonse said, "Just two in your party tonight, Mr. Blackwell?" and then at Roman's nod, led them to a quiet booth in the far corner of the dimly lit space. The intimate table was beautifully set with fine white linen table cloths, expensive gold-trimmed dinnerware and gleaming silver cutlery. Roman didn't miss Hunter's look of concern as he took in the multitude of stem and silverware.

"I have a splendid wine for you tonight. A 1982 Château Lafite Rothschild Pauillac," Alphonse offered.

Roman nodded. "Alphonse, this is a colleague of mine, Mr. Greene. Hunter, this is Alphonse Faroche, the owner."

Alphonse did a little bow and said, "It is a pleasure, Mr. Greene."

As soon as Alphonse left to get the wine, Hunter shifted nervously. "Why did you tell him I was a colleague?"

Roman didn't miss the hurt tone in Hunter's voice and he nearly reached out to cover Hunter's hand with his but drew back at the last second. Hunter seemed to notice the gesture and actually flinched.

"Hunter, look at me," Roman said softly so they wouldn't be overheard.

Hunter lifted his gaze from where he'd been rubbing his finger against the tablecloth.

"I told him you were my colleague because I thought you might be more comfortable with him thinking this was a business meeting rather than a date."

Hunter shook his head slowly. "I'm sorry, Roman. I kept telling myself that we weren't doing anything wrong by being in public together but all I could think was what would happen if people saw me touching you or looking at you a certain way."

"It's okay-"

"No, it's not," Hunter said firmly. "Today was so much fun but it felt like something was missing…it was like I wasn't really sharing it with you because I couldn't be with you the way I wanted."

"Hunter, these things take time…"

"No," Hunter said again. "I don't want to hide how I feel when I'm with you. Even if being gay was a choice, I'd still want to be with you – I'd want people to know how much I love you."

"What?" Roman interjected.

But Hunter continued on as if he hadn't spoken. "I mean, who cares, right? So what if they don't approve of us being together – they can just all go to hell," Hunter said as he got more worked up.

"Here we are," Alphonse said as he reappeared with the bottle of wine.

"Alphonse," Hunter said loudly enough that there was no doubt the people at neighboring tables would hear him. "Roman's not my colleague. He's my boyfriend. We're gay," he added for good measure. "And if you have a problem with that, then we'll take our business elsewhere."

Alphonse looked back and forth in confusion between Hunter and Roman and Roman just shook his head as he bit back his amusement.

"Oh my, these glasses will not do," Alphonse stammered as he suddenly snatched the two wineglasses off the table and hurried off, unopened wine bottle still in hand.

"Say it again," Roman whispered as he shifted around the slight curve of the booth.

"I'm gay," Hunter said softly as he too shifted until their legs were touching beneath the table.

"Hunter," Roman grumbled.

"I love you," Hunter said with a smile as he leaned in to brush his mouth over Roman's. "So much for finding the perfect moment, huh?" Hunter murmured against his lips.

Roman let his hand close over the one Hunter had resting on his thigh. "It couldn't have been any more fucking perfect." Roman didn't give a shit who was watching as he slanted his lips over Hunter's and licked over the seam until Hunter opened to him. Hunter didn't hesitate to kiss him back.

"By the way," Roman said when they finally separated. "Alphonse is as gay as they come."

～

Hunter twisted his hands nervously as he waited for Roman to give the valet his car keys. It had been too dark on their drive up from Monterey to Big Sur to see the sights or even the hotel that Roman owned but as soon as they'd driven onto the lush, beautifully landscaped grounds, Hunter had known the place would be a thing of beauty to behold come daylight.

But none of that was really even on his radar as he thought about the night to come. He'd been telling himself ever since Roman had left for London that he would be mentally ready to take the final step to let Roman make love to him once they were together again, but now that the moment was here, he was struggling to not let that one terrible night in the pool room of the gay club deter him. There was no doubt that Roman would do anything and everything in his power to make the experience a beautiful one but with the nightmares that continued to rattle him, Hunter was afraid he'd panic in the middle of the act and ruin any chance he had at giving to Roman what had been given so freely to him.

"You okay?" Roman asked as he met Hunter on the curb. The bellman had already left to take their luggage up to Roman's room so Hunter nodded and fell into step next to him as they headed for the entrance. After wiping his sweaty palm on his pants, Hunter dropped his hand and brushed it against Roman's. A thrill shot through him as Roman instantly linked their fingers together. No words were needed as they stepped onto the elevator and if Roman noticed how tightly Hunter was clutching his hand, he didn't point it out.

The elevator stopped on the top floor of the twelve story building and Hunter followed Roman down the dark hallway. Everything about the décor was fresh and beautiful but also managed to blend modern style with a rustic feel. Roman had clearly made the right choice to rebuild the hotel using the same unique décor that appeared to set it apart from contemporary establishments.

Roman led him to the end of the hall where there was just a single door that already stood ajar. As Roman was tipping the bellman who was waiting politely by the door, Hunter entered the room and sucked in a breath. What he'd expected was a fancy room with a big bed – what he saw was a full on residence complete with a living room with stylish leather furniture, a gas fireplace and a full sized kitchen off to the right. The whole back wall was made up of glass windows that overlooked the ocean. There was a huge deck with a large infinity pool on one side and a hot tub on the other.

"Roman, it's beautiful," he breathed as he felt his lover come up behind him. Warm lips skimmed his neck.

"I decided to make this my permanent residence a couple of years ago," Roman said as his arms went under Hunter's to wrap around his chest. "You want something to drink?"

Hunter shook his head and then closed his eyes as he felt Roman's lips gently kiss their way down his neck. Hard fingers pulled the collar of his shirt back enough to allow the lips to continue their path over his skin. Hunter lifted one of his arms to curl around the back of Roman's head and he moaned in satisfaction when Roman's lips finally sought his out. Roman's free hand worked the hem of Hunter's shirt up so he could press his hand across the younger man's stomach and Hunter willingly moved back against Roman's body when he used his hand to apply the tiniest bit of pressure. The result was Roman's steely length pressed against his ass. At the contact, Hunter dropped both his hands to reach behind him and close them over the backs of Roman's thighs. But the second he started twisting his hips against Roman's erection, Roman let out a hoarse groan and turned him around. After that, all bets were off as they began tearing at each other's clothes.

"Where's your room?" Hunter asked as Roman nipped at his jawline while his hand stroked Hunter's cock through his underwear.

Roman didn't answer. Instead, he grabbed Hunter's hand and dragged him down a hallway. Hunter didn't have time to take in anything about Roman's room because Roman started kissing him as soon as they walked through the door. Roman was still wearing his pants and as Hunter struggled to get the button loose, he found himself walked backwards until his legs hit the bed. The next second he was on his back and Roman was pinning his arms as he devoured Hunter's mouth. Roman began trailing kisses all over his chest and arms and when he finally released Hunter's arms so he could move lower, Hunter just lay there so he could take it all in. When fingers closed over the waistband of his boxers, Hunter automatically lifted and then waited in hungry anticipation for the feel of Roman's mouth on his cock. But all he got were kisses and licks all around his stomach and upper thighs.

"Roman, please," Hunter whispered as he leaned up on his elbows. The sight of Roman's nose and mouth buried at the spot where his thigh met his groin had him panting but it wasn't until Roman's eyes connected with his that Hunter's whole body drew up tight. There was no single swallowing him down to the root like Roman normally did. No, for whatever reason, Roman had clearly decided to torture him tonight because he zoned in on Hunter's balls. First by licking them, then by drawing each one into his mouth and sucking languidly on them. And even when he was done with that exquisite torture, his mouth moved the opposite way and Hunter felt a mix of fear and excitement go through him as he realized Roman's destination. But it was just another fake out because Roman ran his tongue along the sensitive skin right behind Hunter's aching balls and then set up camp there as he nipped and sucked away until Hunter felt like screaming out his frustration.

"Show me what you want, baby," Roman suddenly whispered and Hunter watched as Roman parted his lips in invitation. Raw lust pounded through Hunter as he sat up and grabbed his dick. Roman's eyes never left his as he waited and Hunter watched them glaze over with passion as Hunter rubbed the head of his dick back and forth over Roman's sleek lips. The pre-come leaking from the crown made Roman's mouth glisten and Hunter quickly leaned down and sealed their mouths together. He licked up the fluid with his tongue and then shoved it into Roman's eager mouth. He only let the kiss go on for a few seconds before he closed his fingers in Roman's hair and pushed him back down to meet his waiting dick. Roman didn't make even one sound of protest as Hunter shoved in as far as he could go. When his slit hit the back of Roman's throat, he pulled out and then shoved back in again. Roman's tongue stroked him as he suddenly sealed his lips around Hunter's flesh and sucked hard. And just like that, Roman once again became the aggressor as he dragged his mouth up and down Hunter's shaft. Hunter was still sitting up so he had a perfect view of Roman's dark head bobbing up and down over his lap and he let his fingers rest on Roman's hair as his lover brought him closer and closer to the edge.

Hunter was sure Roman was going to send him over but at the last second, he pulled free of Hunter and shoved him back down on the bed and kissed him. It didn't last nearly long enough because all of a sudden Roman stood up and shed the rest of his clothes. His dark cock jutted proudly from a thatch of black hair and Hunter eagerly sat up, his mouth watering with need. But instead of Roman shoving into his mouth, he pressed Hunter back down on the bed and then crawled up and over his body. Hunter struggled to understand the new position until Roman finally stopped just above his head, his heavy balls resting against Hunter's chin.

"Open," Roman ordered.

Hunter did as he was told and stifled a moan as Roman's crown pressed between his lips. While the angle didn't allow Roman to go very deep, all of Hunter's nerve endings were firing at the lack of control he had over the situation. It should have frightened him but having Roman fucking his mouth the way he would soon be fucking his body was such a turn on that Hunter was actually reaching down to stroke his own cock to match Roman's smooth in and out motions. Within minutes, Hunter's jaw was aching but when Roman pulled free of him, he actually tried to follow Roman's backward motion. But it wasn't cock he got a mouthful of – it was Roman's demanding tongue. And then Roman was climbing off of him and searching through his nightstand. At the sight of the condom and lube, Hunter bit back the sudden surge of nervous energy that went through him and softly said Roman's name.

Roman glanced at him and then bent over him. "All good?" Roman asked.

Hunter nodded. "Um, I'm ready."

Roman stilled above him but didn't say anything.

"Please, Roman, I really want this…you."

When Roman kissed him gently and then settled on top of him, Hunter couldn't help but smile. As harried and crazy with need that they'd both been just a minute ago, Roman acted like they had all the time in the world.

"Are you sure?" Roman asked between kisses.

"Very," Hunter acknowledged as he wrapped his arms around Roman's shoulders. "Just…"

"What?" Roman prodded.

Hunter could feel the heat flushing his cheeks. "Just don't take me from behind…not yet."

There was just the slightest stiffening in Roman's body but then he began kissing Hunter over and over, each caress becoming more intense and desperate as the last. When he finally pulled back, he whispered, "I want your first time to be something you'll remember forever so if I'm going too fast or I do something to scare you, tell me, okay?"

"You don't have to do that, Roman. It's not my first time."

Roman studied him for a moment and then said, "Yes it is."

Tears stung the back of Hunter's eyes at Roman's words and he closed them just to try to hold the tears at bay. He felt Roman start exploring his body again but this time it wasn't about driving his need higher…no, it was like Roman was worshipping him. But it didn't take long before Roman's kisses became more drugging and his touch more teasing and by the time Roman's mouth closed over his cock, Hunter was begging for relief. The long, hard drags on his dick were slowly driving him insane but when he felt one of Roman's fingers brush over his hole, he couldn't help but tense up. The finger disappeared just as quickly but the sound of the cap on the lube clicking open was like a gunshot going off in the room and Hunter couldn't help but let out a startled whimper.

"Hunter, look at me," Roman said firmly.

Hunter looked down and it wasn't until he saw Roman hovering over his dick that he realized he'd needed to hear Roman's voice to bring him back to the present.

"I'm okay," Hunter said with a nod. "Promise," he added. He waited for Roman to drink his cock back down but to his surprise, Roman climbed back up his body and began kissing him. For a moment, Hunter was worried he'd somehow ruined the whole thing but then he felt Roman's lube covered finger brush his opening again and he stifled a moan as Roman's tongue sought out his at the same time that his finger pressed forward.

~

*R*oman swallowed Hunter's gasp of surprise and kept up the pressure on Hunter's hole until his body accepted the invasion. The second the outer muscle gave way and his finger disappeared inside of Hunter to the first knuckle, Hunter sucked in a breath and his fingers dug into Roman's upper arms. Roman didn't move even a fraction of an inch as Hunter tried to adjust. When his eyes finally opened and he gave him a wobbly smile, Roman leaned down to kiss him. It wasn't until Hunter began voraciously kissing him back that Roman let his finger slide in the rest of the way and while Hunter still tensed, he didn't let up on consuming Roman's mouth. The pressure on Roman's finger was tight and his dick instantly hardened even more in excitement.

He slowly began sliding his finger in and out of Hunter, carefully gauging his reaction for anything beyond discomfort. But when Hunter actually began meeting his thrusts with a subtle shift of his hips, Roman began twisting his finger deep inside Hunter until he found the spot he was looking for. Hunter's eyes flew open at the first brush over his prostate and on the second pass, his shocked gaze searched out Roman's. By the third stroke, Hunter was gyrating his entire body trying to get more of what he was feeling.

"Roman," he panted. "Please don't stop."

Roman had known from the way Hunter had fucked him senseless on more than one occasion that he would be the type to give every part of himself over to the experience and not hold anything back but seeing it actually happen without being lost in his own haze of lust was an incredible, heady experience. Pulling back enough to give Hunter a little bit of space, Roman kept one arm tucked beneath Hunter's shoulders while the other continued to torture his sweet spot. Then he said, "Touch yourself, Hunter. Show me how good it feels."

It was all Hunter seemed to have been waiting for because he quickly began yanking on his dick as he slammed his ass down on Roman's finger. Roman used his distraction to add a second finger which Hunter didn't protest in the slightest. The added pressure had Hunter gasping for air as Roman continued to finger the bundle of nerves and as Hunter's hand feverishly worked to bring himself relief, his whole body began to sweat and shake. Moments later, he wailed as Roman pressed both his fingers against that one spot and Roman let out his own moan as ropes of Hunter's come hit his own body. The orgasm went on and on as Hunter tried to milk every last drop from his cock as Roman continued to draw circles around his sensitive gland. When Hunter finally released his dick, Roman withdrew his arm from Hunter's shoulders and leaned down to clean up the sticky white fluid that had pooled against his abdomen. He carefully withdrew his fingers from Hunter's sated body and then wrapped an arm beneath Hunter to move him farther up the mattress.

Hunter had gone completely lax and his dreamy eyes couldn't stay focused on Roman. Roman used the opportunity to run his hands all over Hunter's soft skin. As lean as Hunter was, his body was actually quite strong and Roman couldn't help but trace every well-defined muscle with first his fingers and then his mouth. By the time he'd made it back down to Hunter's ass, Hunter had started to respond somewhat but mostly just to make it easier for Roman to access his body. So when Roman lifted Hunter's legs up and draped them over his shoulders as he lay near the bottom of the bed, Hunter didn't protest. Nor did he make a sound when Roman's big hands separated the globes of his ass so he could see the little pink hole that was fluttering in nervous anticipation. Since it was clearly begging for his attention, Roman didn't waste any time and as soon as his tongue swiped over the wrinkly flesh, Hunter let out a startled yell.

～

"Roman!" Hunter shouted for the second time as wet heat engulfed his body. But even though his brain was telling him what Roman was doing to him had to be wrong, his body had something else in mind entirely because his ass was lifting of its own accord and his thighs were gripping Roman for all they were worth.

Every lick and suckle went through him like a knife, except instead of pain, it was pure, blissful pleasure. He managed to reach up to grab a hold of a pillow and shove it over his face just in time to stifle another scream as Roman's tongue pressed inside of him. He hadn't believed it could get any better than when Roman's finger had pressed that spot deep inside of him but holy shit was he wrong. His dick was already hard as a rock again and the euphoria from his earlier orgasm had given way to a bone-wrenching need for more. Even though he didn't think more was even possible considering what his first release had done to him.

Roman kept tongue fucking him and then took it up another level by pulling out his tongue just long enough to shove a finger into him and press on his prostate. "Roman, I can't," he cried out as fire burned through his veins.

He wasn't sure if Roman was taking pity on him or if Roman was too turned on himself to continue because Roman suddenly released him and grabbed a condom. The sight should have had all of Hunter's fear coming back but all he could think about was how it could possibly get any better. He watched as Roman spread some lube on his dick and then gently pressed some into Hunter's body.

"Put your legs over my arms," Roman said as he put his hands on either side of Hunter's body. Hunter did as he was told and then licked his lips as Roman used his arms to spread his legs open. He felt Roman's cock against his hole and the tension that he thought was gone came back in full force.

"Breathe out and push down on me," Roman instructed. Hunter followed the gentle order and as soon as the breath left his body, he felt himself being opened and stretched. Pain coursed through him as Roman continued to push forward and Hunter was about to tell him to stop when his body suddenly seemed to buckle under the pressure and Roman sank farther inside of him. He tried to suck in air as the discomfort and odd sensation burned through his ass.

"Hunter, look at me," Roman whispered. Just seeing the love in Roman's eyes had Hunter's body relaxing and then it was like he was drawing Roman in rather than trying to keep him out.

"Oh shit," Hunter breathed when Roman was fully seated inside of him. It felt so strange and so good at the same time.

"Hunter," Roman said again but this time his voice sounded uneven and strained. One look at Roman's face told him why. Sweat dripped from his brow and his whole body seemed to tremble as he tried to keep himself still. With his legs being controlled by Roman, Hunter couldn't easily reach Roman like he wanted to but as soon as he wrapped his hand around Roman's neck, Roman got the message and leaned down to kiss him. As Roman's body pressed down on his, Roman's arms forced Hunter's legs farther open and back and Hunter couldn't stop the cry of pleasure that tore from his lips as the new angle allowed Roman in even deeper.

"I need to move, baby," Roman whispered harshly.

Hunter could only nod but that was all it took for Roman to pull back before pushing forward again. The burning sensation built every time Roman slid into him but it quickly changed to something else as wisps of pleasure started firing under his skin. Roman's lips were hovering just above his and he reveled in the feel of Roman's heavy pants brushing against him as Roman's need grew and grew. His thrusts became heavier and deeper with each pass and at some point Roman released his legs so he could wrap his arms around Hunter and hold him as he pounded into him. Hunter took advantage of the change in position and locked his legs around Roman's lower back, his heels digging into Roman's ass with each lunge. He snagged his arms around Roman's shoulders and held on as tight as he could as Roman's heavy balls slapped against his ass. He sought out Roman's mouth and was rewarded with deep, hungry kisses that turned him on almost as much as the friction that Roman's cock was causing deep inside of him.

"I love you so much," Roman whispered against his mouth.

"I love you," Hunter returned as he released his hold on Roman's shoulders so he could cup his face in his hands. "So much, Roman."

Roman dipped down to sip at his lips a few more times as his lower body relentlessly pounded into Hunter's but then his mouth hung just over Hunter's as he ground out Hunter's name. The feel of

Roman's cock pulsing inside of him set off Hunter's own release and he closed his eyes as the orgasm ripped through him. He clamped down on Roman with every part of his body that he could and held on as wave after wave of pleasure rolled through him. Roman's orgasm was just as strong if not more so because his body kept humping into Hunter uncontrollably as Roman's fingers bit into his skin hard enough to leave bruises. When the haze of pleasure finally settled like a blanket over them, Roman's body pressed Hunter's farther into the mattress. Hunter wasn't sure whose lips found whose first but he didn't care because all he felt were Roman's unspoken words with every tender caress.

CHAPTER 10

Roman was sure he'd never seen anything more beautiful than Hunter on his knees, his beautiful pink lips loving Roman's aching cock as water sluiced down his shoulders and along the curve of his back. And he definitely knew that he'd never felt as cherished as he did when Hunter touched him. Of course, all Hunter had to do was look at him in the way that he always did for Roman to know he'd finally come home. He wasn't invisible anymore.

As the pressure on his dick intensified, Roman leaned his head back against the tile wall and closed his eyes. Sensation after sensation bombarded him as Hunter's lush mouth sucked him all the way down. But when Hunter's fingers dipped between his ass cheeks to play with his hole, Roman gave up the pretense of being able to hold out and he reached down to pull Hunter to his feet. Their mouths fed off each other as Roman searched out the condom and lube that Hunter had openly grabbed from the nightstand before taking Roman's hand and leading him to the shower. He knew Hunter was likely still sore from their passionate encounter the night before so he was all prepared to be on the receiving end this time around, but Hunter took that choice away from him when he reached for the condom and began rolling it down Roman's cock. His movements were slow and drawn out and only served to make Roman more insane with need. As soon as the condom was in place, Roman turned them around so it was Hunter's back pressed to the wall.

Roman reached for the lube but Hunter took the bottle from him, his mossy eyes never leaving Roman's as he put a dollop on his fingers and then reached behind himself. Although Roman couldn't actually see Hunter's fingers at work, he could see the way Hunter's eyes darkened just a little bit and his lips opened on a soft exhale.

"Tell me how it feels," Roman bit out as he slapped his hands on the wall on either side of Hunter's head.

"So tight," Hunter moaned and from the way his hips began to twist, Roman knew he was trying to work his fingers in deeper than they could go. "Hot," Hunter added.

Roman swooped in to kiss him and then reached his hand down to Hunter's crease. He followed the path of Hunter's hand and then began probing Hunter's already stuffed full hole. "Keep them there," Roman ordered as he began pressing his finger in next to Hunter's. Hunter gasped at the added pressure and then let out a whimper when Roman's finger pressed down on both of his and then maneuvered them until he hit his own prostate. Since he knew the angle would be uncomfortable for Hunter to maintain, Roman only held them there for a few moments before pulling his and Hunter's fingers free.

"Put your arms around my neck," Roman said softly and as soon as Hunter had done it, Roman reached down and lifted Hunter up and pinned him against the wall and held him in place as he reached between them to position his cock. Hunter's legs immediately wrapped around him and the position helped Roman search out Hunter's hole. Hunter moaned when Roman slid into him but unlike the night before, Roman surged into Hunter in one long lunge.

"Fuck, Roman, so good," Hunter cried out as his lips searched out Roman's. "Fuck me really hard, okay?" Hunter whispered against his lips.

Since that had been Roman's plan from the get go, he quickly pulled almost all the way out of Hunter and then slammed back in.

Hunter let out a loud curse when Roman did it again but since he began pushing his hips down every time Roman plunged into him, Roman knew he wasn't feel any pain or discomfort. After that, Roman set a ruthless pattern of pounding into Hunter until he was close to the edge and then pulling out until just the head of his dick was holding Hunter open and hanging there until Hunter begged and pleaded with him for more. Then he'd start all over again. He kept up the torment until his own body couldn't take it anymore and then he brutally fucked Hunter until both of them were one body whose only goal was relief. When it came, Hunter actually bit down on his shoulder and the sting of pain had Roman shouting Hunter's name as he unloaded into the condom. Hunter kept slamming his hips down on Roman as his hot release bathed both their bodies just before the hot water washed the evidence of their joining away.

~

*H*unter was grateful for the water raining down on him and Roman because it made the tears easier to hide. He could still feel Roman's pulsing cock deep inside of him and automatically tightened his muscles so that he could feel even more of the mind blowing sensation. Roman groaned at the move and actually shoved into him a little more.

The idea of playing in the shower together hadn't actually hit Hunter until Roman had mentioned needing to wash the sweat from their day away as Hunter had started kissing him as soon as they got back to Roman's place. They'd spent the entire day exploring Big Sur and had spent hours hiking to different spots to admire the view and check out the various attractions. And unlike the day before, Hunter hadn't felt even an ounce of concern about being seen in public with Roman. They'd held hands, kissed, laughed, taken selfies…they'd even asked a couple they'd met on one of the trails to take a picture of them together. If anyone had looked at them strangely or with disgust, Hunter hadn't noticed and he certainly wouldn't have cared because nothing could chase away the feeling of how perfect his life was.

Roman's gentle introduction to what it was really supposed to feel like to have another man buried deep inside of his body had blown every one of Hunter's expectations out of the water. When he'd fucked Roman, he'd reveled in watching Roman come apart beneath him but being fucked by Roman was so much different. It had been exactly like Roman had said...it had been about Roman taking care of him, cherishing his vulnerability that opening himself up to Roman required rather than exploiting it. And if he thought it would be a one-time feeling that came from it being his first time, he'd been wrong because even now with Roman still joined with him, all those emotions were wreaking havoc in his crowded mind. Hence the tears.

Hunter couldn't help the twinge of loss he felt when Roman finally pulled free of his body so he could dispose of the condom. But Roman quickly made up for it by kissing him as he pulled their sated bodies together and stood under the soothing water. It could have been minutes or hours that passed before Roman turned off the shower and pulled him out onto the bathmat and began drying him off with a soft towel.

"Go get dressed," Roman murmured against his lips as he wrapped the towel around Hunter's hips. "We have reservations."

Hunter nodded and then took one last look at Roman's tight ass as he left the bathroom. It was on the tip of his tongue to ask Roman if they could just order room service when he heard Roman's phone ringing where it sat on the nightstand. He glanced at it and called out to Roman, "Roman, it's Gray."

"Can you get it?" Roman called back.

Hunter picked up the phone and answered. "Gray, hi, this is Hunter."

"Hey, Hunter," Gray said, his voice quiet and uneven. A twinge of concern went through Hunter at how off Gray sounded and he automatically began walking towards the bathroom. "Can I talk to Roman?" Gray asked.

"Yeah, here he is," Hunter said as he handed the phone to Roman.

Roman must have seen something in his eyes because he shot him a questioning look as he answered the phone. After that, Roman didn't speak or even move as he listened to Gray. Finally, he said, "Yeah, okay," and then hung up the phone.

"What?" Hunter asked. "What is it?"

Roman put the phone down on the counter and continued drying himself off, his movements automatic and efficient.

"Um, Walt – my father – is in the hospital."

"What happened?" Hunter asked gently as he took the towel from Roman and took over the job of drying him off.

"His heart...Gray said they don't think he has much time left. Hours maybe. Gray and Luke are on their way to the airport."

"Roman, I'm sorry," Hunter whispered as he wrapped his arms around Roman's neck. Roman's arms came around him.

"He's asking for me."

~

*R*oman clutched Hunter's hand in his as they waited for their stop on the right floor. The elevator was crowded and had to make several stops as doctors and other hospital staff got on and off and he eventually lost track of what was going on around him as he mulled over the unexpected turn of events. It had been nearly four years since he'd seen his father and the idea of seeing him now in his final hours both scared the hell out of him and pissed him off.

"Baby, this is us," Hunter said gently as he tugged at Roman's hand. Roman let Hunter lead him off the elevator and down several hallways but with every step that drew them closer to his father's room, Roman just wanted to turn around and go back to his place and crawl into his comfortable bed and wrap himself around Hunter. This was supposed to be their weekend. Every moment of it had been perfect up to this point but somehow fate had deemed that his past should step in like it always did and fuck everything up. He was on the verge of telling Hunter that they were going back to the hotel when he looked up and saw a familiar face staring at him with naked contempt.

Victoria looked exactly as she always did. Perfect. Whatever plastic surgeon she had on retainer made her sixty-three years look like forty-five and her slim figure was perfectly packaged in a silky pants suit that matched her stiletto pumps. Her dark blonde hair was done up in some kind of twist and nearly every piece of exposed skin had some kind of glittering jewelry adorning it. When her frosty eyes lit on Roman, her lips drew into a sneer and she turned her bitter eyes on the young nurse behind the nurse's station. "I specifically told you not to call him," she snapped and Roman couldn't help but wonder how the nurse was supposed to know what she was talking about since she wouldn't have a clue who Roman was.

"Mrs. Hawthorne-"

"What are you doing here?" Victoria snarled as she stepped in their path.

"Mrs. Hawthorne, I'm Hunter, Roman's-"

"I know who you are," Victoria bit out as she glared at Roman. "You're one of his little playthings," she said as she glanced briefly at Hunter. Her eyes went back to Roman. "You and your perversions," she said with a shake of her head.

Her open hatred actually helped Roman snap out of his funk and he tightened his hold on Hunter's hand as he moved in front of him and pushed past Victoria without a word. She let out an outraged gasp and he could hear her venting her anger on the poor nurse as he walked into the room just behind the nurse's station.

He'd expected to see his father hooked up to all sorts of machines but there was surprisingly very little going on around him. There were just the basics – machines tracking his vitals and an IV. It wasn't a good sign.

Walt Hawthorne had never been a big man but seeing him lying in the hospital bed, his pale, wrinkled skin drawn tight over his bones made him seem small and old. Which made sense since Walt was in his early seventies but since it had been so long since Roman had seen him, he only had the image of a fit, well-groomed man who spent most of his days on the golf course to go off of. A twinge of pity twisted in Roman's gut but he ignored it.

His father's eyes were open and staring at some point on the window so Roman slowly walked around the bed until his father noticed him. It seemed to take him several seconds to recognize Roman. The sound of his name being whispered and the small smile that spread across his father's gaunt face had Roman tightening his hand around Hunter's. He felt Hunter's other hand come to rest on his back between his shoulders but there was no pressure for him to move forward.

"Roman," his father said again and then he lifted his hand just a little bit. Bile spread in Roman's mouth at the gesture and while he moved closer to the bed, he didn't reach for his father's hand and he didn't sit in the chair next to the bed.

"Gray's on his way," Roman said quietly. "He said you wanted to see me."

His father's eyes shifted to Hunter but Roman didn't introduce them. No way he wanted Hunter linked to this man in any way.

"I should have done more, Roman," his father said feebly. "I promised her..." Roman stiffened but didn't say anything because he knew exactly who his father was talking about. "She was everything to me."

"If that were true, old man, she wouldn't be six feet under."

His father's eyes closed and Roman felt absolutely nothing when a single tear escaped.

"I couldn't...I would have lost everything. It was all Victoria's."

Roman's rage went to a whole new level at that. "Money? You let her die so you wouldn't lose your bank account?"

"Victoria's father would have ruined me if I left her. But after my sweet Libby...afterwards I told Victoria I needed to bring you home."

"And she just agreed to that?" Roman said sarcastically.

"I...I threatened to expose our marriage for what it was. I told her I would claim you as my son."

Roman felt like he was going to be sick. "So she agreed to let me stay with you."

His father nodded weakly. "As long as I agreed not to tell anyone who you were."

"And to treat me like shit, right?" Roman snapped.

Another tear slipped down his father's face as he shook his head. "There was no other way…"

"There were a hundred other ways, Walt," Roman sneered. "Hell, I would have had a better chance at a fucking childhood if you'd let them put me in foster care."

"Libby-"

"Don't you dare spout some bullshit about doing what you did because of my mother. My mother never would have wanted that for me!"

"Roman, I swear on my life, I loved you."

At that, Roman released Hunter's hand and strode forward until his face was practically in his father's. "You don't know the first thing about love, old man. I hope you rot in hell."

His father let out a whimper but Roman just shoved away from the bed and strode out of the room. He ignored whatever parting shot Victoria aimed at him as he rushed past her and he barely noticed Hunter's fingers closing around his hand. From somewhere behind him he heard the steady, loud signal of a heart monitor and then the corresponding flurry of overhead calls on the PA system. Several nurses and doctors rushed past him towards his father's room but he didn't look back.

$\approx$

"*H*ave you seen him?" Hunter asked Gray as he put his hand on Gray's arm in a silent gesture of comfort. Gray was standing in one corner of the large living room, Luke by his side. As solemn as the wake was, Hunter couldn't help but notice how separate Gray kept himself from his mother as she held court near the long table covered in fancy appetizers.

Gray looked around the room. "No," he said. "We'll help you look," Gray added as he motioned towards the large marble staircase near the entryway to the house.

Hunter had lost track of Roman when he'd gone to the bathroom and he couldn't help but feel a moment of concern when he'd come out only to find the spot he'd left Roman in empty. He'd expected Victoria to go on the offensive as soon as he and Roman had arrived at the church for the service but the viper in heels had stuck close to Gray and played the role of grieving widow. By the time they'd gone to the cemetery for the burial, Gray had managed to escape his mother and sought out Roman but as with Hunter, Roman did nothing more than shake or nod his head at Gray's gentle inquiry as to how he was doing.

It had been a challenge even getting Roman to agree to stay in California for the burial and Hunter could only figure Roman was doing it for Gray because his naked hatred for his father hadn't eased even a little after Gray had confirmed the man was gone. After leaving the hospital, Roman had driven them back to Big Sur but he didn't speak at all and shot down any and all of Hunter's attempts to draw him out. The lack of emotion had frightened Hunter but when they'd gone to bed that night, Roman had made love to him and hadn't held any part of himself back. It had been the same in the days that followed but there'd been no further discussion of his encounter with his father and he hadn't participated in any of the funeral arrangements.

Hunter followed Luke and Gray up the stairs. If the Hawthorne mansion hadn't been so cold and empty, Hunter would have thought it beautiful with all its fine furnishings and expensive artwork and decorations. But all he saw as he moved throughout the home that was clearly meant to be a showpiece was a young Roman trying to figure out where he fit in the strange dynamic that was his new family. How many cruel words had Victoria spat at him in this place? How many times had his father walked past him on these very same stairs and said nothing to the son he supposedly loved?

Gray led him down several hallways to a small room where the door was slightly ajar. Gray pushed open the door, looked inside the room and then stepped back and motioned to Hunter. Hunter nodded his thanks and stepped into the room. A glance behind him showed Gray had entered too but was hanging back and Luke was standing just outside the door.

He found Roman standing in front of the single window that over-looked a wooded area behind the house. He looked beautiful in his crisp black suit as he stood with his hands tucked into his pockets. Hunter glanced around the room and couldn't help but think it looked surprisingly small compared to some of the other bedrooms he'd seen in the place. There was just a single twin sized bed in the middle of the room along with a dresser on the far wall. On top of the dresser were several vases and glass bowls. Boxes were stacked up next to the dresser and the top one was open and Hunter could see more decorative knickknacks resting in it.

Hunter went to Roman's side and put his hand on his arm.

"You okay?" he asked gently, though he knew the answer.

"It's small, huh," Roman asked as he glanced at the room. "It seemed so big to me that first night."

Hunter had figured as much that the room had been the one Roman had grown up in.

"It used to be the nanny's quarters I guess," Roman mused as he looked around the room. "How old were you when they let her go?" Roman asked Gray who still stood near the door.

"Fourteen."

Roman nodded knowingly and Hunter could see the unspoken thought. Roman hadn't even been afforded a nanny to care for him.

Roman moved away from the window and went to the dresser to examine the largest of the three vases. "I'm sorry, Gray, I couldn't do it."

"Do what?" Gray asked softly.

"Keep my mouth shut. Let him say his piece and get out of there."

"You had every right to tell him how you felt," Gray responded.

Roman picked up the heavy vase and cradled it in his hand as if testing the weight. "He said she was everything to him," Roman whispered. Hunter went to stand by his side but just as he was reaching up to settle his hand on Roman's back, Roman flung the vase across the room. It went right through the window and before the glass even hit the floor, Roman snatched up another vase and hurled it at the wall next to the window.

"She was everything to him but he wasn't there watching her die a little every day! He wasn't the one who begged her to get out of bed, who cooked for her so she wouldn't waste away, told her stories about all the places she wanted to see!"

One by one, Roman smashed all the bowls and vases sitting on top of the dresser. Hunter didn't try to stop him, didn't touch him at all. He just wiped at his own tears as he watched Roman break apart, piece by agonizingly slow piece.

"Did he tell you?" Roman suddenly asked as he turned to face Hunter. "Did Gray tell you how she died?"

"No baby, he didn't," Hunter said gently.

Hunter could hear commotion behind him and he was able to pick out Victoria's shrill voice screaming at someone to call the police. Luke's low voice followed and if Hunter hadn't been so focused on Roman, he would have smiled when he heard Luke tell Victoria to shut her fucking mouth or he'd do it for her.

"She took her own life because she didn't want to live without him," Roman said bitterly. "I wasn't enough for her...she needed *him*," he spat. "I told her I'd never leave her, that I'd take care of her forever...that I'd take her to all the places he promised to take her someday but she just looked at me with this sad smile."

Roman's eyes began to fill with tears and Hunter knew in that instant that he hadn't yet heard the worst of it. "I overheard the cops saying afterwards how most women do it with pills or by cutting their wrists in the bathtub. One of them actually said he was glad she hung herself instead of slicing up her wrists because it was easier to clean up. Then he...then he said he hoped she'd broken her neck when she did it because otherwise it would have been a slow, painful way to go."

Hunter swallowed hard as he felt nausea sweep through his system. He ached to reach out to Roman but he could see that Roman needed to finish it.

"She didn't break her neck," Roman announced as tears began to flow unchecked down his face.

Since Hunter suspected what he was going to say, he whispered, "How do you know?"

"Because I fucking saw it!" he yelled. "I was bringing her some soup and I opened the door and saw her standing on this chair in the middle of the room. I didn't know what she was doing at first. Then I saw the cord she had wrapped around her neck. I froze…I just fucking froze," Roman cried. "And then I called her name and she saw me and this look came into her eyes – this empty look – and she told me she was sorry and that she loved me. Then she told me to close my eyes just before she kicked the chair over."

Roman began to sob as he sank to the floor. Hunter dropped to the floor next to him and pulled Roman against him. Roman's hot tears scalded his neck as Roman wrapped his arms around his waist. "I couldn't get the fucking chair back underneath her!"

Hunter couldn't find any words as Roman continued to cling to him so he just held on as tight as he could as tormented sobs ripped through his lover. Hunter began rocking them back and forth as he dropped his head so he could place kisses against Roman's brow. He kept whispering "I love you" against Roman's ear and every time he did, Roman's fingers bit into his body. Hunter had no idea how much time passed before Roman finally calmed but even as the tears slowed, he didn't release Roman. At some point he heard the door behind them snick closed but he didn't look to see if they were alone or if Gray had stayed behind. All he did was hold on to Roman and even after Roman's grip on him finally started to ease, Hunter refused to let him go.

∼

"How much longer?" Roman asked as he tightened his hold on Hunter's waist.

"An hour I think," Hunter responded as he played with Roman's hair.

They were lying on the bed at the back of his jet. Roman didn't remember everything that happened after his meltdown in his child-hood bedroom but he'd pieced together that Gray and Luke had likely helped Hunter get him out of there and arranged for them to fly back home.

"Gray and Luke?"

"Up front."

That surprised Roman. He would have guessed Gray would have stayed behind to be with his mother. "Not exactly the vacation I promised you, was it?" Roman said tiredly.

"I don't know," Hunter said softly. "The beginning...well, I don't even have any words to describe how perfect and beautiful you made it."

Roman glanced up and felt a shimmer of pleasure at the sight of color flooding Hunter's cheeks.

"And the way Gray laid into Victoria at the end there, that was definitely my second favorite part."

"What did he do?"

"He called her a few choice names, told her to go fuck herself and then announced to everyone that he had to go because his brother needed him. Victoria looked like she was going to have a stroke."

Roman chuckled. "How'd I get so lucky?" he asked.

Hunter laced their fingers together. "Luck had nothing to do with it, Roman. We found each other because you refused to give up on me. You have your brother back because you were strong enough to give him a second chance. That's all you."

Hunter leaned down to kiss him and Roman met him halfway. He guessed there would be a time when he would need to deal with the volcano of emotions that his father's death had brought back to the surface, including the truth about his mother's suicide, but for now he had what he needed and that was enough.

CHAPTER 11

*H*unter struggled to focus on his computer but the sound of Roman working on his own laptop was driving him crazy. Not because the sound of the clicking mouse was bothering him but because he'd called an embargo on any fooling around until he finished his English Lit paper. It would have made more sense to stay at his dorm to finish but he hadn't managed to spend more than a handful of hours outside of Roman's company since they'd returned to Missoula and Roman had announced that he wouldn't be traveling for work that week. They'd gotten back late Tuesday night and Hunter had managed to make it to his second therapy session the next morning but only because Roman had insisted that he go.

Whatever demons Roman had exorcised in his childhood room seemed to have extinguished themselves because he seemed surprisingly relaxed. His relationship with Gray hadn't suffered in the least and in fact, it seemed stronger than ever because Roman often spoke with his brother and had driven down to see him several times since they'd gotten back. Luke and Gray had driven up to have dinner with them at a local steakhouse just last night and unlike their previous dinner a couple weeks earlier, Roman was an active participant.

Hunter gave up on trying to concentrate and closed his computer.

He turned around from the desk he'd commandeered and draped his arms over the back of the chair as he watched Roman work. When Roman didn't acknowledge him, Hunter got up and crawled onto the bed until he was straddling Roman's lower legs. Hunter began massaging Roman's thighs but since the laptop was still on Roman's lap, he had very little room to work with.

When he made a move to take the computer away, Roman put up a finger to stop him. "One sec," he murmured. "I just need one more Color Bomb and I'm golden."

Hunter grabbed Roman's laptop and stared at the screen in disbelief. "You're playing Candy Crush?" he asked. "I thought you were working!"

Roman just laughed and took the laptop from him and put it on the nightstand. He dragged Hunter down for a kiss. "I take it the embargo has been lifted?" Roman breathed against his lips.

"Oh yeah," Hunter said as he leaned back enough to work on Roman's jeans. It wasn't often that he'd seen Roman in anything other than dress slacks but the man was positively yummy in the butter-soft denim that clung to his ass and hugged his thighs.

Hunter had barely gotten the button free when Roman's phone rang. But he didn't stop wrestling with Roman's zipper until Roman said, "It's Gray." Hunter hesitated but then figured it could be fun to torment Roman while he tried to keep up a normal conversation with his brother. He started pulling Roman's zipper down but Roman's big hand settled over his and Hunter stilled when he saw the seriousness in Roman's gaze.

"Okay, yeah, give it to him."

Roman hung up the phone and Hunter automatically tensed when his dark eyes held Hunter's.

"What? Are he and Luke okay?"

"They're fine," Roman said. "It's Finn."

"Did something happen to him?" Hunter asked in a panic.

"No, no," Roman quickly reassured him. "They ran into him in town this afternoon and he asked for your number. They didn't give it to him but Gray told him he would ask me if it would be okay for Finn to text me."

Hunter felt his stomach drop out and he climbed off of Roman so he could get up and move around. It had been weeks since he'd spoken to Callan and while he still had every intention of following through with his promise to tell people the truth about what had happened between him and Finn, he'd gotten caught up in trying to get his life on track and then Roman had lost his father.

"I shouldn't have waited…I should have just told the truth that day after I talked to Callan," he bit out. His hand automatically went to his pocket and he cursed when he realized what he'd done. He hadn't had the urge to hurt himself once since the night he'd called Roman when he'd still been in London.

Roman climbed off the bed and grabbed him by the arms. "Hey," he said gently. "You did what you needed to do. He'll understand that."

Hunter didn't get a chance to respond because Roman's phone dinged and Hunter actually held his breath as Roman read the text.

"He wants to know if you'll meet with him this afternoon. He can be here by four."

"Oh God," Hunter mumbled as he sat down on the bed. Two hours…two hours to figure out how to say the two words that really wouldn't change anything for Finn.

"Hunter?" Roman asked.

Hunter nodded. "Yeah, okay."

He left the details of where the meeting would happen to Roman and got up and went to the bathroom. He kept running cold water over his face and arms in the hopes that the itchy feeling would go away but it just kept growing and growing. He looked up and saw Roman watching him with concern in the reflection of the mirror. As Roman handed him a towel, Hunter turned off the water and dried off.

"Did your therapist give you any tips for how to deal with an episode?" Roman asked.

"Some kind of distraction is my best bet. Exercise, a change of scenery – anything to get myself out of that headspace for a few minutes."

Roman smiled wolfishly. "I can think of a few things we can try if you're up for it."

The attempt at levity worked and Hunter felt himself relax. "I'm not sure that's what he had in mind when he suggested it."

Roman's eyes settled on his mouth and Hunter felt his dick jerk as the humor gave way to something else. "Maybe we can test the theory out and then let him know."

"Maybe," Hunter agreed although he was having trouble remembering what they were talking about. Roman's lips descended on his and what started off as a gentle, searching kiss gave way to a white hot burning need. Hunter had no idea if he was more desperate or Roman was...all he knew was that when Roman told him to face the mirror and put his hands flat on the countertop, he did so without question. Roman stripped off his own shirt first but didn't reach for Hunter's clothes next. Instead he disappeared into the main part of the room and then returned a second later with the lube and a condom.

At that point his hands made quick work of Hunter's jeans but he just shoved them to Hunter's ankles instead of removing them all together. His own jeans were next but he didn't take them off either – he just opened them enough to expose his cock and then he was putting the condom on. Something about watching Roman do the absolute minimum needed to bring them together turned Hunter on like nothing else. Even the fact that he suspected Roman would be taking him from behind – something he hadn't ever done since Hunter had asked him not to during their first night together in the hotel in Big Sur – didn't worry him like it should. Maybe because he'd be able to see who it was behind him because of the mirror which was why he assumed Roman had placed him there in the first place. Or maybe it was because he trusted Roman completely and it wouldn't have even occurred to him to confuse the man who loved and revered him with the men who'd brutalized him.

Cool lube was slathered over his hole as Roman stepped behind him and he used his knee to force Hunter's legs farther apart. The heat radiating from Roman's body was intense and the contrast between the cool lube and Roman's hot finger pushing into his body was heady. He watched as Roman's lips skimmed over his neck as he prepped him and then his mouth was sealing over Hunter's. The finger left his body but Roman maintained the connection with their mouths as his cock slid between Hunter's ass. Roman's entry was rough and unrelenting but somehow it was exactly what Hunter needed. There was no pain whatsoever – just the burning, stretching feeling he loved.

Roman only gave him a couple of shallow thrusts before he began ramming into him, his movements forcing Hunter to brace himself on his hands. Hunter's shirt was pushed up enough to expose his back but Roman still didn't remove it. The burning in his ass quickly changed over to a delicious friction that had Hunter moaning with each heavy slap of Roman's balls against his ass. He loved how the hair on Roman's thighs brushed against his own legs and the feel of Roman's wiry hair at his groin scratching over Hunter's sensitive skin had him crying out in delight. When Roman pressed him flat on the counter, Hunter didn't protest and he didn't bother to keep his eyes on the reflection in the mirror because all he wanted to do in that moment was feel. The edge of the counter dug into his abdomen as Roman slammed into him repeatedly but once Roman's hand closed around his dick, Hunter didn't even notice. And then came the weight on his back as Roman leaned over him.

"So fucking tight, Hunter," Roman groaned in his ear. "It's like you were made just for me...a perfect fit." Roman's teeth gently nipped at his ear and then closed over his shoulder. It reminded Hunter of an animal forcing its mate into submission and just that idea alone had Hunter's orgasm building deep in his balls.

"Harder," Hunter ordered as he used his hands to force his ass back onto Roman's length.

"Yes," Roman snarled and Hunter felt Roman's big hand fist in his hair to further hold him still. With all his control taken from him, Hunter let go of everything but the sound of Roman's heavy breaths, the feel of his body covering Hunter's, protecting it, owning it, the sensation of pleasure radiating up his spine. Roman's lunges became so heavy that Hunter actually had to stand on his tiptoes. And when Roman's arm wrapped around his waist to keep him from slamming forward into the counter, Hunter just let his whole lower body go lax so that Roman could fuck him however he wanted, as hard as he wanted and for as long as he wanted.

Nothing about the fucking was gentle or sweet but it was absolutely what Hunter needed and when Roman finally ordered him to come, his body instantly responded and he howled in pleasure as his seed exploded from his body. Roman kept pounding into him long after Hunter came and it wasn't long before another smaller orgasm hit him. It wasn't until the tremors eased that Roman finally took his own pleasure but instead of shooting into the condom, Hunter felt Roman withdraw from him. He felt the head of Roman's dick slapping the spot just above his ass as he jerked himself off and a part of him wished he could watch. But seeing the sweet agony in Roman's features through the reflection in the mirror proved to be a heart-stopping experience because Hunter was usually too lost in his own pleasure to see what happened when his lover came. It was a sight he wouldn't soon forget along with the feel of Roman's hot come hitting his skin and sliding down his ass until it crept between his cheeks. He couldn't help but wonder what it would feel like to have the scorching liquid bathing his insides and he knew that would be his first ask of Roman on the very day his six months were up and he tested negative.

As Roman struggled to catch his breath, he pulled Hunter upright and kissed him. It was only at that point that Roman yanked his shirt off and stroked his hands all over Hunter's chest.

"You're the science geek," Roman murmured against his mouth. "What do you think? Did we prove our hypothesis?"

Hunter chuckled. "I think we did but how about you come to my next session and explain our findings to my therapist?"

Roman laughed and then helped him get the rest of his clothes off before tugging him to the shower.

∾

unter was glad Roman didn't release his hand at any point along the short walk from the hotel to the coffee shop at the end of the block because once he saw the familiar old pick-up truck sitting in the quiet parking lot, he nearly turned around to go back to the safety of Roman's room. To Roman's credit, he had managed to keep Hunter distracted for most of the two hours but everything had come back in a rush as soon as they'd started getting dressed.

Hunter was strangely glad that Roman didn't try to trivialize the moment with empty words of comfort. And he was more than glad when Roman had staunchly refused to let him go by himself.

As Roman opened the door to the coffee shop, Hunter took in a deep breath. The smell of coffee beans hit him instantly but he was too tense to enjoy the aroma. It took a minute to search out the small shop for the familiar blond hair he was looking for. When he did finally find it, he saw that its owner had already seen him. Strangely enough, Finn looked as nervous as he felt. But it wasn't until Hunter's gaze landed on the man sitting next to Finn that his panic went up another notch. He felt Roman stiffen next to him at the sight of Rhys.

It was a strange stand-off – he and Finn looking nervous and Rhys and Roman looking wary. Hunter finally found the courage to get them both moving forward and as soon as he neared the table, Rhys and Finn stood. But it was Rhys who came around the table and closed the distance between them. Roman instantly stepped in front of Hunter – not enough to block him from Rhys completely but enough that he could ward off any blow that might come.

"Hunter, I'm Rhys Tellar," Rhys said quietly. "I owe you an apology."

Jesus, another one. Between Callan and Rhys, Hunter wasn't ever going to be able to catch up. He began shaking his head almost violently but Rhys said, "Yes, I do." His eyes shifted to Roman. "I owe you one as well Mr…"

"Call me Roman," Roman said crisply as he reached out his hand to shake Rhys'. Rhys turned his attention back to Hunter.

"There's no excuse for my behavior," Rhys admitted. "When it comes to Finn and Callan, I tend to think with my heart instead of my head."

Hunter finally managed to find his voice. "You don't owe me any explanations, Mr. Tellar. I deserved what I got and more."

"Hunter-" he heard Roman start to say but Rhys held his hand up to stop Roman though his eyes never left Hunter's.

"It's Rhys," he said. "And no, you didn't." Rhys extended his hand to Hunter. "I'm sorry."

Hunter was too at a loss for words to respond so he nodded his head and shook Rhys' hand. Rhys shifted his gaze back to Roman. "I was just going to get some coffee. Can I buy you a cup?"

Hunter felt Roman's eyes on him and he quickly nodded at the unspoken question.

"You want anything?" Roman asked.

"No, thanks," Hunter said quickly. If he drank anything, it would likely just come back up. Once Roman and Rhys headed towards the counter, Hunter turned his attention on Finn who was still standing next to the table. It was interesting to see how very much the same Finn looked but also how different. He'd filled out quite a bit, probably from the brutal work that ranch life required but his face still had the same innocence to it that had drawn Hunter in from when they were freshmen in high school and Finn had sat ahead of him in their math class. They'd always been friendly to one another but it wasn't until their junior year that they'd started to talk a little bit more. They hadn't exactly been friends but he'd always felt some strange connection to Finn that he couldn't explain.

He hadn't really understood that what he was feeling was attraction because he'd never felt it before – not for any other boy or girl. He'd spent the next two years trying to ignore how his body always drew tight with need whenever Finn was around. And he'd been successful until the day he'd broken down and asked Finn if he wanted to come to his graduation party. He'd expected Finn to refuse since they didn't run in the same circles and none of the guys Finn typically hung out with would be there but, to his surprise, Finn accepted. And then everything had gone to hell.

Hunter forced himself to walk forward. Finn smiled slightly and then said, "Thanks for agreeing to meet with me." Finn motioned to the seat across from him and when Hunter sat, he stuck his hands in his lap so Finn wouldn't see how badly they were shaking.

"How are you?" Finn asked.

Since speech was still eluding him, Hunter nodded.

"I'm sorry for what happened on the sidewalk-"

Hunter wanted to slam his head down on the table. No way he could go through this a third time. "Please," he whispered. "Please don't."

Luckily Finn seemed to know what he was asking because he didn't finish the sentence. "Gray says you're in the engineering program at the university," Finn said.

"Um, yeah, I just switched my major a few weeks ago."

"That's cool. You were always so smart in school...I knew you'd go really far."

Pain lanced through Hunter at the kind words. "I'm so sorry, Finn," he suddenly blurted. Finn looked at him warily – he'd clearly been expecting to ease into this particular topic but between Rhys' apology and Finn's lack of accusation, Hunter was on the edge. Lifting his hand to his mouth for a moment, Hunter tried to get control of himself.

"That night when I saw you arrive, I was so excited. And when I showed you to the pool house so you could change, I just...I just couldn't stop thinking about what it would be like to touch you. And then you opened the door and you looked at me like you knew what I was thinking-"

"I did," Finn interjected. "It was exactly why I said yes when you invited me."

Hunter closed his eyes. He'd never been a hundred percent sure if he'd somehow taken Finn's choice away when he'd pushed Finn back into the pool house and kissed him. At some point Finn had kissed him back and had even started jacking him off but Hunter hadn't known if he'd just gotten caught up in the moment or if he had wanted Hunter as badly as Hunter had wanted him. And then it hadn't mattered because his father had walked in and flipped on the lights and seen his son flat on his back with Finn's hand jammed down his shorts.

"I've spent the last eighteen months trying to figure out what to say to you if I ever got this chance but nothing makes sense to me anymore. I was a coward, pure and simple. I couldn't face what would happen so I put it all on you."

Finn was quiet for so long that Hunter actually started to rise.

"Don't," Finn said gently. "Please don't go."

Hunter dropped back down in the chair and folded his hands together on the table. He didn't realize he was rocking back and forth until Finn's hands closed over his and effectively stopped his forward motion. "Callan says you came to the hospital that night. He said you had bruises on your face."

He'd had them everywhere but he didn't say that. "I deserved them," he responded. "Maybe not for the reason they were inflicted but I deserved them anyway."

"Your dad?" Finn asked.

Hunter nodded. "I didn't know your father was like mine. I swear, Finn. I wouldn't have done it if I'd known. I know that doesn't make it right but I thought he knew about you…I thought he accepted you because you guys were so close."

"We were close," Finn said. "He was my hero. After my mom left, he was all I had. I never told him I was gay because it didn't even occur to me that he would care either way."

"God, Finn, I'm sorry…"

"Hunter, it would have happened at some point. Maybe when I brought home a guy I wanted him to meet or when he caught me looking at a guy a certain way," Finn explained. He laughed and said, "With the way I was always latched on to Callan, I'm amazed my dad hadn't already figured it out."

Hunter couldn't help but smile briefly. But he sobered quickly and said, "It doesn't make it right."

"No," Finn admitted. "It doesn't. But after seeing firsthand what some of the people in this town are capable of and remembering how your dad looked at me when he called me a few choice names, I suspected what drove you to it. How long has it been happening?"

He didn't need to ask what Finn meant. "Since as long as I can remember. He was always real careful to hit me where people wouldn't see the bruises though."

"No one suspected?"

Hunter shook his head. "I got good at hiding it. My mom, she kept telling me it was for the best so between them, I didn't have any reason to think it should be any different."

"And the gay thing?"

"That started when I was twelve or thirteen I guess. If I did anything he deemed too "girly" he'd call me names, smack me around and tell me to "man up." If I spent more of my time playing sports or hanging with the cool kids, he actually seemed proud of me."

"Your mom?"

Hunter shook his head. "I thought she knew about me, about who I was. But she backed him up every time. I begged her to leave once after he'd knocked me around pretty good but she just looked at me like I was suggesting we fly to the moon."

"What about your grandmother?"

"I never told Gran and Pops about what was happening. Gran called me a couple days after I lied about you and told me I should tell the truth. I was so ashamed that I never spoke to her again after that."

"I see your grandmother all the time, Hunter. She's been up front about not believing what you said that night but she's never once condemned you. I know she'd love to hear from you."

Hunter nodded as a lump of emotion got stuck in his throat. "I will...I'll go see her soon." Hunter forced his eyes up and said, "I'll tell everyone the truth, Finn. I've fixed things so my father can't touch me anymore, and I'll go back to Dare and admit what I did. I'll go door to door if I have to."

Finn was quiet for such a long time that Hunter began shifting nervously in his seat. He had no idea what else to say to Finn to convince him of his intention to follow through.

"That day on the sidewalk when Rhys went after you," Finn began. "You didn't try to stop him. He was about to hit you a second time and you didn't even blink. It was like none of your instincts to defend yourself even kicked in."

God, this was not the direction he thought Finn was going to take. "I don't know what you want me to say, Finn."

"I don't care if the whole town ever hears the truth or not. I have exactly what I want. Two men who love me more than anything else in this world, an extended family that most people would kill for and a future doing work that I love. What I want is for you to have those things," Finn said gently.

"My guess is you've got the love part covered if the guy you came in with is anything to go by and I'm hoping the fact that Luke and Gray are already very protective of you means that you're well on your way to getting the family part. And I have no doubt that you won't have any trouble with the work part. But what I want most is for you to forgive yourself for what happened that night because I'm afraid that when I tell you that I forgive you, it still won't be enough for you to stop punishing yourself."

Hunter felt like his heart was being ripped out and he couldn't stop the tears that stated to fall. A hoarse cry erupted in his throat but he managed to stifle it and accepted the napkins that Finn slid across the table. Finn's hand settled over his and he said, "I forgive you, Hunter."

At his words, a sob tore free of Hunter's throat and he wasn't surprised when Roman appeared and sat down next to him and pulled him against his chest. He had no idea if other people were watching or not but he didn't care either way because he couldn't stem the tears that fell. Finn's words had released some kind of dam inside of him and he doubted anything he did would put it back. And in truth, he wasn't sure he wanted to.

"Okay?" Roman murmured against his hair once he settled. Hunter nodded and then used the remaining napkins to wipe at his face. He looked across the table to see Finn's chair was empty. "He's getting a refill," Roman said as he slid a paper cup with a cover on it in front of Hunter. "Vanilla latte."

Right. Because they were his favorite.

Hunter felt in control of himself enough to take a sip of his latte. "Did you and Rhys make nice?" he asked, hating how his voice still sounded shaky.

"We did but only after he agreed to let me take a swing at him for him sucker punching you."

"He did not," Hunter said in dismay.

"Well, it wasn't like you were going to do it yourself, so I'm your champion," Roman said.

"My what?"

"Haven't you ever watched *Game of Thrones*."

"Yeah," Hunter said, still completely confused.

"Remember that episode where the dwarf guy has another guy fight for him in his trial?"

Hunter couldn't hold back his smile. "Yeah."

"That guy was his champion."

"Wait, didn't the guy die? Like horribly?"

Roman seemed to have to think on it before saying, "That's beside the point."

"No, the big guy he was fighting like crushed his head. It was disgusting."

"Oh, hey, are you talking about that scene from *Game of Thrones*," Rhys interjected as he appeared with Finn at the table and sat down. "Because that was fucking epic!"

"I know, right," Roman said. Hunter and Finn exchanged smiles because even as their men began dissecting the infamous fight scene, they both maintained some kind of contact with their lovers. Rhys' hand was covering Finn's and Roman was still holding Hunter pressed up against his chest and had his arm draped over his shoulder. Hunter reached up to lace the fingers of his free hand with Roman's and then looked at Finn and mouthed the words, "Thank you."

∾

"*W*hat are you doing?" Hunter asked as he put his toothbrush away and crawled into bed next to Roman who was looking at something on his tablet.

"Looking for a house," Roman said.

"You're buying a house? I thought you liked living at the hotel in Big Sur."

"Not in California. Out here," Roman responded. "And I'm thinking we should just rent a place until you finish school and then we can decide where we want to live full time."

"What?" Hunter said. When Roman didn't immediately answer him, Hunter grabbed the tablet and tossed it aside. "You're staying here?"

"I'll have to travel for work still but I think I can figure something out so I'm only gone a week or two each month."

"But...but are you sure that's what you want?" Hunter asked even as he crawled over Roman's body so he could straddle his lap.

"Do you really have to ask that?" Roman murmured as he kissed Hunter. "And did you hear the part where I said 'we'?"

He had but he hadn't let himself believe what he was hearing. Roman kissed him again and said, "Hunter, that was my way of asking if you'll move in with me."

Too overcome to speak, Hunter nodded vigorously and then crushed his mouth down on Roman's. He maneuvered Roman until he was flat on his back and then proceeded to torture him until Roman was begging for relief. But it wasn't until Roman threatened to rescind his offer that Hunter took pity on him and surged inside of him with one hard thrust. Roman reached down to grab his ass as Hunter started pounding into him and even though he was topping, he happily gave control over to Roman whose fingers dug into Hunter's cheeks as he set the pace he wanted. Hunter focused his attention on Roman's needy cock and spit into his hand and then wrapped it around the pulsing flesh and then adjusted his motion to match Roman's. Brutal and fast one minute, slow, deep and twisting the next.

As Roman increased the speed, Hunter pulled Roman's cock against his own abdomen and held his palm flat over the flushed shaft. He leaned forward just enough so that his own body could act as a counterpoint for his lunges into Roman's body. Every time Roman pulled him forward so that he was pressed as deep into Roman as he could go, the cocoon he'd created with his palm and his gut slid down Roman's length. When he slid out of Roman, Roman's cock surged through the tunnel his hand had created. As soon as Roman realized what he'd done, his movements became frantic and he began desperately slamming his body against Hunter's to increase the tension. Roman ended up coming first but even as his come spilled onto Hunter's stomach and down his hand, Roman kept dragging Hunter's ass forward and back until Hunter let out a wail of completion. Then Roman held him as tight against his ass as he could and groaned every time Hunter's body convulsed inside of his. When the aftershocks finally stopped, Hunter carefully pulled free of Roman's body and got out of bed just long enough to get cleaned up and to bring a washcloth back to bed for Roman. Then he crawled under the covers. He snatched up the tablet and handed it back to Roman so they could look at the available houses.

"Would you come with me to Dare tomorrow?" Hunter asked.

Roman put the tablet down on his lap and turned to look at him. "Sure. What for?"

"I'd like to see my grandmother and I want you to meet her."

A wide smile passed over Roman's mouth and then he nodded. "I'd like that."

Hunter settled against Roman's side as he picked the tablet up and began scrolling through the different screens.

I forgive you, Hunter.

With those words, Finn had somehow released him. It was something Hunter had staunchly refused to believe would happen even if he ever did hear those words come from Finn's mouth. But it was one time he was a hundred percent glad to have been in the wrong. He still had every intention of making things right for Finn with the town but knowing that Finn didn't hate him had lifted an additional weight off his shoulders that he hadn't even known was there. And while he wasn't sure if they could ever be friends, the four of them had had a really good time at the coffee shop the day before. But if there was even the remote possibility of that happening, Hunter had to take the final steps to fix things. And that meant it was time to go home.

CHAPTER 12

*R*oman pulled his car into the driveway of the Victorian style home and parked it next to a black SUV that was sitting near the porch stairs that led up to the house. A police cruiser was sitting next to it and from earlier conversations with Luke and Gray, he knew it belonged to Dare's other deputy, Jax Reid. Neither he nor Hunter had seen the deputy since that day that Finn and Hunter had run into each other for the first time so Roman had no clue if the guy was going to be receptive to their visit or not. Gray had said that Hunter's grandmother babysat for the couple and since she hadn't answered when they'd driven to her house, Roman had figured she was on duty for the vet and his cop boyfriend. He really hoped Jax and Dane turned out to be as open-minded as Rhys and Finn because he doubted that Hunter would be able to take any more emotional trauma at this point. Even though the visit with Finn couldn't have gone any better, Hunter had still been wrung out by what had happened and continued to struggle with the feeling that he'd somehow gotten off too easy. Roman had no doubt that those feelings would ease as time went on but he definitely didn't want any more shit dumped on Hunter by people who didn't know what a good heart he had.

Roman and Hunter got out of the car and started walking towards the house when they heard a commotion coming from the small building near the house. A door opened and then there was a shout. All of a sudden, an almost entirely white puppy raced out of the building and across the driveway, its big ears flapping around its wide head.

"Jax, he got out!" someone yelled.

Hunter knelt down on the ground and called to the puppy who quickly changed course from where it was headed towards the road and ran straight into Hunter's arms. He scooped it up just as a man came out of the building and frantically began searching the grounds. He already had a puppy under each arm and was struggling to keep them in his hold.

"He's here," Hunter called as he showed the man the puppy and the man slumped in relief.

"It's okay, Jax! We got him!"

Roman recognized the deputy as he hurried out of the building, also carrying two puppies. "Oh thank God," Jax said as he shifted the puppies to get a better grip on them. All of them were white but had splotches of black on them. They also appeared to be bigger than the one in Hunter's arms.

"Thank you," the slightly smaller of the two men said. Roman stepped forward to take one of the puppies from him. His eyes shifted to Jax who was studying Hunter. He clearly recognized him. Roman automatically stepped back so he was standing slightly in front of Hunter and he didn't miss the way Jax's eyes took in the move.

"Dane, this is Hunter Greene," Jax said. "And I'm sorry, I don't think we actually met the other day," Jax said as he tried to reach out a hand but then abandoned the idea when the puppy tucked under his arm started squirming.

"Roman Blackwell," Roman supplied.

"Roman, Hunter, this is my fiancé, Dane," Jax said.

Dane's whole countenance lit up at the word 'fiancé.' "It's nice to meet you both," he said as he reached out his hand to shake both of theirs. "Hunter, your grandmother has told us so much about you."

Hunter stiffened at that and Jax quickly said, "We didn't tell her you were back in town."

Hunter relaxed. "Is she here?"

"Yeah, she's inside with Emma," Dane said. "You mind helping us take these guys inside?"

"Sure," Hunter said as he snuggled the puppy in his arms. "Do they have names?"

"All of them except for the one you're holding," Dane said. "We're letting their adoptive owners name them."

"They're not yours?" Roman asked.

Dane shook his head. "We've been fostering them after someone found them abandoned on the side of the road when they were only a few weeks old. The one you're holding, Hunter, is the runt so we're having a little more trouble finding him a permanent home. He's got a few health issues that means he'll be on medication for a while and not a lot of people want to have to deal with that."

"Poor baby," Hunter murmured as he dropped a kiss on the puppy's head. He got a kiss for his trouble and chuckled as they followed Dane and Jax up the stairs.

As soon as Dane opened the door, a shrill voice called, "Those puppies better not have dirty feet like last time because I spent all morning mopping the floor."

Hunter froze in the doorway as his eyes focused on the stairs leading to the second floor. An old woman with a baby in her arms was carefully walking down the stairs. Her eyes were focused on each step so she didn't see Hunter until she reached the last one and then she froze, her mouth open in a wide O. The woman was as thin as a stick and had her silver hair piled up in some fancy look that almost reminded him of the beehive hairdos women used to wear. She was wearing a black and white linen dress with a matching jacket and a pillbox hat. With her perfectly applied makeup, she looked like she should be sitting in some fancy tea room somewhere eating watercress sandwiches. Well, except for the shoes. Because instead of matching, dressy shoes, she was wearing a pair of sneakers that had some kind of jewels bedazzled on them.

175

"Oh, my darling boy," she cried as she moved forward and handed the baby to Dane who ended up shoving the puppy he was holding into Roman's arms.

Hunter didn't move or make a sound as his grandmother's arms went around him and neither reacted when the puppy began squirming between them.

"Gran," Hunter finally whispered. He succeeded in pulling the puppy from between them and somehow Jax managed to take it even though his hands were full. Jax gave Roman a quick nod and he followed him through the kitchen to a small laundry room where a gate was set up to keep the puppies in the room. Roman carefully put the puppies he was holding down on the other side of the gate and then hurried back to the front door. Hunter and his grandmother were still hugging but Hunter was anything but lax as he held her close.

"Come, come sit," his grandmother urged as she began leading him towards the living room.

"Gran, um, there's someone I want you to meet," Hunter said as he held out his hand to Roman. Roman took it and watched Hunter's grandmother for any sign of contempt as Hunter said, "Gran, this is Roman Blackwell, my boyfriend."

The old woman looked him up and down several times before saying, "You got a job?"

"Yes ma'am, I do."

"A savings account?"

"Uh, yeah," Roman replied.

"You aren't hiding some wife and kids somewhere, are you?"

"No ma'am."

Her sharp eyes flashed back to Hunter before settling on him once more. "You love my grandson?"

"More than anything else in this world."

She studied him for another long moment before nodding her head. "Okay, you'll do." Then she was wrapping her spindly arms around him before turning her attention back to Hunter and leading him into the living room. Roman wasn't sure where Dane and Jax had disappeared to but he was glad for the privacy. Roman wasn't sure if Hunter wanted him present but he didn't have to ask the question because Hunter held out his hand expectantly. Roman took it and followed Hunter into the cozy living room and settled down next to him on the couch. His grandmother kept patting Hunter's face as if to confirm he was really there.

"My baby, what happened? Where have you been?"

"I've been at school Gran."

"You never came to visit. You didn't call me back."

Roman had his hand on Hunter's thigh so he felt him stiffen at his grandmother's heartbroken tone. "I know Gran, I'm sorry. I was too ashamed to face you."

"Oh my dear, I shouldn't have been so hard on you. I never took time to listen to your side of things," his grandmother said softly.

"I've been pretty messed up about everything, Gran. I didn't want you to see me like that. But I talked to Finn, told him how sorry I was and he forgave me."

"He is a sweet boy. I knew you two would work it out."

"I'm going to set things right with the people in town too. Tell them what really happened."

"Well, if any one of them gives you a hard time, you tell them to come see me, you hear?"

Hunter laughed. "Okay, I will." He hesitated and then sought out Roman's hand for support. "Gran, I need to tell you something else."

"Okay, honey, you can tell me anything."

"That night that I lied about Finn…I did it 'cause I didn't want Dad to hurt me again."

It seemed to take his grandmother a minute to understand what Hunter was saying. "Hurt you?" she whispered.

"He'd been doing it for a really long time, Gran. I knew if he found out I was the one who kissed Finn, he'd hurt me really bad. He ended up doing it anyway. That's why I didn't want to come see you that morning when you called me, do you remember?"

Hunter's grandmother seemed to be in shock because she nodded and said, "I wanted you to come have breakfast with me so I could ask you what had happened at your party."

"I had no way of hiding the bruises so that's why I said no."

"No," his grandmother finally said. "No," she repeated though it sounded like less of a denial and more anguished. Tears began spilling out of her eyes as she leaned in to hug Hunter. "My baby, I'm so sorry, I didn't know."

"It's okay, Gran. No one did."

"Your mother," his grandmother said.

Hunter just shook his head and his grandmother covered her mouth as another round of tears hit her.

"Gran, I'm safe now. They can't hurt me ever again. And I'm so happy, Gran. Roman…Roman, he saved me and he loves me. I have what you and Pops had."

"Oh baby, I'm so glad," she said as she pulled a tissue out from under her sleeve and dabbed at her face. She struggled to compose herself and said, "How did you two boys meet?"

"Roman's thinking about buying your land, Gran. We met while I was showing it to him."

Hunter's grandmother's face fell and then she shook her head and looked at Roman. "I'm sorry, but there must be some kind of mistake. That land's not mine anymore."

"What?" Hunter said in shock. "You sold it?"

"No," she said as she shook her head. "It's yours, Hunter."

"What?" Hunter asked.

"The land – it's yours. Your grandad and I talked about it before he died. He knew I'd never want to live there without him so we decided that if something happened, the land would go to you. He set it up as a trust until you turn 21 and then you can do whatever you want with the property."

"Why didn't you tell me?"

"I wanted it to be a graduation present – that was one of the reasons I asked you to come over for breakfast the morning after your graduation."

Hunter glanced at Roman.

"Mrs. Greene, are you the trustee until Hunter turns 21?"

"I was along with Hunter's mother. But Hunter's father-"

Hunter's grandmother suddenly went silent.

"He what, Gran?"

"He...he convinced me to sign the trusteeship over to him." Her eyes widened in horror. "He said you hated me for not believing you..."

Hunter's grandmother looked so forlorn that Roman actually wanted to give her a hug himself. But Hunter folded his arms around her and said, "It's okay, Gran." To Roman he said, "As trustees, do my parents have the right to sell the land?"

"They do," Roman nodded. "I got an email from your dad this morning saying he had another buyer. I had already planned to buy it but I was going to talk to your grandmother about cutting your father out as the realtor so he wouldn't get the commission."

Roman noticed Hunter's crestfallen look and realized the cause. He gently grabbed Hunter's chin and forced him to look at him. "Baby, I decided a long time ago that I wasn't going to develop the land. I wanted it for us...either to live on it someday or just to go there because it's our spot."

"Really?"

Roman nodded. "I can easily outbid any other sellers but that land is yours and they shouldn't get to profit from it. As co-trustees and your parents, they wouldn't have much trouble accessing the funds until you turn 21 – they can say it's all in your best interest."

"Is there any way to stop them?"

"Mrs. Greene, do you still have the document you signed when you transferred the trusteeship to your son?"

"It's in my safe deposit box at the bank. I can get it in the morning."

Roman focused his attention on Hunter. "We'll need to challenge the trusteeship in court. If we can't break the trust early, at least we can try to get it so it's just in your grandmother's name."

"Hunter, I'm so sorry I let this happen," his grandmother said as she hugged Hunter again.

"I shouldn't have waited so long to talk to you, Gran. I should have known you and Pops would have taken care of me."

Roman sat silently as Hunter and his grandmother talked about all the changes in his life but Roman only half listened because his mind was racing with what he needed to do to get Hunter back what was rightfully his.

～

*H*unter smiled as his grandmother waved the little girl's arm at him from the doorway. After they'd finished talking, his grandmother had introduced him to Emma, Dane and Jax's ten-month old baby girl and he'd fallen instantly in love with her chubby face and animated gestures. He'd gotten to hold and play with her for a while and he'd felt Roman's gaze on him more than once. It had opened up a whole new realm of questions about what their future would hold and he couldn't wait to find out.

The revelation that his father had duped his grandmother into signing over complete control of his trust didn't surprise Hunter in the least. And he had no doubt that his father would fight tooth and nail to keep control of the property, especially after Roman had told him that it was worth millions of dollars. He'd been staggered to hear that but hadn't even once considered selling it if Roman could help him get it back. And the idea of sharing it with Roman, maybe someday living there like his Gran and Pops had planned to do, well, there was just no price that could be put on that.

Hunter gave his grandmother and Emma another wave as he stood next to Roman's car to wait for him. He watched his grandmother disappear into the house and then glanced at his phone. He'd assumed Roman had gone back into the house to make a pit stop but at ten minutes and counting, Hunter had to wonder if the man had gotten some bad chicken or something when they stopped at the small deli on the outskirts of Missoula for lunch.

Hunter was about to head back up the stairs when the door opened and he saw Roman backing out of it. He wondered at the strange position but only for a moment because as soon as Roman turned around, Hunter gasped at the sight of the squirming puppy in his arms.

"What did you do?" Hunter asked as Roman handed him the puppy.

"Us runts gotta stick together," Roman said as he gave the puppy a pat and then leaned down to kiss Hunter. "We need to bring him back for his shots in a week and Dane's going to get his medications together for me to pick up tomorrow."

Hunter knew he was grinning like an idiot as he carried the puppy to the car and got into the passenger seat. "Thank you, Roman," he said as Roman got the car started.

"You're welcome," Roman returned as he brushed another kiss over Hunter's mouth. "I love you," he whispered just before the puppy's wet tongue covered both their mouths in a trail of slime. "He needs a name," Roman said as he backed the car up.

"Already got one," Hunter said.

"What?"

"Champion. Champ for short."

Roman smiled. "Champ it is."

~

"*R*oman, it's fine. Just put him down. She won't hurt him," Gray urged.

Roman wasn't as confident as Gray as he watched the way Ripley was eyeing the puppy in his arms. He'd learned from Dane that Champ was some kind of Great Dane mix and that even as the runt of the litter, he'd likely be close to 150 pounds easily when full grown. Not that that would do the puppy any good right now with the huge German Shepherd who looked like she could kill him with one good bite.

"Roman, trust me," Gray said.

Roman finally put the puppy down but remained squatted next to him as Ripley came up to sniff him. There were some tense moments as the two dogs worked out some dominance ritual that Roman didn't have a clue about but then they were off and running through the huge backyard.

"Where's Hunter?" Gray asked as they began walking toward the spot by the water where the dogs could play.

"He's driving down a little later. Some of his classmates were meeting at the library to prep for an exam on Monday. He's going to go meet his grandmother to pick up the trusteeship papers and then he'll meet us here for dinner."

"I'm glad they worked things out," Gray said. "Sounds like things went well with Finn too."

"They did. I don't think Hunter was expecting it so he's still struggling to accept that he can put this whole thing behind him."

"Sometimes the things we think we left in the past are just waiting to catch up to us when we least expect it."

Roman chuckled. "Don't worry, Dr. Phil, I've decided to talk to someone about the stuff that happened with my mom…and Walt."

Gray slapped him on the back. "Man, I rock this big brother shit."

Roman laughed but sobered when he said, "How are you doing with things?"

"It's hard to miss someone who wasn't really there, even when he was."

"And Victoria?"

Gray shook his head. "Don't really want or need that in my life. I've got all the family I need right here." Once they reached the log by the stream, Gray said, "A little birdie told me that you were thinking about setting up roots around these parts."

"Did that little birdie happen to be wearing bedazzled Nikes?"

"It may have," Gray acknowledged.

"I found a couple of rental properties between here and Missoula that have a lot of land for Champ to run around on and the commute isn't too bad. When Hunter's done with school, we'll see what happens next. But to answer your question, I think we've both found exactly where we want to be."

Gray wrapped an arm around him and dragged him in for a long hug. "Welcome home, baby brother."

Roman smiled as Ripley and Champ both began jumping against them with wet, muddy paws. "Better late than never," he murmured as he reached down to pull Champ up on his lap.

~

*H*unter parked his car in front of the hair salon and climbed out. He couldn't help but scan the sidewalk outside his parents' realty office at the end of the block. He had yet to make any kind of contact with them and had decided to hold off until after Roman had gotten the process of challenging the trusteeship underway. Hurrying into the salon, he easily found his grandmother sitting near the entrance. Her little brown dog, Teddy, was on her lap as the woman behind her did something to her hair that involved covering it in a strong smelling blue cream that reminded Hunter of the *Smurfs* cartoons he used to like to watch when he was little.

"Hey Gran," he said as he came around the chair and leaned down to kiss her cheek.

"Oh, my boy, how are you?" she asked. Before he could answer, she looked at the woman behind her using the reflection in the mirror and said, "Felicia, this is my grandson."

The young brunette smiled at him. "Hi, it's nice to meet you," she said as she held out her hand.

"No, no, don't bother," his grandmother said as she reached her hand up to push Felicia's hand back. "My Hunter only likes boys who like boys," she said crisply. "And he doesn't need a beard," she added.

Although Hunter wanted to disappear into the floor before he died of embarrassment, the brunette took it all in stride and let out a little laugh.

"Gran, do you have the papers?"

"I do," she said as she pointed at her purse which was hanging from a hook underneath the counter in front of her. Hunter grabbed it and gave it to her and waited patiently until she pulled them out and handed them to him. "I went down to your father's office to give him a piece of my mind."

"No, Gran, we told you not to."

His grandmother waved her hand as she gave him the purse back. "Don't worry, he wasn't there. But I made sure to tell that wife of his that they're not getting what's yours. I also told her that come election time next year, I'm going to find someone to run against him. And if I can't, well then I'll just do it myself."

Hunter groaned. So much for the element of surprise. He leaned down to kiss her again and said, "Stay away from him, okay, Gran?"

His grandmother dismissed him with a wave but not before she planted a kiss on his cheek. Once he was back at his car, he tossed the papers on the passenger seat and began searching his pockets for his phone so he could let Roman know that the cat was out of the bag. The sound of a rumbling motor caught his attention and he looked up to see Finn's truck on the other side of the square pulling into a spot in front of the police station. Finn and Rhys both waved to him and then Finn was motioning him over. He left his car where it was and trotted through the park. By the time he reached Finn, the young man and Rhys were sharing a heated embrace as they said their goodbyes.

"Hey, Hunter," Rhys said as he slapped Hunter gently on the back before brushing one last kiss over Finn's mouth. "See you later," he murmured.

"Bye," Finn said dreamily. It wasn't until Rhys was out of sight that Finn finally focused on him. "Hey, I heard you saw your grandmother."

Hunter nodded. It still felt so strange to be talking so openly with Finn but he wasn't going to miss the chance to connect with the young man who could have become a good friend if circumstances had been any different. There was absolutely no residual attraction between them so that was one less obstacle to deal with.

"I did," he said. "I almost forgot what a force of nature she can be."

Finn laughed but his humor suddenly died down as his focus went to something behind Hunter. Hunter turned around and saw Clem Henry, the owner of the local hardware store, eyeing them as he swept the sidewalk in front of his shop. Even from a distance, Hunter could see the open disdain that was focused entirely on Finn. The man disappeared inside his store and when Hunter returned his attention to Finn, the young man tried to brush off what had happened.

"So I was talking to Callan and Rhys and we were wondering if you and Roman wanted to come to dinner on Sunday. Gray and Luke will be there. Jax and Dane, too. Your grandmother said she'd come if she hadn't managed to find a date between now and then so I think it's a pretty safe bet that she'll be there too-"

Hunter reached down to grab Finn's hand and began dragging him to the hardware store.

"What are you doing?" Finn asked.

"Something I should have done a long time ago," Hunter responded. He shoved open the door to the surprisingly busy store and led Finn to the checkout counter which Clem Henry was busily cleaning off with some paper towels. He stilled when he saw them and his lips twisted into an ugly frown. The man had to be in his late sixties with thinning hair and a serious pouch going on. He was wearing a striped, short sleeve button up shirt along with a pair of brown slacks.

"Mr. Henry, do you remember me?"

The man nodded and said, "You're the mayor's boy."

"Hunter."

"Right."

"And you know Finn?" Hunter asked.

A sharp nod.

"You don't like him much, do you Mr. Henry?"

Mr. Henry didn't respond so Hunter continued. "What don't you like about him? The fact that he works just as hard, if not harder, than any of you?" Hunter asked as he glanced at the few people who'd stopped to listen in on their conversation. He recognized one of the men as one of his father's poker buddies but he didn't dwell on that fact.

"Or that he'd give the shirt off his back to help any one of you out if you needed it?" Hunter said. "In fact, didn't he do just that when you had that fire in the back of your store a few years ago, Mr. Henry? Wasn't Finn one of the few people who showed up to help you clean up the water damage?"

Mr. Henry's eyes shifted to Finn and a glimmer of guilt appeared and Hunter knew that the man hadn't remembered Finn from that time.

"I'm going to take a leap here and guess what bothers you about Finn is who he loves."

"It ain't natural," Mr. Henry snorted.

"You like my dad, right? You respect him? Admire him?"

"Your dad's a fine, upstanding citizen. God-fearing. Respectable."

"So your definition of a good, God-fearing, respectable man is one who beats the shit out of his kid because he got a B on his homework instead of an A or because he didn't make the Varsity football team on his first try or because he spilled cereal on the living room rug while he was watching his favorite Saturday morning cartoon. Tell me, Mr. Henry, is that natural?"

"Well, no…"

"Was it the natural thing for Finn's dad to beat him unconscious because of a lie *I* told just so I wouldn't have to admit to people like you that I couldn't make my body react to girls the same way it did to boys?"

Hunter looked at the people milling around the counter. "Finn never assaulted me. I lied to protect a secret that I was too ashamed to admit because I didn't want to lose the only people who were supposed to love me. That's what's unnatural, Mr. Henry," Hunter said as he turned his focus back on the clerk. "That God-fearing, fine upstanding citizen that you admire and respect so much would rather his son be rotting in a grave somewhere as a straight man instead of living in this world as a gay one. There's nothing more fucking unnatural than that."

Hunter shook his head and finally said, "If you can't accept who Finn and I are, then just leave us alone to love whomever we want."

The store was so silent that Hunter could swear he heard crickets. Finn shot him an "I told you so" look and Hunter gave him a little nod. They both moved for the door when Mr. Henry called out, "Wait." He leaned down to pull something from beneath his counter and Hunter actually wondered if the man was about to pull a gun on them or something. But to Hunter's surprise, Mr. Henry pulled out what looked like a small picture, the kind that people used to carry around in wallets before everything went digital. It was wrinkled and bent like it had been handled countless times. Mr. Henry reached across the counter and handed Hunter the picture. He took it and then lowered it enough so Finn could see it too.

"Her name was Billie…Wilhelmina actually but she liked it when I called her Billie."

Hunter studied the picture of the young black woman. She appeared to be in her late teens or early twenties and from the dress she was wearing he guessed the picture to be from the sixties or seventies.

"I met her in college in Georgia. I asked her to marry me on our second date. She said yes," Mr. Henry said as a slight smile spread over his lips.

"I took her home to meet my folks."

"What happened?" Finn asked when Mr. Henry fell quiet.

"They were real nice to her, polite, asked her about school, her family. When I told them we were getting married, they congratulated us. Billie and I were so happy that we started making plans for our wedding as soon as we got back to school. The next weekend I went home to talk to my folks about where we should get married. They told me I couldn't marry Billie and that if I did, they'd stop paying for my school and kick me out of the house. I told them I loved her and that I wanted to spend the rest of my life with her but they didn't care. They said they didn't want no…"

Mr. Henry hesitated, his voice breaking. "They called her a real bad name and said they didn't want her as a daughter in law. They said the same thing about the kids we were planning on having."

To Hunter's shock, Mr. Henry reached up to dab at his eyes. "I was only nineteen and didn't know how I'd support Billie with no job and no money. So I told her we couldn't be together. She cried and begged me not to leave her...that we could figure it out together but I was too scared to go against my parents. She transferred to another school a few weeks later and I never saw her again."

"I'm sorry Mr. Henry," Hunter said as he handed the picture back.

The man traced his finger lovingly over the picture and Hunter actually heard him whisper, "My Billie," before he looked up at them. "I can't say I understand why you boys are the way you are, but we ain't got no problems between us any more, you hear?" His eyes settled on Finn as he spoke the last words.

Hunter figured it was as good as they were going to get. "Thank you, Mr. Henry," he said as he turned to leave. The old man let out a non-committal grunt in response.

As Hunter followed Finn towards the door, he glanced over his shoulder and noticed his father's friend talking on his cell phone. The man's small eyes connected with Hunter's just before he turned and disappeared down an aisle.

"Hunter," Finn called from where he was holding the door open.

"Coming," Hunter said and he followed Finn outside.

"Wow, that was...wow," Finn said once they reached his truck. "Thank you for that."

"It was a long time coming," Hunter said. A contented feeling went through him as Finn hugged him and as he watched Finn climb into his truck, Hunter felt his spirits lift. Even if Roman couldn't work a miracle and get him his grandparents' land back, he had a hell of a lot to be thankful for.

Hunter waved at Finn as he drove past and headed back out of town. He took his time walking across the park towards his car but stopped when he heard the loud rumble of an engine behind him. He could tell it was a diesel truck from the way it sounded and as he looked over his shoulder, he saw the vehicle in question stop in front of the hardware store. A niggle of uncertainty went through him as he recognized his dad's poker buddy come out of the hardware store and climb into the bed of the truck. The truck was too far away to make out the driver or the passenger so he started walking back towards the store so he could get a better look as it passed. None of the occupants seemed to notice him as the truck drove past him but he sure as hell recognized the passenger. Fear went through him as he trotted across the park to the other side to watch which way the truck went and the second it turned right at the stoplight, Hunter raced to his car. He already had his phone out and was dialing Roman's number as he put the car in gear.

"Hey," Roman said as he answered on the first ring.

Hunter slammed on the gas and barreled through the intersection. "Roman, I need you to call Rhys or Jax for me."

He could tell that Roman was on instant alert because he said, "Why? What's going on?"

"I'm not sure, it may be nothing," he said as he quickly explained the visit to the hardware store. "I didn't have time to stop at the police station."

"Hunter, are you following them?"

"Yes, but I don't see them. They're too far ahead of me. I need to see if they're headed to the CB Bar."

"Hunter-"

"Please Roman, make the call. Call Callan too – even if he's out checking the herd, he might have his phone. I'm going to call Finn."

"Okay," Roman said quickly. "But if you see something, wait for Rhys and Jax, do you hear me?"

Since that was a promise Hunter couldn't make, he simply said, "I love you, Roman" and hung up. He dialed Finn's number but cursed when it went straight to voicemail. He pressed the gas down as far as it could go and when his phone rang again a few minutes later, he didn't dare answer it for fear of losing control of his car.

By the time he reached the dirt road leading to the ranch, he could see a dust trail from whatever vehicle had been there ahead of him. He hoped to God it was from Finn's truck but in his gut he knew it wasn't. His suspicion was confirmed a few seconds later when the dust cleared as he reached the barn. The same black truck he'd seen in town was parked right next to Finn's.

Terror shot through him as he slammed his car into park. He reached beneath the back seat and yanked out the lever action rifle that he always took with him to the lake and then ran through the barn. He found what he was looking for almost immediately. The three men and Finn were along the side of a storage shed near the corral that the big white horse, King, was in. The animal was in a panic as it tore around the enclosure.

Two men were holding Finn's arms as Hunter's father punched him in the stomach. Even from the distance, Hunter heard Finn groan and just as his father drew back his arm to hit Finn again, Hunter pointed the gun in the air and pulled the trigger.

The two men holding Finn immediately released him and Finn dropped to his knees. There was a bruise on his face but otherwise he appeared unharmed. His father seemed surprised to see him but his face quickly pulled into a sneer and he actually had the balls to pull his arm back as if to hit Finn again. This time, Hunter didn't bother with aiming into the air. He aimed directly at his father's feet, pulled the lever back to reload the gun and pulled the trigger in one smooth motion. The dirt at Malcom's feet flew up and Malcom froze mid-punch. Hunter yanked back the lever and watched in satisfaction as his father swallowed nervously as the empty round was discharged from the gun and a new one was loaded.

"You," Hunter said to the two men. "Walk towards me slowly."

The men did as they were told and once they were within a few feet of him he said, "Stop and lay down on your stomachs, hands behind your head." He kept his gun pointed at his father. "Finn, you okay?"

"Yeah," Finn managed to wheeze.

"You guys have a gun out here?"

Finn nodded and climbed to his feet. It took him a couple seconds to catch his breath and then he was hurrying past Hunter and into the barn. He reappeared moments later with a shotgun.

"Watch them," Hunter said as he motioned to the two men on the ground.

"With pleasure," Finn drawled as he drew back on the barrel of the shotgun. Hunter could hear sirens in the distance but he kept his eyes on his father as he closed the distance between them.

"Big man with the gun," his father bit out.

"Get on your knees," Hunter ordered, his anger barely leashed as he stared down the barrel of the gun at the man who'd taken such pleasure in tormenting him. When his father ignored his order, Hunter fired again. The bullet actually took off the very tip of his father's boot and his father screamed and jumped back. "On your knees," Hunter said again as he reloaded the gun. When his father continued to balk, Hunter warned, "You know I'm nowhere near out of bullets."

His father's eyes narrowed but he finally dropped to his knees. Hunter got to within a couple feet of the man who'd sired him. "No heart, isn't that what you said when I wouldn't shoot that whitetail when you took me hunting for the first time?"

"Your mother would have thrown less of a fit than you did."

Hunter ignored the barb and said, "Why come after Finn? Your buddy there must have told you I was the one who told everyone in that store about your dirty little secret...and mine. Why not just come after me?"

When his father's eyes hardened, Hunter nodded his head in understanding. "I was next, is that it? Finn was an easy mark because you knew where he was headed and that Rhys was on duty today and chances were good that you'd catch Finn on his own so you figured you'd take care of him and then come after me as soon as you got the chance."

"Hunter."

The sound of Roman's voice washed over him like a caress. He glanced out of his peripheral vision and saw that Roman wasn't alone. Both Jax and Rhys were with him. Jax was busy cuffing the guys on the ground and Rhys was examining Finn's injuries.

"Roman, please tell me Jax and Rhys aren't going to have to arrest you for reckless driving."

"I was on my way to Dane and Jax's to pick up the medication for Champ when you called."

"You know who this is, Dad?" Hunter asked as he motioned with his head in Roman's direction.

"He's the developer looking at my land-"

"Your land? Don't you mean my land?" Hunter asked.

"That land is mine you worthless little shit-"

Hunter fired the gun and heard his father yelp as the wood behind his head exploded. For the first time, his father actually looked scared and Hunter couldn't help but enjoy how good it finally felt to have the tables turned.

"Hunter," Roman said softly. "Please don't do this."

"Why not? It's no less than he deserves for everything he's done. To me. To Finn and Rhys and Callan."

His father paled and Hunter knew his guess had been right. "Deputy Reid, might I suggest that you take a look at my father's financial records and see if maybe he didn't make a contribution to the accounts of those guys that burned down Callan's barn and killed his herd?" His steely gaze locked with his father's. "And shot Finn."

"I think that's an excellent suggestion," Jax said casually.

"Hunter," Roman said again and Hunter finally took his eyes off his father long enough to connect with Roman's.

"You see, Dad, he's not just some developer," Hunter said as he held Roman's gaze. He hated the fear he saw there…for him. "He's the man who loves me above all others. Who would give his life for mine without question and without fail every time. And he wants me to put this gun down not to save your sorry ass but because he doesn't want me to have to live with the guilt of killing my own father."

Hunter slid his eyes back to the man on his knees…the man who no longer owned the title of father. "Look around you. Not one of these men would lift a finger to save you. In fact, I bet every single one of them would help me bury your body without me even needing to ask. Because out here, you're the one who doesn't matter. You're the one who doesn't fit."

Hunter lowered his gun and stepped back. It didn't feel like enough, just walking away. But he found that in that moment he wanted something else more than he wanted revenge. And with that thought in mind, he turned his back on his father and began walking towards Roman. Roman's features relaxed as he began moving forward but suddenly they pulled tight just as his mouth opened to yell Hunter's name. He saw both Rhys and Jax going for their guns but they hadn't gotten them past the holsters when a gunshot rang out. Hunter froze as his eyes locked with Roman's and he heard him scream the word "No."

But in the second it took Roman to reach him, Hunter said, "I'm okay."

Roman's hands grabbed him by the shoulders to yank him around so he could check his back and Hunter quickly noticed two things. The first was his father still on his knees with a silver revolver lying in the dirt next to the hand that used to be attached to his father's arm. The second was the sight of Callan Bale about a hundred and fifty feet away riding his horse slowly towards them, a rifle in his right hand.

His father's screams of agony pierced the air as Roman dragged Hunter into his arms. It vaguely registered that someone would probably need to apply a tourniquet to his father's arm at some point to keep him from bleeding out, but Hunter didn't really give a shit if that actually happened so he just took Roman's hand in his and then went to check on Finn to make sure his friend was okay.

EPILOGUE

ix months later
"You okay?" Roman breathed against Hunter's lips.

Hunter nodded but seemed incapable of speech as Roman surged into him again. The pleasure that Hunter was feeling was written all over his face but there was more there too. And Roman knew exactly what had put that look on Hunter's face. He could feel it actually. The small, white gold band was pressed against his own skin as Hunter's fingers clutched his.

Roman pulled back until his cock nearly slipped from Hunter's body. He held himself there for a moment, reveling in the feeling of Hunter's depths trying to hold on to his naked cock. He pushed forward again and watched Hunter's eyes close as his head dipped back on the sleeping bag and Roman used the opportunity to kiss his neck. As soon as Hunter lowered his head again, Roman kissed him and then drew his cock back again. His next glide hit Hunter's prostate and Hunter groaned at the contact as his legs tried to wrap around Roman's ass to keep him from pulling out again. But he did it anyway and swallowed Hunter's answering moan. Over and over he let Hunter's body draw more and more of his release to the surface as he made love to Hunter's mouth with his tongue.

The evening air was cool as it washed over their naked bodies but Roman barely felt the chill because his need for Hunter kept building and building. As with every time they made love, Roman's intent was to draw their coming together out for as long as he could but as soon as he buried himself inside of Hunter's heat, he knew it was a promise he wouldn't be able to keep. And when Hunter lay beneath him, his eyes acting as windows to his soul, exposing every thought and emotion he was feeling, Roman knew he didn't stand a chance.

Roman increased his thrusts until Hunter was panting against his mouth and then he released one of Hunter's hands so he could use his arm to hold their bodies together as he rolled them so Roman was on his back. Hunter didn't even hesitate for a second as he sat up and began riding Roman. He linked their hands together again and Hunter used the connection as leverage as his hips twisted over Roman's. The engagement band on Hunter's left hand stood out in stark contrast to his pale skin and Roman couldn't help but run his fingers over it.

There hadn't been a doubt in his mind that Hunter wouldn't say yes to his proposal but he'd still been overjoyed when Hunter had fallen to his knees and whispered yes as he'd wrapped his arms around Roman's neck. The eight months since they'd met hadn't always been easy as they'd both had to adjust to being apart when Roman was forced to travel for work. Hunter's therapy had done wonders but he still had to deal with the occasional trigger that left him frustrated that he hadn't been completely cured of his need to hurt himself. Roman had also talked to someone about the way he'd responded to his father at his death and the memories of his mother that the event had triggered. Throughout it all, Hunter and Roman had drawn on each other when they struggled with trying to heal the wounds their pasts had left behind.

Dealing with the trusteeship had been easy once Hunter's father had been convicted of multiple felonies including conspiracy. Hunter's guess that Malcom Greene had been involved with the men who'd vandalized Callan's property and nearly killed Finn after burning down Callan's barn had been spot on, and Malcom had been sentenced to more than twenty years in prison. His trial for attempted murder was scheduled to start later in the summer. Hunter's mom had given up her role as trustee and left Dare to go live with a distant cousin somewhere in the south. Roman had urged Hunter to consider saying goodbye but in the end he'd decided against it. Once the land was back in his grandmother's care until he turned 21, they'd started talking about the house they wanted to build. They'd settled on a cabin that would look much like the one Pops had planned to build but it would include all the creature comforts that would make the place uniquely theirs.

"So beautiful," Roman murmured as Hunter's body rocked back and forth over his. Hunter leaned down to kiss him, releasing his hands so that he could cup Roman's face.

"Love you," Hunter whispered against his lips.

Roman surged upwards and wrapped his arms around Hunter's waist to support him as they continued to kiss while Hunter began riding him in earnest. "Love you, soon-to-be husband."

A gasp escaped Hunter's lips at that but before he could do anything, Roman grabbed him and rolled them again and slammed into Hunter over and over. Fingers twisted in his hair and clamped down on his shoulder as Hunter began grunting with every powerful thrust. Roman's own control was shot to hell so he just kept barreling into Hunter until he shattered into a million pieces as his orgasm ripped through him. As his come began to coat Hunter's inner walls, his gliding motions became easier, freer and he used the added lubrication to shuttle in and out of Hunter at a relentless pace. Hunter's hips lifted to meet his and as soon as he began bucking wildly beneath Roman, Roman reached between their bodies and gave Hunter's cock several hard tugs. Hunter cried out in relief as he came and even before he was finished shooting, Roman pulled free of his body and leaned down to suck Hunter's cock deep in his throat. He swallowed the last of Hunter's essence and then lifted up to kiss Hunter as he slid his cock back into Hunter's silky depths.

The fire kept them warm for only so long so Roman reached out to search for the edge of the sleeping bag to tuck over them. He could already see the sun starting to peek over the horizon which didn't surprise him since they'd been making love to each other all night long. And since their only plans for the day were to join everyone at the CB Bar for dinner, they had the whole day to sleep, fuck and sleep some more. And somewhere in between, they'd manage a trip to the hot springs which inevitably would lead to more fucking.

"Any idea how we're going to choose our best men?" Hunter asked drowsily.

Roman chuckled and gently pulled free of Hunter's body before saying, "I get to play the brother card so I think that puts just you in the hot seat."

Hunter groaned and Roman knew exactly why. For the young man who'd been isolated ever since leaving Dare, coming back had somehow had the exact opposite effect and he'd built lasting friendships with every single man in their extended family. He and Luke often snuck out to Luke's shed which at some point had been re-coined his woodworking shop and played around with all the new toys Luke had stocked it with. Hunter had managed to get just as sucked into Gray's books as everyone else but had inadvertently set off a firestorm when he'd let it slip that he'd managed to convince Roman in his own unique way to tell him what had happened to the harried detective. His friendship with Finn had flourished as they reminisced about the better parts of their high school experience. Rhys still had some epic guilt about the shitty way he'd treated Hunter so he always went out of his way to make sure Hunter knew how much he liked him and between Callan and Dane, Hunter had started working with the various rescue animals that the vet and the horse trainer always seemed to have on hand. Jax had been the easiest nut to crack because all Hunter had to do was work his magic on little Emma and the big man had easily accepted Hunter into the fold.

"You think I can flip a coin?" Hunter asked as he pressed up against Roman.

"Sure, but I can guarantee you'll never hear the end of it if you do."

"Maybe we should elope. I've never been to Vegas."

"Your grandmother would kill us."

"We'll take her with us."

"Your grandmother in Vegas?" Roman suggested.

"No, Vegas isn't ready for that," Hunter agreed. "Okay, putting a pin in the best man selection. What about location?"

Roman looked at him and said "Here" at the exact same time that Hunter did.

"When?" Hunter asked.

"Tomorrow."

"Okay."

"What?" Roman said as he leaned up on his elbow to look down at Hunter.

"Let's do it."

"Are you serious?"

Hunter levered up to kiss him. "I've been waiting my whole life for you, Roman Blackwell. Even one day more seems too long."

Roman smiled and settled back down on top of him. Hunter's arms wrapped around his neck. "We're getting married tomorrow."

"Yeah we are," Hunter said with a big smile. "Don't we need to get blood tests and a license?"

"We'll do the ceremony tomorrow and do the rest of that stuff next week," Roman said. "What about the best men?"

"As long as all of our friends are there, I don't care where they stand. Beside us, behind us…just as long as they're all with us."

"Your grandmother is going to flip."

Hunter thought about it for a moment. "She can officiate. She got ordained online for Dane and Jax's wedding just in case the reverend got into an accident," Hunter said as he used air quotes when he said the word accident.

"You know what that means, right?"

"No, what?" Hunter asked.

"It means no sleeping in," Roman said as he gave Hunter one last hard kiss and threw back the covers.

"Fuck, that's cold," Hunter said as Roman yanked him to his feet. "Hot springs?"

Roman was about to say they didn't have time when Hunter arched his brows. "Thirty minutes."

"I can work with that," Hunter said as he began yanking on his pants. He paused when he heard some rustling in bushes behind them.

"Shit, what is that? A bear?" Roman asked. Hunter automatically reached for the rifle next to the sleeping bag but his hand hadn't even closed around it when Champ came tearing through the woods and jumped onto the sleeping bag. The dog had gotten much bigger than Dane had thought he would and was still growing.

"Holy hell, Champ," Roman groaned as he tried to yank his pants from underneath the dog's heavy bulk. He was just righting himself when Champ jumped off the sleeping bag and took off towards the lake. Roman's jeans snapped back and he nearly fell on his ass. Hunter began laughing hysterically.

"Damn dog," Roman muttered. He was distracted by some more rustling and looked up just in time to see a patch of black and white waddle up to their campsite. "It's just Lucy," he called to the fleeing dog.

"Uh, Roman," he heard Hunter say.

"Yeah."

"That's not Lucy."

"What?" Roman asked as he looked up from the pants he was still trying to get on.

"Not Lucy," Hunter called as he darted past him.

Roman looked down at the skunk, dropped his pants and took off running, stark naked, after Hunter.

The End

A NOTE TO READERS

This book was particularly personal to me because of the way in which Hunter chose to deal with his pain.

As a survivor of self-injury/self-harming, I can tell you it is a very serious and traumatic condition and I would urge anyone who is suffering through it in silence to seek help. You have absolutely nothing to be ashamed of and there are many resources out there that can help you deal with the underlying issues that cause you to turn on yourself to seek relief from your pain.

Talk to a friend or a parent or a trusted loved one. Don't be afraid to talk to a medical professional. What you are feeling inside is very real and there is no shame in asking for help.

This is just one of many sites that is a good place to start:
http://www.mentalhealthamerica.net/self-injury

Please take care of yourself. You're worth it.

Sloane Kennedy

ABOUT THE AUTHOR

Dear Reader,

I hope you enjoyed Roman and Hunter's story. This was the last planned book in the Finding series but I suspect at some point I will need to revisit the men of Dare, Montana.

As an independent author, I am always grateful for feedback so if you have the time and desire, please leave a review, good or bad, so I can continue to find out what my readers like and don't like. You can also send me feedback via email at sloane@sloanekennedy.com

Join my Facebook Fan Group: Sloane's Secret Sinners

Connect with me:
www.sloanekennedy.com
sloane@sloanekennedy.com

f 𝕩

ALSO BY SLOANE KENNEDY

(Note: Not all titles will be available on all retail sites)

The Escort Series
Gabriel's Rule (M/F)

Shane's Fall (M/F)

Logan's Need (M/M)

Barretti Security Series
Loving Vin (M/F)

Redeeming Rafe (M/M)

Saving Ren (M/M/M)

Freeing Zane (M/M)

Finding Series
Finding Home (M/M/M)

Finding Trust (M/M)

Finding Peace (M/M)

Finding Forgiveness (M/M)

Finding Hope (M/M/M)

The Protectors
Absolution (M/M/M)

Salvation (M/M)

Retribution (M/M)

Forsaken (M/M)

Vengeance (M/M/M)

A Protectors Family Christmas

Atonement (M/M)

Revelation (M/M)

Redemption (M/M)

Non-Series

Letting Go (M/F)

29847819R00129

Printed in Great
Britain
by Amazon